A Dangerous Trade

STEVEN VEERAPEN

First published in 2018 by Sharpe Books.

ISBN: 9781793044631

TABLE OF CONTENTS

A DANGEROUS TRADE

PROLOGUE

He has no idea he's being watched. Idiot. Carefully, almost daintily, he picks his way down the slope of the hill, his arms outstretched for balance. He moves with all the grace of a crippled donkey as he picks through the carpet of burnt orange. His face is a curious mix of exertion, boredom, and disgust at his task. It's a smug face, self-satisfied. Hateable. Stopping to mop his brow, he spits, looks back up at the castle on the hill, and then removes a paper from his doublet. He nods his head slowly, before turning skyward and exhaling relief. Back into his breast pocket goes the paper.

He has no idea he's being stalked. His hunter has the measure of him, even from the occasional peek out from behind an old oak: a gentleman, playing at the art of spying. That was the way of it in England, regrettably – class over competence. The busy Secretary Cecil will learn the hard way how the game must be played.

The gentleman spy sits down on an old log and unwraps a cloth. A little jumble of bread and cheese scatters across his lap. He sets to it. His Adam's apple is quivering when an arm snakes around his neck. He has no time to cry out; his head snaps back and his food flies free. His killer holds on, squeezing the throat until life has fled too. Now he sets to work.

Firstly, he thrusts his hands into the doublet and retrieves the paper. It's the only one. That, at least, is clever. The writing is not cyphered; in fact, it's written in a remarkably clear secretarial hand.

Item: Tutbury. Divers entrances and exits. This is no fit place to keep a fallen dame secure. Another keeper and another lodging are most heartily recommended, or who can say what might fall out? Ever in Your Honour's humble service, William Pursglove.

William Pursglove, thinks the man who has felled him. Probably it was his real name. Cecil's men don't yet seem bright enough to have even understood the need for false ones. He produces his own paper and holds it up. They're a close enough match – both without any special mark of their origin. He chances a look around before dragging the man behind the oak tree and producing his own stoppered inkwell, pen, and a cheap wooden pounce pot. Copying the hand of Pursglove, he writes his own message. He stutters at first, then the pen moves rapidly, the ink bleeding out.

Item: Tutbury. A suitable place for a dame.

The first two words are almost exact replicas, and he allows himself a smile as he scatters the thick flecks of sand on the ink and lets the wind take the rest. Now, the body.

Firstly, he puts his new note in place of the original. Deep into the man's pocket it goes. But the dead man is still warm. The eyelids and lashes quiver in the stiff breeze. He presses down once again on Pursglove's windpipe, staring off into space as he does so. Once done, he pulls a knife from his belt and begins to saw at the finger joints – a good, sloppy job. He doesn't particularly want the corpse's rings, but it all has to look real. Throwing the fingers deeper into the woods, he gives a few quick jabs around the abdomen, the chest, each haphazard. He takes the purse of money too, making a thoroughly bad job of tearing and sawing at its string.

He pauses to catch his breath. How stupid the corpse looks, gawking at him. In irritation he kicks it; no, he corrects himself – not irritation. It's all for the good of making the whole dispatch seem like mischance. When he has a good lungful of wind again, he begins to drag the dead spy away from the castle, away from the woods, and towards the nearest stretch of brigand-haunted road.

It's an astonishingly freeing thing, to kill without qualm or conscience. Whether it was the dogs and cats he'd dispatched as a child or his slattern of a wife. Once you accepted it was God's will, that he had gifted freedom from conscience, it was easy – it meant being a chosen one. Now to see if he can convince others to enter that light and liberty: to see if he can make others kill.

Part One: Winter Beckons

1

An autumn breeze carried the chill of the season through Hampton Court's park. It did not carry the whispered conference Jack Cole knew was taking place amongst the emaciated trees and frost-coated statues. He waited on the edge of the park, watching his breath as it puffed out and dissipated against the sky. A risky place for a meeting, he thought. Stupid, almost. But then why should a duke and an earl not meet wherever they choose?

'Hunting in December,' tutted Tom, Jack's colleague. 'My balls are freezing off.' Both men knew that the hunt was a ruse. Somehow, though, it felt necessary to keep up the pretence, as though the bushes around them had ears. The building behind them did. It had a hundred windows, a thousand ears, a thousand eyes. Every chimney was a lurking menace. Jack gave himself a shake. It was too easy to become frightened when your master was doing something dangerous – it was like being a child caught raiding a bread stall. He pushed away that thought, before memories of his own childhood could rise up and taunt. No thievery, for sure, but –

'Hold up,' said Tom, his peppery beard folding down on his chest. 'Listen. Aye, they're coming in.'

Before he saw anyone, Jack's ears picked up the steady thud of approaching riders. They changed in quality as the hooves moved from grass to gravel. He tossed his head, sending his unruly brown fringe out of his eye as the duke of Norfolk appeared, a retainer at his back. The earl of Moray had presumably departed by some other route. A little cleverness, at least.

As the senior man, Tom went ahead to take the duke's bridle and speak with him. Jack kept his head bowed. The horses were his business, not the great men who sat on them. Still, he could make out a whispered conference, although the words were indistinct. It was a few seconds before he realised they

STEVEN VEERAPEN

had grown louder. Tom was hissing his name.

Jack stepped forward, his head still lowered. He had begun moving towards the retainer's horse when he felt Tom's grip on his arm. Out of the side of his mouth the older man said, 'the duke wants you.' There was awe in his voice. Jack's stomach shifted, and he felt his mouth run dry, but he stepped forward, his thick boots crunching. He thought of walking on eggshells, and then bones, before he chanced a look up.

'Cole?' The duke's voice was high-pitched, a trace of the north rounding out his vowels. Rich north was what all the servants called it – proper-bred north. Jack kept his head down. 'You are Jack Cole?'

'I am that, your Grace.' He swallowed.

'Good man. Look at me when I speak to you.' The duke's command sounded more like a petulant entreaty. But Jack's chin tilted.

The only duke in England was not an impressive man; Jack had never thought so. His presence all came from the clothes. He wore a rich purple suit, with a riding coat trimmed in thick fur. A medallion hung round his neck, the chain links golden. All of it was designed to impress, and to detract from the thin, permanently-surprised face. 'Good. I would talk with you, lad.' As he spoke, Norfolk's eyes darted first up, then down, then side-to-side. They seemed to go anywhere but in the direction of Jack's. 'You have been in my service some time, I understand. In lowly degree.'

'Yes, your Grace.'

'Yes. And you have a wife?'

'I do.'

'Mm-hm. That is a fine thing, to be wed. A fine state. Enjoyed it myself and hope to again. But you have no children.'

'None, my lord. Not … not yet.'

'God give you some soon, then. A young married lad with a fair wife. You shall want advancement. All young men do.' Norfolk nodded at the last, as though in confirmation of his words.

Jack said nothing, lowering his head again. He wondered

6

what might have brought about a sudden promotion. He'd done nothing save shovelling horse shit in the stables and occasionally bringing in the duke's friends' horses when no one more salubrious was available. A little sliver of excitement passed through him. Maybe the duke was going to travel abroad, and he wanted a team of horses and their boys. 'I have in mind for you to move your service elsewhere. It is good that a young man with no ties should move around. Move up.' Evidently the duke did not think of a wife as a tie. 'Would you like that? Would you?'

'I … you wish me to become a chiefer groom?' A sudden crunch on the gravel announced Tom's attitude to that idea.

'What's that, lad? Speak up!' Jack repeated himself. 'Yes, in a fashion. You are aware … you know of the earl of Shrewsbury?'

Jack had heard of him: one of the richest men in England, by all accounts.

'That fine lord has a great number of houses as fine as Arundel, and as great a number of horses. Houses even as fine as this.' Norfolk's arm rose under his cloak, the furs bristling, as he gestured in the direction of the palace. 'I should think there's a place for one such as you and your woman in his household.'

Jack swallowed. Move to the service of another earl? Be thrown into another household? 'Your Grace isn't … uh, displeased with me?' An iron fist clutched at his heart, turning his voice to a petulant squeak. He bore no particular love for the duke of Norfolk, but the thought of being cast out, unwanted, thrown away, was intolerable. It made him feel like an outsider. For a moment he imagined what the duke must see: a whiny boy. Colour crept into his cheeks in a rosy blush. He despised himself for begging - he'd always wanted to be off somewhere, to have a fresh new start, and here it was, in a way. And he was railing against it. Coward.

'Not at all, lad. I mean to give you a chance – advancement. Though he is but an earl, he's a fine one. And a privy councillor before January, if the rumour-mongers speak true.' Norfolk's voice changed; he began to sound like a frustrated schoolmaster, eager to be gentle but already weary of a particularly stupid student. He stopped. Hesitated. 'And you shall still receive my favour. What you get by Shrewsbury … I shall continue to pay. But privately, you understand?' Now he was a man-of-the-world sharing secrets with a lesser mortal. 'You shall tell no one that you are my man. To all the world's eyes and ears you are a gift from me to my friend; I send you with a fine horse and you and your woman are an annuity – a surplus to the gift.'

Jack sensed that the duke was trying, in the way of a stupid man, to make a curse sound like a blessing. 'All I ask,' added Norfolk, 'is that you keep me informed of what passes in my friend's house. He is … he is to have a guest soon, in all likelihood … and I should very much like to correspond.' His eyes were darting more furiously than ever. 'If my letters should arrive … well, you shall see that they get to where they are meant to go. You will be rewarded. If you hold your peace. Do you understand me, la- Jack?' Finally, he looked down at him directly and his narrow eyes blazed.

'Yes, your Grace.' It came out more sullenly than he had intended. He knew he had no choice. When the master commanded, the subject obeyed – it was the same the world over. He was being asked to shift himself and Amy from a comfortable place in a ducal household to the service of some other man, to spy and to make sure letters arrived for some other wealthy patron. All under the guise of being the gift attached to a fine horse. 'Is that all, my lord?'

'That is all, that is all - no more. Unless it haps that you discover anything there that you think it meet I should know, of course. But I leave that to your tender years to judge. Do you take my meaning?'

'Yes, my lord,' lied Jack.

'Capital,' snorted Norfolk. He briefly reached out a gloved hand before retracting it, as though thinking better of touching a young servant. 'Oh, ho!' His hand found better service in a salute, aimed at someone else. Instinctively, Jack turned.

Out of a path further down the edge of the park, another rider was emerging. It was the duke's riding companion, the

Scottish earl, Moray, followed by a brown-bearded retainer. Jack's eyes were sharp. He could see that Moray's brows drew together in irritation at being hallooed so publicly. The Scotsman managed a curt nod in Norfolk's direction before turning away. His shoulders sloping, he pulled his hat low and rode away, gravel flying behind him.

The duke said into the air, 'a fine man for Scotland. Until its right ruler ... Almost one of our own. Come, let us take our own leave of this place. You, boy, you can write your wife, wherever she is – you can write?' He did not wait for an answer, even though Jack opened his mouth to speak. 'And tell her to prepare herself to be presented to the earl. I understand she is one of my laundresses. Soon she might be laundress to that furtive fellow's sister. Advancement, tell her.'

***

'You know who he means?' said Tom, his eyes popping out of his florid face.

They were in the stables at Howard House, the great complex of buildings often still called the Charterhouse: the monastery it had once been. It was the first chance they had had to speak since Jack's talk with the duke. Or the duke's talk at him, he corrected himself. 'The murderess! The Scotch murderess, that's who he means. That Moray's sister ... it's the queen of Scots, that's who he's writing to.'

Jack kicked out at the rush matting and then flopped down on a felled and dressed tree trunk that had been converted into a bench. He flicked away his fringe before speaking. 'So what? It's not fair.' Tom ignored him and he ignored Tom as they launched into two separate, one-sided conversations.

'See, I wondered what he wanted with the Scotch-man. I thought he was done here. The wench's trial will be over and she'll be dead soon enough.'

'I don't see why I should have to go anywhere. Advancement. I got enough of that getting a place in the duke's stables. I ...' he faltered. He had got into the duke's

9

stables by means of his father's office in Norfolk's household, lowly though it was, and he had promised himself long ago never to think of that old tyrant again. Dead and gone. He was glad Tom was barely listening; Tom, like everyone else, knew what his father was like. Instead, he said, 'England's meant to be liberty, not – not slavery. That's what this is, slavery.'

'But why send her to Shewsbury? Why not let her die the death here? Worried it'll bring a rabble out, probably. Better to her keep her head a while yet until the dust settles. Reckon the Scotch don't want her anymore. The French neither. Our master does but.' Tom turned a sly look towards Jack. 'My master, should say.'

Jack thumped a fist on the bench and then drew his knees up. It was a childish gesture and a childish pose, but he didn't care. He still felt like he was being kicked out. 'I dunno what that face is all about, boy. I heard what he said. You'll be getting paid twice.'

'Pfft. What can I do with two men's pay?'

'For Christ's sake, I'll go then! Ungrateful – you're going to a rich lord and having your pockets doubly filled, and you look like you've just been kicked in the balls.'

'I … I know my place here,' said Jack. 'I have …' He was about to say 'friends' and closed his mouth. Tom knew his reputation better than that. No one wanted to be friends with the bland-faced moon man. He had tried, God knew, but he had mucked it up somehow. 'I know where I am here.' He knew the weakness of that, and he knew that Tom knew it.

'You know where you are anywhere in England,' sniffed Tom. 'And skirts are skirts anywhere. You can make new fellows and chase new women.'

The word drew Jack back. 'And Amy – what am I supposed to tell Amy?' Tom shrugged, as though that was unimportant.

'That she can dunk some other folks' piss-stewed bedsheets in another river. What does that matter? You're married five minutes and you're already pecked by thoughts of your wench?'

Jack gave a sour look up at the portly old man in front of him. He knew Amy was just an excuse. They barely knew one another – they had only been married the previous April. He had proposed because she was pretty and made him feel liked, and she said yes because ... he supposed because she really did want and love him. What was important was that she had freshly come up from the country and he could be anything he wanted to be with her. A poet; a warrior; a hero brimming with confidence; a jack-the-lad. She was – she is, he thought – an open book in which he could write his own story.

Tom folded a towel, laid it on the floor and placed some brushes on top of it. Then he sat down too. He reached to the floor and picked up a loose piece of straw, inspecting it as though it were a joint of meat before popping an end in his mouth and chewing. 'Look here,' he said at length, settling a hand on his round stomach. 'You're young yet. All life is about moving around. It's like ...' he struggled, looking around the cavernous stable. 'It's like we're all horses, us lot. Some run wild in the fields and starve in winter. Others get mastered, and polished up, and made good. But we go where our masters direct us, see? We don't run wild. And sometimes they give us away, or what-have-you. And by-and-by we accept it. Cos if we don't, we'll have to run wild, and starve, and go without shoes. So don't worry. Think on what you're getting, not what you're losing. A new start. You can let all the old shit be shovelled clean away. All of it. A chance to be where no one knows anything about ...' He trailed off.

Jack turned, still unsmiling. In his own way, Tom was a kindly man. He treated him almost like a nephew, and so, of course, that was what Jack had tried to be in return. 'I ... yes. I know what you're on about.'

'Do you, clever-boy? What I'm on about is saying you should be scrubbing down those brutes and shovelling their shit. Come on now, look sharp.' He clapped him on the back, half in jest and half to force him up. 'Go on now and tell that pretty wench of yours that she's off to serve the queen of Scots, and ... wait.'

Jack turned, reluctant amusement written on his face. It was a rare thing for him to smile at anyone other than Amy. From the moment he had been old enough to work he had smiled on everyone, until eventually the taunts started: that he was a mad moon-man, a grinning simpleton. He had lost his reason to smile at the world. 'Son ... I know old Norfolk meant you to write to her – he didn't know she was here. But ... only, don't write anything about this business ever, even if you're ever separated. This thing the duke's on at you for. Just be careful what you say. To anyone, wife or not. It's ... well you heard what brought the Scotch queen down. Letters. And that's what you'll be looking after. If they can clap a queen in irons think what they can do to a stable lad.'

2

They had two rooms at Howard House, tiny and mostly empty of things, but a real luxury. You can bet, thought Jack, they wouldn't get that in Shrewsbury's employ, no matter how rich the old man was. He entered the first one, done up as a parlour, and took off his dirty jerkin. On the little uneven shelf Amy had put up a few sprigs of holly. He could hear her whistling in the next room, but he didn't greet her right away. The right way of announcing his acquiescence to a move hadn't formed in his mind. A button fell off as he wriggled out of the coat and skittered away across the floor. Damn it! He held up the ruined garment to see if it was still serviceable, but the two sides wouldn't come together. Urgh! In a swift movement he tore the whole thing asunder.

Instantly, shame crept in, the sudden flare of annoyance gone. It had been a stupid thing to do. Now Amy would have a harder job of mending it, all from a split second of temper. It was a bad sign, the inability to control the temper. He feared it a little. People always said that that kind of madness, sudden and wild, could run in the blood like a poison. He ran a hand through his hair sheepishly before picking up the tattered garment and crossing to the low door and into the next room.

Amy had her back to him. Her hands were thrust deep into a huge bowl of frothy water, her forearms stained grey. 'Sweetheart,' he said. The word still tasted odd. Her whistling stopped, and she half turned, her cheek dimpling, so that she is in profile.

'Husband,' she said, her voice light but pert. 'What news?'

'I've ... I've torn my coat.'

'Throw it on the floor there.' Her skirt jerked as she kicked out at the floor. 'I'll have a look later.'

He did as she said, then smiled. Hers was infectious, and he went to her, circling his hands round her waist. 'Hey – I'm all grimy, leave off!' But her voice was full of laughter. When he didn't let go, she took a handful of the dirty water and threw it around her side at him.

'What have you done today?'

'I've taken in some linen, cleaned it, got it out to dry. Mad stuff.'

'Is Parky still at you?' 'Parky' was Mrs Parkin, the duke's chief laundress and scourge of the female staff. A necessary evil in a widower's house.

'You wouldn't believe – see when we're anywhere near London, she thinks she's the queen herself. Listen to this...' He did, as Amy launched into one of her tales of Mrs Parkin's depredations. He didn't just nod and smile, but became animated as she spoke, taking her part. That, he had begun to think, was how you knew you were in love. The aimless tales, the daily struggles, the minor woes: no matter how much you heard the same dull stories, you didn't tire of them. It was the singer you heard, not the song.

At length, Amy finished, wiping a grubby hand on her skirts. 'There we are, another one to clean,' she said, looking down with amused regret before shrugging. 'What a life. Anyway. I've been prattling like a fool. What have you been doing this morning?'

'Ah,' he said, pulling out a stool and beckoning her to sit. She looked amused again. 'You're being awful gentlemanly. I could get used to this.' Then a furrow creased her brow. 'You said you tore a shirt – did something happen? Has that old Tom been nagging?' He sat close by her, on their low bed.

'No, it wasn't my ... never mind the coat,' he said, a little crisply. He was clearly wearing his shirt, and she knew he never removed it unless it was full dark. 'Or Tom. It's ... well, the duke was out hunting today, with that Scotch earl. He ... afterwards he asked to speak to me himself. Man to man.' One of her fair eyebrows arched. 'The thing is, he said he wants us to leave his service.' He swallowed, unsure what to expect.

'He's given us the boot?'

'No, no. No – nothing like that. No, he ordered – he's commanded – that we move to a different household. Shrewsbury, wherever that is.'

'The earl of Shrewsbury?'

'Yes, he's … he's giving the earl a horse, a gift. And we're to go with it. But to stay on, in his service.'

Amy's gaze fell to her hands, still wet, and she clasped them as she digested the news. 'Is that all?'

'Yes. I tried to say we were very happy here, that we didn't wish to go anywhere, but –'

'Are you?'

'Am I what?'

'Happy here.'

Jack shrugged. 'I … it's not bad. I know my job. I know the people.'

'And they know you,' she said, and he thought he detected an odd note in her voice. 'And me. So we know people. We'll get to know people in Shrewsbury. It's all well away from London anyway, is it not? So what does it matter? We'll go together, it's not like he's tearing us apart, is it? He'll be a married man, Shrewsbury. I just bet that the wife's a dragon.' Something seemed to light up her face – realisation. 'Hold, he's married to Bess, isn't he? Of Hardwick? The woman with many husbands. Oh, Jack – we shall be well enough with them. A mistress, eh? Better than working for a widower.'

'Right,' said Jack, putting an arm out. She got up off the chair and collapsed on the bed beside him. It sagged even closer to the floor as she folded into his arm.

'Changing service in one big house for another. What does it matter?'

There was wisdom in her words, Jack felt. Neither of them had any real family left. Being part of service meant you made your own family wherever you fetched up. 'So, Mr and Mrs Cole go off to join the earl of Shewsbury's house, from the duke of Norfolk.' She giggled as he spoke. 'What?'

'Mr and Mrs Cole,' she echoed. 'We sound so old. Proper married, respectable old folk.' He liked the sound of that, though he had always detested his name. He let the image wash into his mind, as he had often fantasised when lying beside her in bed these past months. Mr and Mrs Cole – a good married couple, hard-working, he fearless and calm and she kind and a little colourful. Preoccupied with children, maybe. A perfect family, devout and well-liked, no secrecy between them and no past behind them. It was what every other family in Christendom seemed to have, save his own.

'We'll be gentlefolk before you know it – arms, the freedom of any town, you wait and see. Think on that. What would you want on our arms? A kitten for you?' He touched her nose lightly.

'I don't think – why a kitten?'

'Well then, what? What would suit me, eh?'

'I … a chameleon.'

'A what? A lizard?' asked Jack, drawing away from her with a puzzled look. 'Why a lizard?'

'Well a bird then – I don't know – this is foolishness.' Her laughter flattened and died and she changed the subject, a little too quickly, Jack thought. 'Anyway you know what I'd be happy with.' He did. It was Amy's dream to have enough money one day to leave service and open a little shop somewhere, where she could sew things up and he could sell them. He had claimed to agree wholeheartedly with her that it was an excellent plan. It was what she had wanted to hear. 'Here. Why the earl of Shrewsbury? Why does the duke want to favour him all of a sudden?'

'I dunno. I couldn't exactly go asking him that.'

'Mmm. I suppose not. When do we go?'

'He didn't say. Just to be ready, like. The horse is a new year's gift. The rich folk always like those in January, new year or not.'

She nudged her head against his shoulder once and then stood, kneading the small of her back. 'That soon, eh? Well, that's plenty of time enough, weeks and weeks yet. How long does it take to get there? Will it be dangerous?'

'I dunno,' he said, rubbing at the side of his nose. 'I'll watch over you, Mrs Cole.' She smiled at that, and it was a smile free of any kind of mockery. He liked that. He could be anything to Amy; that was what had first attracted him to her when she had arrived as a junior laundress at Arundel. He'd heard whispers about the new girl: that she had altogether too much to say for herself – 'too broad-mouthed by half, that little mare, but fit for riding' – but that was good. He liked to listen more than he liked to talk. She knew nothing about him, about what a weak little child he had been. To her he might be a great hero, bold, from a loving family. He could remember the words of courtship he had used to her: 'whatever you want me to be, Amy Wylmot, I will be that'. He had meant them.

***

A few days before Christmas, on solstice day, the wind that carried frost into the courtyard of Howard House brought with it song and the stench of wine. All over London, wealthy merchants, nobles, and young lawyers were already looking forwards to making merry. The poor, too, were eagerly anticipating downing tools, burning yule logs, and sharing bread with their neighbours. Added cheer, too, came in speculation. 'Mary Queen of Scots shall have her head chopped off' sang the religious-minded, their cheeks aglow. The religious-minded of the other persuasion said nothing. It was better that way, especially in London.

With the news that the fallen Queen Mary was having her fate deliberated by the Queen and her council came wilder tales. More monstrous fish had washed up on the Thames; a two-headed calf had been born somewhere in the north; a woman had given birth to a cat. People were going from house to house crying out that the signs of portent were upon England – although what was portended nobody quite knew. Still, it felt like 1569 was going to be a year of wonders.

The gossip has reached Howard House too, but the staff said little. The lives and deaths of the great were for their master to chew over, not them. No one liked a servant with an opinion.

Amy Cole, never much interested in the glossy personal lives of their superiors, had, too, other things on their mind as the house was stocked with Christmas fare and rumours of plague in the outer reaches of London swirled.

You could fit your whole life in an armful of packages. That is exactly what Amy found when they'd gathered their things together, folded them into sackcloth, and secured them with string. It was no different really, from moving from one great house to another during a sweetening: the faces at the destination might change, but you were still on the road. Amy had put on a travelling cloak with a hood, and fancied that she looked quite dashing and mysterious in it. Jack, however, looked very young in his mended jerkin and outsized gloves. She watched as he tossed his head back, flinging away the fringe that always hung down over one eye. It was a gesture she loved. It was one of the few that she felt was truly his.

They were gathered in the courtyard, ready to leave the duke of Norfolk's service. There was no farewell party; everyone had work to be getting on with. Mrs Parkin, though, had given her a sovereign and wished her well. The other girls – the shallow-minded team in which she worked – did likewise but without the money. It was an easy parting. Amy liked them – most of them – but they weren't her family. Her family had all departed the world, her mother last of all, gifting her a lifetime's worth of useless platitudes. It was over a year since Nan Wylmot had been sewn into the winding sheet that she'd put together herself, and still she lived on in the little things. They made Amy feel that part of her past still lived.

 Chief amongst the pearls the increasingly eccentric old woman had given Amy was that she ought to marry a man in need of a mother. 'Be their mother, and they shall never leave you, and you shall never be their slave', she had said. Amy had never really understood what that meant until she met Jack Cole.

 She looked at him as he stood by the new horse, at his youthful, always-frightened face, and thought she had begun to understand. Her husband, she knew, was a chameleon, his personality still unstamped. He had as much as told her that he would be anyone to her, if she willed it, like a man of clay. He'd reached out to her like a drowning man when she'd arrived at Norfolk's house with a letter from her aunt protesting what an expert seamstress and washerwoman she was. She didn't know why at first – she had never been one to stir great emotion in any man in the village, pretty without beauty, she thought – until she realised that he'd been waiting for someone just like her. Fresh from the backside of nowhere-in-particular and looking for advancement, work, and wonder.

Yes, he was a chameleon – but one who had been found out and shunned for it, the poor fool. That was the thing about living in a great household. Once gained, you wore your reputation like your master's badge, right there on your chest and back. Once you were known as a man who had nothing to say for himself, and who would give the same fair words to all, you soon found yourself with no one. She had pitied him his awkward attentions. They were endearing, in a way. And in the course of her digging about the household for stories about him, well –

'You ready?'

'Ready,' she said, sparked out of her memories.

'It's just the road we take down from the north for part of the way. The earl's household should be waiting for us by now. The duke's given me papers.'

'That's good.'

'Yep,' he said, patting at the big white stallion he'd be riding. She could see the pride on his face and thought for a moment she was seeing the real him in the boyish excitement.

'Can you control that big beast?'

'Of course,' he said, giving her a grin. His teeth were all very white. Today he was trying out his cocky, impressive guise – the one she found far less endearing than the lost boy. That was the problem with men. They seemed to think that their most tiresome personas were the ones women found most attractive. Absurdly, a snatch of verse her mother used to recite rang in her head: Why is our life so cruel and dark, that men no longer speak to friend, why does evil so clearly mark, the monstrous government of men? She shook it away.

'A stallion fit for an earl. Or a queen,' she smiled.

'What? What d'you mean?'

'Just what I say,' she said primly, enjoying her own chance to be mysterious.

'You … you know what all this is about?'

'I'm not deaf,' she laughed. 'Jack, the whole household has

been abuzz about where the queen of Scots is likely to fetch up, and it's not Scotland. Us girls were drawing lots on who would have the charge of her.'

'But ... this is the duke's ... I don't think I was supposed to ...'

'Don't worry, I didn't say anything much. I played dumb. I bet down that she'd go to the block. I mean, she killed her husband, didn't she?'

The question rang out into the morning and was lost in the ringing sound of metalwork and splash of buckets being slopped out. All of London knew that the Scottish queen had killed her husband, been tried for it, and found ... well, no one really understood what Queen Elizabeth had decided – which, if the gossip floating around was true, was nothing yet. A decision might be published after Twelfth Night said those who were keeping their ears to the ground.

Whether Mary Stuart was guilty or not guilty didn't really matter to Amy. If one rich woman killed a rich man, what did it matter? She shivered at the thought. Still, it would be an exciting thing to be part of a household with a scandalous woman hidden away in it. It would be interesting enough to see her in the flesh, the famous Mary. If she had to wash her sheets – well, you could learn things from people, especially people reviled as whores, from their sheets.

'Keep your voice down, Amy. Here, let me give you a hand up.'

Once they were both mounted, they began their trot out of the courtyard, leaving behind the duke of Norfolk's household. Once outside, the cobblestones gave way to sucking mud, and smoke filled the air. The high walls of Howard House sat cheek to cheek against hovels. Elizabeth's London was down to their right, thought Amy, glancing that way – and she had never liked what lay within it. Everything was crooked, from the people to the streets to the dwellings. No style matched, and outside the big estates there was no symmetry or prettiness to please the eye. The southern people barely seemed English. They seemed instead Londonish. Coarse. Constantly fighting over scraps and hostile to anyone who didn't sound like them.

She took one hand off the bridle to knead the small of her back. It was an old gesture of her mother's: 'crack your back; it chases away the agues before they can start'. As she did so her stomach arched forward, small and hard. In a new life she might not be a mother to Jack but might become a mother to his sons, she thought. He had never mentioned children to her, but she assumed that he had married her to get some. Partly, at least. Strange how changes made you think of other changes. But no; one thing at a time. She knew she would have to keep an eye on her husband in this strange new world they were being sent to. Oh, not in the way some women keep hawkish eyes on their men – he was no roving bawd – but in his endless desire to please, to be all things to all men … well, who knew what the servants of the earl of Shrewsbury might be like.

3

The people of London hated working, it seemed. There were days to go until the first of Christmas, and already it seemed a fever of festivity had infected the people. In country households the revelries during the festive period jigged onwards, but someone was always doing the cleaning. In Norfolk's household they took turns. One day the laundresses would drink sack, and each have a bite of a fruit tart whilst the stable lads swept up; the next day the stable lads would pass around ale and put their feet up whilst the laundresses served them. In the city, business started to grind to a halt and the middens began overflowing even before the festive season properly began.

Jack led Amy through a tribe of masked men thronging Aldersgate Street. 'Ho, fellow, what a horse!' called up the leader. The mask was black. It seemed you couldn't set foot outside in London without being accosted. Whether they were brigands or simply young lawyers practising their festive foolery a few days early was unclear.

'Thank you,' nodded Jack.

'And what a wench.' Jack crimsoned, knowing he should say something valiant, defend his wife's honours. Instead he said, 'right, let us pass. We're on business.'

'There's no business on a holiday!'

'The duke has business every day.' He took advantage of the brief conference the duke of Norfolk's name brought to urge the horse forward, turning to make sure Amy was behind him. She was, and she didn't look put out.

'Ho, you owe us passage,' shouted the leader of the masquers. 'It's tradition – you owe us!'

'We owe you the sight of our horse's arses,' shouted back Amy.

'You … a stranger-bitch with fire in her guts!'

They didn't follow, moving on to unmounted marks. Jack

kept his head down as he rode forward; Amy held hers high. 'You're not sad about missing the revels, are you?' he asked her, feeling the need to say something.

'More than a week of making merry with folk I already have to look in the face every single day? No, thank you.' He turned ahead again, pleased by her impish smile.

The pair had been commanded to meet with the earl of Shrewsbury's train on the Aldersgate, where it met Pickaxe Street. The large group could be heard before they could be seen, and when they did rise into view, it was as a palette of colours. Some men and women were mounted, others were wading through the muck and passing around tankards. At the head of the procession was a sturdy-looking little man, leaning down from his horse to converse with a slighter, lankier figure.

Jack led Amy towards the group and resisted a smile as the white stallion drew gasps and slight cheers. He drew level with the line of men and women and fumbled in his breast pocket for his letter. Or had he stowed it in the pocket hanging from his belt? No, it was between his shirt and doublet. He was still digging when the lanky man detached himself from his conversation and skipped lightly through the mire towards him.

'Yes?' he asked through his nostrils. He wore a livery with the earl's badge prominent – the outfit of a secretary or official of the household.

'I come from his Grace the duke of Norfolk,' said Jack, trying consciously to deepen his voice. 'I have been commanded to bring this horse for your master as a token of his Grace's deep affection. His ... his deep affection towards the earl.' Damn it, he though; he had started out so well.

'Is that so?' The man's eyes ran greedily over the horse. It stood stock-still, almost seeming aware of its breeding and value. 'I am Woodward – Thomas Woodward – the earl's steward. You have some writing from the duke?'

'Yep – yes, I do.' Jack fished out the letter and handed it over. Woodward took it without looking at it. Instead he studied Jack with detachment. An awkward silence fell between them, neither man sure exactly what to say.

Eventually Woodward broke it.

'My master will be most thankful. Can I help you down from the brute? I fear the earl does not have the duke's gift ... here ... he had planned to send it on the first. He is only returning to Chatsworth for a brief spell to see the countess – he will be back at court after Twelfth Night.'

'Begging your pardon, Mr Woodward, but it's in the letter that my wife and I are to go with the horse. We're to join the earl's household. I am a master horseman and my wife a laundress. It's ... it's in the letter,' he repeated lamely.

'What? I ... I wasn't told. More servants, more? The earl's household does seem to be getting busy this day. Ugh...' Something in the man's tired, thin face seemed to give. 'Ah, well - if anyone serves me, he must follow me; and where I am, there will my servant be also. So says the gospel of John.'

'What is this, Thomas?' cut in a new voice. It was the man who had been mounted before Woodward had come down the line towards Jack. With surprise Jack realised it must be the earl of Shrewsbury. He was a man of about forty, his hair receding at the front but only on either side of a wispy fringe which hung doggedly down his forehead. He had more the look of a friendly merchant than a magnate, and he stood in the muddy road with his hands clasped behind his back as he leant forward: the pose of an older man. 'A fine, fine horse,' he said, warmth radiating from his eyes.

Woodward passed him the letter, his head bowed. He slipped open the seal and read aloud. The duke had written that Jack was a master horse keeper and Shrewsbury emphasised the words with a questioning inflection. Then he smiled again, a little wearily, and said, 'you are welcome to my household then, Jack Cole. And Mrs Cole. I hope you will give me good service and for my part I will reward it. I'm afraid I have a master of horse, but ... yes – Mr Woodward, you are worthy enough of your own horse man. Mr Cole here can be your man, in name at least. Until he has proven himself.' Then again, 'what a fine, fine horse.' Jack felt awkwardness envelope him. He liked Shrewsbury instantly, and yet knew he might be required to do things under the old chap's nose.

24

Further, although he had removed his hat, he was aware that he was sitting mounted whilst his new master stood in the muck. Monstrous fish and two-headed calves swam and skipped briefly through his mind.

'Well, let us be off,' said Shrewsbury, clapping his hands together. 'I have promised my wife in faith that I would be with her before Christmas Day. Woodward, see to my new people. See that they are well tended on the road.' He gave the horse one last lingering look and then strode back towards the front of the group.

'Right. Well.' The steward looked behind him to the departing back of Shrewsbury. 'As a rule I should say I don't like female servants. You did say you are married? Properly, in the eyes of God?'

'We are, sir.'

'Yes. Good. Well then, you are come from a great house. You know the rules. It's for your woman to see to such menial work as might be required. Mr Cole, you know your duty. Be ever ready with good answer, ready to serve, and gentle of cheer. So that men may say "there goes a fine officer". Be courteous of knee, soft of speech, keep your hands clean and nails – take care of the earl's livery when you have it. Do not cough or spit too loudly and keep your fingers out of your ears and nose. Keep your countenance fair at all times and above all, young man, do not lie. Ever.

'You, Cole, you can ride abreast with Mr ...' he paused, biting on a lip as though he couldn't quite remember, his mind so filled with his new recruit speech. 'Mr Heydon. Your wife can ride with the laundresses. At the back. We must move now to make the most of the day. I shall have to find some place for you at Chatsworth when we get there. Of course, you realise that it might be a tight fit. We were given leave to expect a horse, not the servants with it.' His lip curled downwards in silent rebuke at the last. 'Still,' he added grudgingly, 'I extend you our master's welcome.' With that he turned on his heel and loped after the earl.

'Well,' called Amy over the noise of the street, 'that's us told.'

'Yes,' said Jack, turning in his seat. 'You go with the women at the back.' As she nudged her little horse towards them, Jack thought: who the hell is Heydon? He began asking around until eventually he was pointed towards a man his own age, clean-shaven and dressed in grey. 'Mr Heydon?'

'That's me.' The inflection of his voice was strange; there was something flat and unaccented in it. He sat his horse with one hand on his hip, the other holding the bridle as though it were a napkin and he at a grand dining table. Cropped brown hair showed under a plumed hat, and a silvery-black short cloak was pinned at one shoulder.

'Mr ...' Shit, thought Jack. He had only just heard the steward's name and already it was out of his mind. 'The earl's steward said I'm to ride with you.'

'Good – I was getting worried I'd have no one to talk to all the way north.' Heydon gave him a long look up and down and then something seemed to break, light pouring into his face. It transformed him. 'Well then, we might as well be friends. Call me Philip.'

'Philip – I'm Jack. Jack Cole.'

'Well, Jack Cole, that's some horse you have there.'

'A gift from the duke of Norfolk,' he beamed, his chest expanding.

'I see. And you?'

'A gift from the duke of Norfolk,' said Jack, and both men laughed. There was something freeing in laughter, something that put one at ease. 'I'm newly come to help with the horses.'

'So, a new man. Well then, you and I will get along just fine. Come, fall into line and you can tell me about yourself.'

'I'd rather hear about this household. Since I'm a new man. You know, who to watch out for, who's fierce and that. What do you do?'

'I'm ... a secretary. Ha – nah, man, that sounds too grand. No, I'm a man of letters, really. I can tutor in the classics and write, stamp, and seal.' Jack had the vague impression he was being read the man's wares. Privately he wondered why the earl of Shrewsbury would require a tutor; perhaps he had children. As though answering his thought, Heydon said,

'There was some trouble with the countess's old tutor. Well, her children's old tutor. He left. Left a gap for a gentleman to fill, though the children are now off into the world. Every great house can do with a spare reader and scribe. See, my old man, gentleman he was, he wanted me reared in a noble house. To learn the ways of England, he said – the old ways. But I was a rakehell of a lad and went off my own way. But better late than never – and the earl never refuses a northern man of good name. How about you – you a married man?'

'I am that. Wife's riding with the women.'

'I see.' Heydon looked vaguely down the line of people before turning back to Jack and dropping his voice. 'I'm acting as a secretary but hoping for better things.'

'Aren't we all?'

'All what?'

'Hoping for better things.'

'I suppose so. What do you hope for, Jack? What do you and your wife hope for?'

Jack thought for a moment. He considered parroting the usual lines about providing good service and being a good and honest man. Instead he said, 'I dunno. I'd like to travel one day.'

'Oh, travel. I've travelled. It's a rare thing.'

'Where? Where to?'

'Everywhere. You name a place and I'll tell you if I've been there.'

'I don't … France?'

'Oh yes, I've been to Paris. The Sorbonne, the student quarter. Good wine, but some of those students and their foolish ideas … But the women.' He clicked gloved fingers, giving no sound. 'Not like here. Not half so timid. Where else?'

'Italy!'

'Italy,' said Heydon, his eyes clouding. 'You don't ask much, do you? Haha – yes, I've trod the Via Appia Antica once or twice. Is that where you'd like to go?'

'I dunno. Haven't thought that far ahead. The world. The whole wide world. That's where I'd like to see. Not just

England, I mean.'

'There's a fine thought,' said Heydon. 'I share a bit of that myself still. The fever for travel still rages, though I've done it aplenty – grows hotter, in fact. Well it's natural, isn't it, that young fellows should want to see all the noise and the hurly-burly of the wide world. To furrow our oats in foreign ground and yield to God and fortune.'

'God and fortune,' echoed Jack. He liked the sound of that. 'Yep, a fine thought, like you say.'

'You'll get a bellyful of God from Woodward,' smiled Heydon. 'Likes his Bible. They all call him the preacher.' Jack filed that away: a nickname for his master might make Amy laugh. Then he frowned at the thought of having to listen to sermons endlessly. Heydon seemed to read his face. 'Oh, don't worry; I'm not like that. No, no, no. No time for hot gospelling.' Something intense seemed to fire up the man's eyes. 'I reckon you wouldn't find that out in the wide world, eh?'

'Maybe not,' said Jack. His smile, he knew, had become fixed. The conversation was already drowning him.

'Well let's not turn down that path. Look here, we're moving out. Make tracks, beast!' Heydon's horse refused to move. 'Would you look at that? A horse who says nay and means it.'

Jack laughed. He leant over and clapped the horses rear, which made it stumble forward. Heydon smiled an embarrassed smile and Jack silently recorded the weak joke in his mind. He might be able to pass it off as his own if he ever needed to be witty.

And so they were off. The cavalcade had picked up on the earl's lead and begun to trot forwards in unison. Tankards were hastily placed in saddle bags and the murmur of conversation changed in pitch as people began to focus on avoiding the more miry patches of ground. Behind them London fell away, and the poor came out to grab at the horses and cry up for alms.

Jack Cole began to think that the new life he hadn't asked for and had only dreamily wanted might just be the start of something good after all.

***

At the back of the little procession of animals, men, and women, Amy had joined her fellow female servants. There were few of them; most women had apparently remained with the countess whilst a small team had accompanied the earl to do the menial tasks. Mostly they were matrons. That was her lot now and she welcomed it. Better to have a little status as a married matron than be a feather-brained girl amongst feather-brained girls. Still, it was to her disappointment that, as the earl's people moved out, the almost-offensively polite women servants seemed to have no inclination to talk about anything other than her husband. Some women, she thought, seemed to wish to talk about nothing else when they got together than men.

She dutifully answered questions in as vague a manner as she could; it wouldn't do to get her new colleagues' backs up. However, as she made answers like, 'Jack wishes to be a good and honest servant to the earl'; 'no, the duke was a kind and good master, as will be the earl'; and 'no, we heard nothing about the Scotch queen or her husband in the duke's household', her mind sharpened and focused elsewhere.

At first, she thought it was her imagination. The road out of London was bound to be well-travelled and busy, especially when everyone seemed to be ducking work. But no, the further they rode, as the buildings fell away to open fields, the surer she became. Someone was following them.

She had spotted the fellow out the corner of her eye when they had waited to move out from Aldersgate: it was his costume which drew her. He was swathed in dark dun, the colour of mud; a rough brown hat hid his upper features, and a brown scarf buried his lower ones. He had been lurking between two buildings, peering out at them. When they had moved off, she had thought him to have been no more than a thief awaiting a chance. If he was, he was a persistent one. And he had a horse.

At the troupe moved northwards towards Derbyshire, the man in brown followed, never actually joining them, never passing them, and always seeming to pause when the earl's steward called a rest. She considered telling the other women; she couldn't tell the steward or any other man, for they would not listen. But the women seemed lost in their own chatter about London; about their husbands; about children growing up; about how prettily Chatsworth was coming to be; and, when excitement overtook them, about the mysterious Scottish queen and whether she would live or die. And so the man followed.

It was an unsettling feeling. She began to wonder exactly what kind of frightening and ill-portended life she and Jack might have been thrust into.

4

Chatsworth was not Arundel. It was not Howard House, or Hampton Court, or even Nonsuch Palace. It was something different and something new. It had the word 'modernity' built into its stone and timbers. It was the newness that appealed to Jack as the earl and his servants led the way into the straight, square-fronted building's courtyard on Christmas Eve. Scaffolding stood about, abandoned in the late afternoon darkness. Shrewsbury was helped down from his horse and immediately vanished into the house, apparently eager to be reunited with his wife. The servants began to dismount and disperse. Well, thought Jack, this was it. A new start.

The few days' ride out of London had been an illuminating one. At each rest stop he was reunited with Amy as the pair slept together on pallets in the inns the earl commandeered, but during the ride he was side-by-side with Philip Heydon. His new friend – and friend he really seemed to be – had regaled him with stories of his adventures abroad and promised Jack that one day they would go out and see the world together. Like brothers, he had said. He had told him also of the Shrewsburys: how they were very much in love; how the countess's children from a previous marriage were betrothed to the earl's; and how it was all but confirmed that the loving couple would soon have custody of the Scottish queen. He seemed dismayed that Jack had no opinion on the Scottish queen and dropped hints that he would soon know her better – they all would. Only when Heydon asked about Norfolk and Jack's role as a horse keeper did the latter grow evasive. Taking the hint, Heydon always turned the subject back to more innocuous things. It was a nice feeling to have a friend. Hitherto Jack had only known older men who spoke down to him or men his own age who scorned him as two-faced and double-dealing when he tried to show friendship equally to all.

'Get yourselves into doors,' said a harried-looking Woodward, his clothes mud-splattered but his face alive with authority. 'You shall have a chamber above the stables, a single room. I suppose your wife will want to lie with you rather than with the other maids on the laundry floor?' He didn't wait for an answer. 'But remember that it is not your property but the earl's. You might needs have to leave it at any point if it is needed for someone greater than a horseman and his wench. And get that bloody great beast housed and seen to. I must attend on the master.' He gestured in the direction of one wall of the house, lined with real glass windows, and then hurried on, issuing directions and commands as he went.

Jack had dismounted, and Amy had joined him. He noticed that the other servants, each seeming to know what they were doing, had abandoned their horses and realised with a start that he was now expected to deal with them. He gave a frightened look to Amy, but it was not her who answered it. It was Philip Heydon.

'Jack, the stable is over there. If the earl's master of horse is absent, then there will be some boys about. Don't be afraid to show them your authority.'

'Yes, Mr Heydon.'

'Please, call me Philip when we are just us. Ah, this must be your lovely wife. Mrs Cole, yes?'

Heydon swept off his cap and bowed to Amy. Jack had told her all about him, but she had, annoyingly, avoided every opportunity on the road to speak to him herself. 'Yes,' she said. 'I'm Mistress Cole. And pleased I am to meet you.' Jack didn't like her tone. It was cold, distant, not like her at all.

'I think we shall get to become friends, mistress, in time. You have a fine husband and you do him proud. Although I confess I had preferred the pleasure of riding here with you rather than your husband.' He paused his suddenly eloquent flow when he saw Amy pulling a face at him. 'At present I must go and find where I am to lodge. Good morrow to you.' Again he bowed, clapped Jack on the shoulder, and strode off as if he owned the place.

Silence had descended on the courtyard, the twilight and the cold making it seem a crystalline, self-contained world. 'Your friend,' said Amy, 'is a man of charm.'

'You were a bit rude to him, Amy – don't you like him?'

'I don't know him. He's your friend.'

'He's a gentleman and a scholar. How about that? Us friends with a gentleman – that' a fine thing, isn't it?'

'That depends on the gentleman. Though I think he's not as witty as he thinks he is.'

'Well … maybe his jesting is a little …' Jack struggled, a little needle of conflicted loyalty stabbing at him.

'Me, I think I'd laugh harder at my own funeral than his jesting. Why, I wonder, should a gentleman take such interest in a man who works in the stables?'

'Philip's a traveller, he says he doesn't think of the world of rank and all that. He says in all the world we are one people and one faith.'

'What? One faith? And Philip, is it?' Amy's brow knitted.

'Ugh, he just means that there need be no stout walls of rank between friends. He thinks we're his friends.'

'He thinks you are his friend.'

Jack folded his arms. He did not care for his wife's strange show of dislike, and he didn't want to encourage it. That wasn't how he'd imagined their new life starting out at all. 'I can't leave the horses out here,' he said, hoping to stop an awkward silence in its tracks. 'Can you shift for yourself and find our chamber?' He hoped she would take care of that for him – the thought of having to enter the great house without knowing exactly where to go brought on an extra wave of anxiety.

'Yes, husband,' she said. There was no humour in the use of the word this time. He wondered if something else was on her mind.

'Here, did you see a man in brown when we set out? And again on the road?' she asked, as though in answer.

'A man …' Jack cast his mind back. 'Yes, I think so. Once or twice. A pedlar or something. All muffled against the cold. 'Some silvery hair under a cap, I think.'

'Did he? I just saw the cap and scarf.'

'What about him?'

'Just didn't like the look of him, that's all.'

'Well we got here without him robbing us. So that's something, isn't it?'

'I suppose,' she said, a little reluctantly.

'Good girl.' He paused, before adding, 'I love you, Amy.'

'I love you too,' she said, and the warmth of her smile cracked the ice that had started up between them.

***

Amy asked her way to their chamber up an outside staircase and along a wood-panelled corridor. There was a sprawling collection of rooms some way above the stable block. As she had discovered from speaking with her fellow matrons on the road, there were few female servants. Instead, there was the usual male chain of command, with steward, butlers, ushers, waiters, cupbearers, servers and carvers each vying for authority. It was the steward, the haughty Mr Woodward, who attempted to run the place as a military operation.

On finding their new home, a tiny chamber with two separate beds, she sat down and put her head in her hands. The mysterious man in brown seemed to have given up – or got better at hiding – by the time they had reached Derbyshire, but still he poked his head into her thoughts. She could not escape the feeling that something unpleasant was about to happen, that she and Jack had been led into something much bigger than themselves. She looked around the bare chamber, more akin to a monastic cell than a bedroom. She supposed it was designed to be a place for heads to droop at the end of the day and nothing more. It was all plastered and clean, but soulless. Well, she would just have to change that. Sighing, she got up off the bed, wincing at a loose straw that poked through the rough canvas. Typical. The beds were as rough as possible, the better to prevent people oversleeping and shirking work. She worked it back in and, when it proved stubborn, kicked the bed.

She had taken her pack from her horse and began to unwrap

it. Onto the beds went her spare sleeves and her mother's trinkets. On tiptoes, she placed the sprig of holly she had brought above the door lintel. Tomorrow would be Christmas, she mused – the start of the days of revelry. A good chance to meet the new folk when they were all drunk and happy, and to take advantage of being new herself.

One man she did not trust yet was Mr Philip Heydon. For all her husband had raved about what an exciting man he was, she had no interest in a much-storied young gentleman. Annoyingly, Jack hadn't taken up her attempts to belittle the man with anything like the enthusiasm she had expected; normally he would read her attitude and mirror it. Something about Heydon must have been stronger than her own will. Everyone knew about the hijinks, the madcap schemes, that such young fellows got up to. Wenching, carousing, politics: if her husband got himself in thrall to this man, she knew he would eagerly join him in anything. She would just have to watch out for him, that was all. She would just have to be his mother.

It was some time later that Jack found her. 'You were a time,' she said. 'Are the horses seen to?'

'Yes,' he said. His arms were laden with bread and cheese. 'Look!'

They ate a while in silence. 'What do you think of the place? It's fine, isn't it?'

'It is,' she said, one cheek distended. 'A fine place. The other women seem pleasant enough.'

'We'll like it here, don't you think?'

'I hope so.' She realised she was being moody. 'Yes, Jack, I reckon we'll like it here. Food, a roof, work, each other – what else do we need?'

'Nothing,' he beamed. 'I knew you would like it here. I like it.'

'Did you meet the earl's horse master?'

'No. No, he wasn't there. In fact, the stable lads told me that he never is, not except on special days. In truth, they said the earl has been in need of a new man to tend the horses. So, it's like a step ahead for me. For us. That's good, isn't it?'

'Yes, Jack,' she said, patting his head. 'That's very good.'

'What's better is that tomorrow's Christmas. So we don't even have to start working straight away. Who gets a holiday right before starting a new job of work, eh? Mr and Mrs Cole, that's who.'

Before she could reply, the door opened without a knock and a little head popped in. 'Mr Woodward says to say the earl wants all the house in the great hall now,' said the page. Then, 'you have to put this on, Mr.' He thrust out a bundle. Jack got up, took it, and the boy was gone before he could thank him and ask him where the great hall was.

With his back to Amy, Jack changed out of his dirty doublet and slipped the livery over his head, brushing a hand over the rough-sewn badge. She laced on fresh sleeves and, taking her little brush, wiped off the worst of the dust that had got under her riding cloak. 'Come on,' she said, inspecting him. 'That looks good on you. Better than the duke's.' Then a sharpness came into her eyes. 'Though they could do with finer seamstresses here, I reckon. Anyway, they told me where the hall is. Let's go.'

Thanks to Amy, they found the great hall on the east side of the courtyard. It was a cavernous room and still it was filled to capacity. The smell of fire mingled with sweat and the chalky scent of broken rushes, all of it emanating in a hot, heavy wave out of the double doors. They filed in through an antechamber, where a tubby little man in a tabard ostentatiously checked their names against a ledger and inspected their hands and shoes. 'Hey! Out, you brute, out!' the usher hissed, making them both jump. A dog had attracted his attention and he manoeuvred his froglike body around them, clapping his hands until he had chased it outside. Shrugging at one another, Jack led Amy into a press of warmth, light and heat. Conversation rippled. 'It's all settled'; 'he's going to tell us tonight'; 'no, he'll wait until after the revels'. A few heads turned in their direction, giving them appraising looks, but no one tried to engage them.

'What's it all about?' Amy asked, grabbing at the sleeve of an older woman she didn't know. She felt Jack stiffen, as he sometimes did when she was pointed, but if she let that bother her, the two would live in silence and dumb ignorance all their lives.

'Who are you?'

'The new laundress. Is the earl to wish us a happy Christmas?'

'Yes. No.' The woman's jowls bounced, her skin loose and leathery. 'I mean yes, he will – but he's going to tell us what to expect. They say the Scotch queen is coming into his care – under this roof. Herself! He'll have to say something about that, I reckon. Hush!'

The whole room seemed to obey the woman's command. The usher had entered the hall, and he strode sedately forward, his chest out. 'Give place, give place. Speak softly, now. The earl comes.' He moved towards the front of the hall, the crowd parting for him. If there was one thing you could be sure of, thought Amy, it was that ushers were puffed-up toads in every great house.

From a private entrance the earl emerged, leading a stout, handsome woman. He led her to chairs on the raised dais at the end of the room and waited until she sat before he addressed the crowd.

'My good people, I bid you welcome,' he said, his hands clasped behind his back. 'And the countess and I wish you the very best of the season to come.' He licked his lips. 'We find it fitting that you all hear about what is to come before you begin your revelries. When your work commences in full after Twelfth Night, it is likely that there shall be some slight changes. We are to expect a guest.' No one spoke, but silent excitement shivered through the room. 'Yes. In fact, the countess and I shall be taking a journey immediately after the festivities. We think it meet that you should know now that we shall require stout men and a number of womenfolk to come with us to our castle at Tutbury as soon as the revels are ended. We shall decide in our course who and how many of you we shall need. Until then, we discharge you of your right duties to us until the feast days are ended. Please, good people, make merry and rest. We all of us have a time of trial coming to us. But a time of the highest honour too. Remember that, all of you.'

He stood back and smiled at his wife. The countess returned it. She looked tired, though, thought Amy. Shrewsbury held out a hand and she took it, rising from her chair. Together they left the servants to their gossip.

'Tutbury,' shrieked the old woman Amy had accosted at no one in particular. 'Jesus, what a place. Did you not hear, there's been murder done around there lately? I'm not bloody going there!'

Jack looked down at Amy. 'What was that about then? The queen of Scots isn't being sent here?'

'I suppose not. Where on earth is Tutbury?' Jack shrugged. Their new friend seized her chance.

'It's one of the earl's castles. Away out in Staffordshire somewhere. An old place, falling apart, they say. They've never taken us out that way – it's a ruined place. I tell you, that's where they must be taking Queen Mary to put her to death.' She had begun to babble, and Amy wondered if she was a little drunk. 'They can't make us go out there, though I swear in faith I'd follow the countess to ends of the earth. You, you're the new girl – you can go!'

Amy felt a chill run through her, but with it a little thrill of excitement she couldn't account for. 'Do you think they'll want me?' she asked Jack. He shrugged again. 'I mean, I'll go if I have to. But … well, I reckon they'll want you here if it's just a few going. If the horse master is so poor.'

'I don't know,' said Jack.

'Well, we might be getting broken apart come January.'

'I hope not.'

'And,' whispered Amy, 'what the hell is this about murder?' She looked around for the gossiping woman, but she had moved deeper into the throng, and seemed to be repeating herself to others.

'Who knows? Probably nothing. People die all the time and it's blamed on something or other.'

'But murder!'

'Stop it, Amy. Stop talking about that. Please.'

38

She drew back, reading his face. It had paled, even in the flickering light of dozens of candles and a roaring fireplace. 'Sorry,' she said, unsure why. 'I only … I only hope that this thing, whatever it is, with the Scottish queen is done and over quickly.'

5

Jack tightened his coat against the chill. Winter had sunk its teeth in and January was turning out to be a colder, darker, wetter month than December. He had set the stable boys to doing what he used to do: sweeping, brushing, and cleaning tools. It felt good. He could take to the job of a superior, even it was usurping the job of the horse master. The old man, a friend of the earl's, stuck a florid face into the stables every few days but otherwise stretched out his dinners and began his suppers early. The rumour was that he spent most of his time in the village, courting local women. Knowing that he now had a new man come from the duke of Norfolk seemed to have enabled his lack of care more than ever. The other horse keepers, too, had shown deference. Knowing that he came from a ducal household and was nominally the steward's man had brought him respect – a new thing.

Jack stepped away from the stables, out into the courtyard. Every so often the smell of horses and their mess required it. Messengers had ridden in and out of Chatsworth since he had arrived, and he had kept an eye on all of it. The only thing of interest had been a letter from the earl of Leicester, stamped from the privy council. That was none of his concern. Nothing had come from Norfolk and all that had gone out to him were letters of thanks and several haunches of venison killed during the Christmas hunts and sent out as a new year's gift. Dimly he wondered how the extra payments would be doled out to him, but he could certainly not write to the duke himself. His job, as he understood it, was to be a watcher, not an interferer. Thus far, there had been precious little to watch. He hoped it would stay that way.

Yes, he liked being part of a big house, he thought, letting his eyes wander up the neat glass and stone of the buildings in front of him. You knew what you were and what you were supposed to be doing. But sometimes he liked to take a little walk and close his eyes and imagine being his own man. That was one role he had never got to play. It was a fantasy, of course – being your own man meant being out in the world, scratching a living, starving if a crop failed or fire hit you. But it was a nice thought. Amy would be by his side, of course, because were else could his wife be? Maybe marriage hadn't brought him the sense of duty and normalcy and acceptance he had hoped would arrive overnight, but she was his now and forever. He let the image come: he and Amy in some village together, hidden from the world, not having to think about precedence and hierarchy and the ruthless efficiency of a noble house. That's what travelling offered, he thought. You could live somewhere under a burning sun one day and move on before people pried and came to expect you to open your mouth and your heart to them. You could be whatever you wanted to be and someone else when you arrived at a new home. 'I'm Jack and this is my wife, Amy,' he imagined himself saying to some smiling foreigner. 'We are wealthy merchants. We seek adventure in the Holy Land. We are from the New World and have seen marvellous wonders. We are lately come out of the Indies.'

'Good morrow to you, Jack.' He started and turned, smiling when he saw Philip Heydon marching towards him, his black coat flying out.

'Mr Hey- Philip. How do you fare?'

'Very well indeed. How is that wife of yours?'

'Amy? Amy's gone with the earl and countess.' He frowned a little. He knew he had told Philip that before. Amy had left right after Twelfth Night, when a small group of men and women accompanied the noble couple to inspect Tutbury. It had been a wrench, not only because he would miss her, but because he disliked the idea of being left alone amongst people who were still strangers. He had gotten to know names and faces, but a couple of weeks wasn't time enough to make friends. Besides Philip.

'And no word from her? Can she write?'

'She can write a fair bit,' said Jack, a little defensively. 'But … why should she? She shall have her hands full.'

'Quite, quite.' Heydon waved his hands in the air in a dismissive gesture. 'Are you very busy, my friend?'

'Busy enough. How about you?'

'Me, I haven't enough to do, mate. With the earl away, there are no letters for me to read through. Shockingly poor grammar, the earl has. No,' he said, tapping his nose, 'all that's come in is a letter from the privy council. Saying that the Scottish queen is to be locked up in Tutbury, the poor lady. Nowhere else, no matter the complaints the earl might discover about the place.'

'There's something,' said Jack, unsure of himself. 'So, we'll have to go there?'

'So it seems, more's the pity. From what the servants say it is a poor sort of a place. But let's not linger on that. I'm sure your wife will make it up good and pretty for us. Do you have time for a talk?'

'Yes, if it pleases you. Something troubling you?'

'No, not at all – apart from all the talk about this Scottish queen and what it'll mean for … for us all.'

'It excites everyone, I suppose. What she'll be like, I mean.'

'Have you thought on it?'

'Not really.'

'I suppose you know she's of the old faith?'

'Yes, that's why she fetched up here isn't it? The Scots are reformers, aren't they?'

'They are that. Some of them. The ones who govern now, at any rate. A barbarous and stiff-necked people. Yet many aren't. Reformers, I mean.' Heydon paused, giving Jack a measured look. 'You know, in Europe most prefer the old faith. If you travel you have to stick hard by it, else you're apt to get a dagger in the back in some nations. The Spanish, the French, the states of Italy. It's only on this isle that the root of the new faith has taken in each corner.'

'I hadn't thought about it,' said Jack. In truth, he tried to think of religion as little as possible. Yet he could sense that Heydon expected something from him. 'The duke of Norfolk is of the new faith.'

'Is he, though?'

42

'Yes,' said Jack flatly. 'My fath- my family, they were hot on the new faith too when I was a boy. Very hot on it.' He did not say that his father had been a fanatical reformer, amongst other things.

'And you? Are you so hot on it?'

Jack shrugged. 'I believe in God. I think He understands what goes on and judges as He can. Can't really know much more than that.'

'A noble sentiment, mate. An answer worthy of a Sybil. Yet it's no crime to prefer the old faith, no crime at all. I mean – the new one's only going to be around as long as the queen lives, so you needn't sell your soul for it for long. Tell me, would you like to hear how they worship in France, and in Italy?'

'I ...' Jack struggled, not sure how Heydon wanted him to answer. Heydon leapt on the silence.

'I don't mean to force you. It is just that ... well, with this noble household about to undergo a change, it might be worth your understanding better of the mysteries of the Catholic faith. It's no crime – you won't be doing anything wrong.' He gave a big foolish smile, as though he was explaining something to a child. 'As long as you attend the household services in the chapel you are doing your duty by the queen.'

'Would you like me to?'

'I would – I don't ... there aren't enough folk to talk to. You can only rely on men you can call friends, you know.'

'When?'

'Whenever you like. This evening. Your wife will be away a while yet. Do you think she should like to open her mind to workings of the world? I mean, you won't be led by her of course.'

'I think ... my wife would wish me to do as I wish.'

'Splendid. I'll visit you in your chamber.' He flapped his hands in an exaggerated flourish. 'And there I'll introduce you to the world without your even having to set foot on a boat. You'll smell the scents of French cathedrals and taste the wine of Rome. Jesus, it'll be good to relive it all myself, stuck here.'

Philip Heydon walked away without looking back, leaving

Jack standing in the courtyard alone and cold.

***

Everything that Chatsworth was, Tutbury was not. Where Chatsworth was modern and inviting, Tutbury was ancient and surly. Where Chatsworth sang of a bright new world, Tutbury brooded on its hill and whispered of secrets. It was, Amy thought, like looking into the past. Not in the way that some people did – it was not a place of verdant fields and polished yellow stones, of knights and fair ladies. No, it was not a place of the imaginary past, gilded with honour and virtue, at all. It was the real past. Crumbling, washed out, stinking.

The sight of it had filled Amy with dread, not helped by a growing sense that it was unwise to leave her husband at home. She had hoped that he might be required to come along on the visit, but the earl and countess had brought only a skeleton crew of workmen, a gentlewoman, and women to clean. Something of the Shrewsburys' disgust and anxiety had communicated itself to their servants. When they had rode into sight of the castle, a feeling of gloom had sunk into everyone's bones. The earl rode ahead with the men whilst the countess, known to all as Bess, had stayed with the women.

Bess looked like a mother bear in her furs. She spoke with an unashamed Derbyshire accent that one could cut with a knife. 'Right, my girls,' she said, reining in. It came out 'me gehls'. 'You're all going to have a job of work getting this old mausoleum fit for company. The men are gone on ahead to see what we need. They'll see to the furnishings. They'll strip Chatsworth and Sheffield bare if they have to. You will have to get on your hands and knees and scrub, scrub, scrub. I hope none of you are afraid of hard work.'

A little murmur of nervous laughter animated the women.

'Good,' said Bess. 'I like that. Now have a care here. You'll have heard there's been murder done about these parts. You're not in Derbyshire now. This is Staffordshire, where they breed 'em to kill and respect none but themselves. Speak to no man and keep your heads down. Come, the earl should have opened up the place by now.'

They wound their way up through the village, ignoring the appearance of curious locals, and up the hill and through the curtain wall to where Tutbury Castle crouched. It was an old L-shaped building with a tower at the corner. The shorter arm of the L comprised an old timber and plaster hunting lodge, its wooden joints cracked and splintered. Some of the stones from the tower had fallen to the ground. The hill on which it sat sloped down to wooded parklands, and the narrow windows were either empty sockets or hung with rotting wooden shutters. Amy wondered how even the full household at Chatsworth could ever have hoped to get such a place in order.

They left their horses with one of the earl's men – one of Jack's stable hands – in the courtyard. If there was a stable, it would likely be overgrown and dangerous, as the courtyard felt. Amy turned to one of the young maids who had accompanied her, Alice, and whispered, 'we can't make this place up. It looks like it could fall down tomorrow.'

Bess turned, her ears apparently sharp. 'What was that, girl?'

'I said we'll have a job getting this place fair. It looks like it could fall down.'

Anger passed briefly across the countess's face and was replaced by a grin. She looked odd in her finery. Her face and body seemed made for openness and honesty, whilst the rich clothing was meant for severity and imperiousness. Little pearls on her hood and a diamond collar around her throat framed a face that, when she smiled, looked only motherly. 'Well said, wench. A good thing then I don't fear hard work, nor any of my folk. Is that right?'

'Yes, my lady.'

'Let us look inside. Perhaps it shan't be so bad.'

It was worse. Bess seemed to acknowledge it herself. Her husband had paused inside with the men and stood peering at a window in what looked like an ancient great hall, his hands behind his back as he bent forward. 'I really do not see how it can be done, my dear heart.'

'It'll be done because it has to be done and there an end to it, my lord.' The countess had one hand on her hip. She nodded curtly, apparently to convince herself. 'Your men, my girls. We'll do it. You see if we can't. If I can see the rest of the place I should have some idea. Wait but a moment, my lord.'

She gathered her skirts and strode through a door in the hall and further into the chain of rooms, leaving her husband and servants in her wake. Everyone stood their ground, unsure what to do. Bess's gentlewoman looked close to tears. Shrewsbury gave an awkward smile and had turned his attention back to the window when she reappeared, her face set. 'I can see how it could be done. Yes, I can see how it could, but not that it should. We should have to fetch every stick of furniture from Sheffield and bring it here.' She put a hand to her temple and kneaded it. 'Days ... weeks ... In fact ... In point of fact, Sheffield would be better altogether. Save the men the job. Yes, husband. You write the queen and you tell – you ask her to have the Scottish queen sent to Sheffield. We will entertain her there. She shall be quite safe there, tell her.'

A light went on behind Shrewsbury's eyes and shone out towards his wife. 'Yes, my dear. Yes, I really think that would be best. I will write the queen and ask her.'

'Do you not think it better to go to her, husband? To go and make plain your view of the matter?'

'Yes, my dear. A most worthy suggestion. I shall go forthwith to London. In truth I shall be glad not to tarry in this evil place longer than a day's hunting.'

'Fine, fine. And I shall make haste back to Chatsworth and await the queen's pleasure. Just leave me one man to watch over us and keep the horses. Now make haste, husband.' Her words began to spill over one another. 'My girls and I shall take some refreshment in the village and then be off.' She stepped forward and embraced him, in full view of the assembled servants. Amy felt relief wash through her, not at the thought of shirking hard work, but, like Shrewsbury, of being free of the foulness of Tutbury Castle.

The earl rode off with his men whilst the women descended

upon the village inn. There, Bess gave way to her rank and took a private room with her stony-faced attendant, where she could dine and be waited on in peace. The tavern keeper was almost lost in his own bowing, despite the countess's constant attempts to shrug him off. As she left the big open front room, she paused, beckoned the man over, and preceded him into the private chamber. Before the door banged shut, Amy heard her say, 'this man who turned up dead. I don't like it. The earl don't like it. Smells of popery. Who was he?'

Left in the gloom of the tavern, the girls nibbled at some bad cheese and dried fruit, none in the mood for talking. Amy's mind soared at the thought of being reunited with Jack. It was a strange thing, being separated from someone you saw every day. You thought you might welcome it, welcome a chance to have a break, but the opposite was true. You found yourself turning to say something to them and they weren't there. Or you imagined what their response to something else might be but heard it only in your head and wondered if you had got them right or wrong. Soon enough she could stop wondering. Only ... only, what might that strange Heydon man have been up to in her absence? She did not trust him. She did not like him. Throughout the Christmas revels he had courted her, paying her foolish compliments. Each time she would turn to see Jack, a stupid eager look on his face, as if thinking, 'isn't he nice, Amy? Isn't he?' Rather than endearing Heydon to her, that look always made her even more wary. No gentleman befriended the son of a yeoman without wanting something in return. Jack might be willing to believe it could be so, but she was not. The man had some other motive.

She was still musing when Bess and the tavern keeper came out of the private room. 'My thanks, my lady, my humble thanks. You've done me such honour today, I can't tell you.'

'Fine,' snapped Bess, one hand on her hip. 'My thanks to you, tapster. Your goodwill shall be remembered hereafter. And ...' she dropped her voice, 'recall what I said. If there are any further whispers about anyone coming here and taking anything, you tell me. Or my husband. But I should like to hear of it.'

'Of course, my lady, at once. The smallest bruit, yes.'

'Good man.' Astoundingly, she clapped his shoulder as a man might before turning her back on him. 'You are refreshed, my girls? Good. Let us make haste then, there is no sense in wasting any more time. And let us hope none of you have to return.'

As the women remounted their horses and began their journey back towards Chatsworth, Amy began to feel the oppressiveness that the castle had brought over her dissipate. On the road outwards, she turned to give the place one last look when she spotted something that made her heart leap. Her old friend, the man in brown, was standing in an alley between two of the village houses, watching them go.

***

'And voila,' said Heydon. 'With that, the fellow's sins are shriven, and his soul purified, and he can go to purgatory with a clear conscience and the path to Heaven clear. That is what they believe anyway.'

They were seated in Jack and Amy's chamber, Jack on his own bed and Heydon on Amy's. 'Is that what you believe, Philip?'

'A leading question, mate.'

'Sorry.'

'No, no – I don't mean it as a criticism. It is a good question. Yes, it is what I believe. Though I was raised as much in the new faith as you were, from when I was ten years old and the queen came to the throne.'

'I was ten or so when she came to the throne too,' said Jack. He thought that was about right. He didn't know his birthday exactly.

'And so we missed out on the Catholic faith of the queen's sister.'

'Those were bad days, I heard. Burning, pers –' he struggled with the word. 'Deaths. It was the Protestants she burned. I sometimes wished...'

'Yes?'

'Nothing. How did you get to be a Catholic? Was it travelling?'

Heydon lounged back on Amy's cot, his eyes rising to the ceiling. He was a young-looking fellow to have been travelling. He gave the air of a worldly man, but in appearance he didn't look dissimilar to Jack himself. He just seemed to carry himself with more ease. That, thought Jack, would be the gentleman in him, the breeding. 'A little. Yes. I think so. And education, learning about the history of the world and what an old thing the Catholic faith is and what a new thing the new one.' He sat up. 'But listen to me, Jack – discovering the old religion – it has altered my life. I was like a lost and lonely sheep, alone in the world with my parents gone. Your parents are gone, aren't they? And then I found this great thing: order. Fathers who never die and are never cruel. The mother of Christ who was mother to us all. No ranting hot gospellers, no beatings with bibles and all of that tripe. Just a brotherhood of faith.'

'It sounds good,' said Jack, not wishing to offend. And, in truth, it did sound good.

'It is good. Do you know, Jack, I felt when I met you that you were good enough to be one of us. I honestly did.'

'Wait, Philip – I didn't say –'

'No, don't put yourself down, Jack. Believe me, it's not everyone I could speak to so openly about this. The queen grudges no man his conscience, provided he keeps to her faith in public – and I do.' Jack's mind turned, and he tried he tried to think of some polite, friendly means of drawing the conversation to a close. But he had spent too long thinking and missed the natural pause in Heydon's speech to say anything. 'And I will, as long as she sits down there in London and tells us what to do up here. But I felt an honesty in you, a truth. I don't,' he added, a little huffily, 'take these things lightly. I'm a light man, to be sure, but not in matters of faith and friendship. It's only that when you said you desired to travel, I saw that I might be of some service. Of course, if you didn't mean it…'

'No – I did. I do.' Jack sat up and leant forward himself. He

49

felt that somehow he had offended, and wished to take it back. 'I am very, uh, flattered that you'd ask me.'

'I'm no flatterer, sir.'

'I didn't mean that.' He scrabbled for the words. If Amy were here, she would know what to say – she was always better with people than he was. But then, Amy didn't like Philip for some reason. To his dismay, his new friend was getting up and brushing down the front of his doublet, as though talking to him had soiled it.

'I'm sorry, Philip – please, just … maybe let me think about this. It is a lot to think on, this religion.'

'Yes, Jack. And it is I who's sorry. I didn't mean to push you, not at all. As I said, I only heard from you a desire for something and sensed in you the light of God. Such things should not be ignored. I only ask that you speak of this to no one. Friends … well, they're open with each other, but they keep their confidences close.'

'I won't,' said Jack, a firm nod punctuating his assent. 'I won't say anything.'

'Not even to your wife. Perhaps especially not your wife. She doesn't,' he shrugged, 'like me.'

'That's not true, Amy is –'

'Don't worry,' said Philip, smiling. 'I like her all the more for it. She is watching out for you. But I shouldn't like to get either of you into trouble if she starts talking to people about religious matters. A woman doing such things … it can be troublesome.'

'I could – I suppose I could teach her, like you're teaching me. About the faith.'

Heydon seemed to consider this, leaning back and studying him. 'You'd like that, eh? She is your wife. You might just tell her what you want her to be and that's the end of it. Yet…' He tilted his head and gnawed on his cheek. 'I think your wife is … I think she won't come quietly on your travels.' Jack hung his head, knowing the truth of it. It was a shameful thing to have a wife with opinions. 'No. Not yet,' Heydon went on. 'Not until … well, one day soon she will join the multitude in being brought to the light. Let this be our secret. But please, do think on it. Soon enough a Catholic queen will be in our midst. I have no doubt letters shall arrive for her from all quarters.' He let a pause draw out, and his lips curled in a smile as Jack's eyes darted around. 'Mmm. I tell you, it'll be my heart and soul's joy to serve this royal lady when she joins the earl. I would really be hurt if a friend should spoil that.'

'I won't. I won't spoil it.'

'Thank you, Jack. Well, then, I'll bid you goodnight now. But remember that you have a light in you. Can you feel it? Can you feel the light?' He was teasing, and Jack smiled.

'Yes, like a torch.'

'Like a torch. Thanks for listening. It's a good friend you are to do that.' He gave a little bow before leaving the room.

Jack lay back on his bed, his stomach churning. So Philip was a Catholic. He wanted him to become a Catholic. He had no objection to that in principle, so long as it didn't involve having to do anything above his duties. He tried to imagine a light burning inside him, and then he imagined it in a sea of other lights. All of them set on an altar in a great cathedral in Rome, or France, or Spain. How different could that be from a bare, unlit, whitewashed church in Norfolk. How much such an image would have disgusted and angered his father.

He knew that the Catholic priests said they could forgive impure thoughts and past sins. But how far could that extend? How much could one even say to a priest without that priest running off to an authority? And did they hear and judge, as normal men, or were they so used to hearing confessions that nothing shocked them?

Something in the back of his mind told him that he should ignore such questions. The idea of a holy man granting absolution through the offices of a bishop in Rome was foolish. But ... but ... then surely the whole of Europe was foolish. Surely his grandparents and their grandparents and all men and women right to the beginning of time were foolish? Amy would probably tell him to ignore Philip, perhaps even to report him or avoid him. It wasn't illegal to be Catholic in your conscience, that was true, but Jack was fairly sure that trying to make more Catholics was a dangerous thing. It was trading in souls. But why shouldn't a man convert his friends if by doing so he believed he could make their lives better, perhaps even make their afterlives better? Amy would see it all as something sinister rather than something born of friendship. And she couldn't keep her mouth shut, bless her. No, he wouldn't tell her. Some things had to be kept quiet, put in a box and hidden even from a wife. God knew he was experienced enough in that.

He drifted off to sleep with the candle in his mind still burning.

Part Two: Spring's Dawn

1

February was a nasty month. Each year it seemed that winter resented its death and each year it spat one last gob of ice, snow, and freezing rain at the world it was soon to leave.

They waited in the courtyard of Tutbury Castle, a large, decorous band of household servants – the men and matrons at rapt attention, the junior maids and pages fidgeting in the cold. Ordinarily they'd all be at work, in their own stations, their butteries, their pantries, their stables. Instead they had been ordered to muster, in their cleanest clothing, to welcome the Scottish queen. The sourness of fresh whitewash fought a battle against the deep-set smell of the sewer middens. A cold wind seemed to blow it in every direction at once.

The earl and countess had failed to convince Queen Elizabeth to change her mind about Mary Stuart's prison. In January had come the announcement that nothing had been proven against the Scottish queen; but still she was to remain in England, her brother Moray returning to Scotland to govern in place of her infant son. An advance messenger had arrived to state that the royal party was approaching – later than expected, but on their way nonetheless. Still nothing was really ready. The servants waited outside to greet the new arrival mainly because most of the rooms were still in shambles.

Life had a way of letting you down, Jack mused. If at first it failed to do so, you could always let yourself down. That was how it seemed as he considered his first few weeks with the Shrewsburys. He and Amy had weaved themselves into the fabric of the household, and yet he had not emerged the strong, powerful protector he had hoped. Instead he had been frozen in impassivity. That would have to change – it might change, with the coming of Queen Mary. He would have more to do, anyway – they all would.

Jack turned, scanning the crowd. Eventually he spotted

Amy at the back, standing amongst some gossiping maids. She looked bored. He had scarcely spoken to her since the move to Tutbury. They slept apart, the servants bunking down wherever they could until more permanent sleeping arrangements could be built; at mealtimes, the horse men had cold food carried down to them in the stable which clung to the outside of the curtain wall. He tried to catch her eye, but she didn't look over. Instead he caught Philip Heydon's. His friend gave an exaggerated yawn, and Jack smiled at it. He knew Heydon was anything but bored. For weeks he had spoken of nothing but Mary Stuart: how beautiful she was said to be; how wronged she was; how devoted she was to what he called the true faith – the faith of France and Spain and Europe and the world. But Philip had been doing more than that. He had admitted that he had written to Queen Mary's secretary, although only on matters of business, to find out what might be needed for her personal offices. He had promised again and again that he would see Jack and Amy off on their travels one day. After all, Jack had offered that desire up to Philip himself. It had been his own idea – his own desire and goal. He had not pressed him into going Catholic, but he had wondered aloud many a time if Jack's life wouldn't be better if he were to convert. How much easier the job of travel would become! The thought of travel focused his mind on the supposed arrival of the Scottish queen.

How long had they been waiting? An hour at least. His earlobes were stinging. Noon had passed, and there might not be much daylight left. Whenever restlessness threatened, though, the usher cried out 'speak softly, speak softly' as he made his way up and down the massed ranks, looking for all the world like a round little bowling ball passing over a decayed green. Jack felt a bead of moisture forming at the tip of his nostril. He chanced a look around before cuffing it away.

Eventually the sounds of approaching horses came, splitting the cold air: the jangle of bells and, cresting the hill, feathered plumes, banners, and mounted riders. The usher disappeared inside, leaving the crowd to murmur. There were dozens of them – a whole troop, perhaps sixty people. At their head rode soldiers in leather jerkins, and another company brought up the rear. As one, the assembled servants fell to their knees, as they had been instructed to do.

As the new arrivals poured into the courtyard – which had been partially mown and swept – the earl's horse master stepped forward. Around him hung a mist of pure liquor, and Jack winced. Sickening. The man, Amy said, looked like someone had put clothes on an uncooked chicken. Worse, he was a drunk, kept in office only because he had been Shrewsbury's friend during long-gone Scottish campaigns. If there was one thing Jack could not tolerate it was a man who drank. He did not object to much, did not feel strongly about much, but drinking to excess was an exception.

Still, the master's shuffling movement was the signal for Jack and the other stablemen and grooms to get up and move forwards: a whole team of them – grooms for the stirrups, the palfreys, the reserve horses. The stout master moved towards the group and, Jack saw, he made for a moustached man who sat near the front of the group. That was bad. He was supposed to attend immediately upon the Scottish queen, not the man, Knollys, who escorted her.

'I bring you your guest,' said Knollys to the horse master. 'And this for your master.' From his doublet he produced a letter and handed it down, before allowing the horse keeper to help him dismount with a creaking of harness and stirrups. 'Ah, here is the fellow.'

From the castle stepped Shrewsbury and Bess, both glittering with jewels. The former bowed deeply, and the latter dropped a curtsey before they moved forwards. Shrewsbury let his eyes run over the company. He looked exhausted, Jack thought, and he seemed to have lost weight over winter rather than gaining it. A cloud crossed his face when he saw that his master of horse was busying himself with Knollys, leaving the queen of Scots mounted. Jack looked up at her.

Mary Stuart was in her twenties, and, sitting atop a horse, she looked like a figure from a classical story. Her face was flushed with the ride, although her riding habit seemed remarkably clean. Even her hair, jet black, remained unruffled, arranged though it was in an elaborate swirl of curls. Jack felt his heart begin to race as she turned from the castle and looked down at him. She smiled, her cheek dimpling, and held out her bridle. Acting on instinct he stepped towards her and took the reins, holding out an arm for her to dismount. She leant on him and stepped down – a tall woman, but graceful. As she gained the ground, she whispered, 'merci,' her breath coming hot in his ear. Then she moved forward, following Knollys, and the other grooms began to help her party off their horses. They had all been told to wait until the royal party was safely indoors before taking the animals down to the stables and safely locking them up.

Mary joined her gaolers, her back to Jack. So that, he thought, was the much-storied Scottish queen. No murderess there. A woman who had plotted the death of her husband would be swarthy, crooked, and sly. Here was a young woman of manners – a queen.

'Welcome, your Majesty,' said Shrewsbury, his voice carrying over the din. 'We bid you welcome to our home.' Mary said nothing but inclined her head. If she was appalled by Tutbury, as Jack felt sure she must be, she did not show it. 'Please, your Majesty, won't you come in and warm yourself. It is the greatest honour that my household and I can express to serve your turn.'

'Thank you,' she said, as though with difficulty. Her words were gilded with a French accent. 'My lord, I have but ten horses and not so much grooms. If it please you I require muckle more of each.' She turned, tilting her head. 'Until I have my own master of horse, perhaps this bon jeune homme might serve me.' She nodded briefly at Jack.

***

'She likes you – she wants you to serve her!' said Heydon. He was standing in the small cubby where Jack slept, just off the stables; a men's dormitory had yet to be built. 'Mate, she wants you!'

Jack tried not to let the excitement show on his face, but he could not resist a grin. 'Just for a while, Mr Woodward said. Just until the earl has sorted her household out. Her own people will be coming, he said.'

'Bah!' Heydon waved an arm. 'The earl will want to lessen her household, not increase it. I'm telling you, you're in. You know what that means? You'll be off on all kinds of adventures.'

Jack's face lit up at the words. 'You think?'

'Of course. She's a queen without a kingdom. She'll have all kinds of correspondence, things needing fetched.'

'Correspondence,' echoed Jack, forming the word slowly. 'You could help with that, though, couldn't you? Does she have a secretary, do you think?'

'You read my mind,' laughed Heydon. 'Have you met Thomas Morgan?'

'I don't think so. Should I have?'

'He's one of the earl's secretaries.' Heydon dropped his voice even though the cubby was empty but for some rats. 'He's one of us. Of the old faith.' The word 'us' brought a glow to Jack's cheeks, although he wasn't entirely sure he could count himself a Catholic yet. 'He intends to work for the Scottish queen in the art of spiery. I have given him my word I should help him. We are a brotherhood, Jack.'

'Spiery?'

'The art of watching. Of listening. Come now, you are in it already.'

Jack's spine stiffened, and he began spluttering. 'You were sent into this household by the duke of Norfolk, were you not?' Heydon went on. 'I'm no fool, my friend. The world knows that the duke hopes to marry with this queen. Some on our side hope he will thereafter turn to the true faith. The others – the earl – yes, he knows all about it – think that the duke will convert Queen Mary to heresy and keep her in thrall.' He shrugged. 'If you ask me it's all a foolish notion, but you must play your little part.'

'I … I don't do anything. I don't say anything to anyone, I just see that letters get where they should go, that's all. There's nothing bad in that, is there?'

'No, no, of course not. Yet … if you are to be a true friend and a loyal man of Rome – if you wish to travel and really see the world – then you might open your eyes a little wider.'

'What to see?'

Heydon grinned, a big, open, friendly grin. 'Wonders, mate. This year will be filled with them.' He put a hand on Jack's shoulder. A friendly gesture. Jack always heard that about the gentry and those above them: that they could shift their speech and their gesture to their audience. That they could bind men to them. That they could command and be obeyed by the force of their natures and fair speech. In his experience some had it and some didn't. Philip Heydon, he decided, did. 'This year shall see the north rise, a damned heretical Jezebel deprived of life, and the true faith restored.'

'I don't know about any of that,' said Jack. 'I – what is it you want me to do?'

'Do? You don't have to do anything but be a good friend. Pledge your loyalty to this fair queen and let your brothers do what they must.'

A shiver of fear ran through him and he suddenly wanted to be with Amy – to listen to her little tales about the women servants and work. Heydon seemed to read his mind. 'But you mustn't say anything to anyone – not that wife of yours nor the earl and his folk nor anyone. That is the thing about men in our trade,' he sighed. His voice had turned lofty, eloquent. 'We must trade in the comforts of loose tongues for guarded ones. It's why women are ill fit for this work; they talk loosely. Alas, a man on such secret service must trade his right to speak freely for the … ah, the rewards of doing the right thing. But the rewards – the salvation of our souls and the adventure of it all – that makes it all worth it.' Again, he clapped Jack's shoulder. 'You're a good man, Jack Cole. You stick by me and I'll see that you get all that you want out of this life.'

***

So that was the Scottish queen, thought Amy as she walked towards the room off the laundry where the female servants had set up a temporary camp. What on earth did men see in her? Too tall by half, and with a baby face. Some men probably liked that, though – that look of innocence and pretty helplessness. But then men never knew what was good for them.

She paused at the low doorway to the hall. There was no actual door, but some rough material hung from the lintel. Even working through the nights for weeks, it had been impossible to make Tutbury fully habitable. Instead, teams of servants had toiled to furnish and freshen a small number of chambers and halls, leaving the others to continue festering. Living in the few hastily assembled rooms felt like being on a little collection of islands amid an unfriendly sea. And despite everything the place still stank, the reek recognising no boundaries.

She raised her hand to pull back the dividing curtain when she heard voices within. 'I don't like her,' said one. She recognised it as belonging to one of her fellow maids, Alice. 'You can tell she's a bitch without her even opening her mouth.' So, thought Amy – her colleagues were no more enamoured of the famous Mary Stuart than she was.

'Well see, there's the problem. She's a shrew into the bargain.'

'What's the husband like, though?'

'The horse lad? I think he's handsome.'

'I think he's odd – looks like she's broken him down with the wagging tongue of hers. You heard him talk? You can barely hear him. I reckon he's lost his tongue through listening to hers. Why are they even here anyway?'

The conference dissolved into laughter and Amy felt her ice grip her heart. It melted as anger flared. She threw back the curtain and flounced into the room, her skirts trailing. 'A fine right you have to speak ill of anyone,' she snarled. Flustered, the two gossiping maids dropped their eyes to the ground. Alice looked up and began, 'we weren't speaking of you –' but Amy cut her off.

'I don't give a damn who you were speaking of. Prating tongues that speak ill turn black and drop off.' That was one of her mother's warnings. 'Although I'll have you know my husband is worth ten of each of you. If he speaks softly it's because his tongue isn't so fat nor so stupid as yours.' Then, knowing it was petty, she added, 'maybe if you spent less time talking about other people, you'd be able to find husbands of your own. And not be such a pair of fat little pigeons.' There, she thought. Bridges burnt. But she was still too angry to care. She threw herself into gathering as many bedsheets as she could and, with her arms laden, she turned on her heel and kicked the makeshift door aside.

Once she was back in the hall, she felt tears sting and blinked them away. She had been nothing but nice to her fellow maidservants since she arrived – and they had seemed happy to rub along with her. Why, she wondered, why did people always have to be so false? And why did she always have to rise to it?

She marched out of the castle with her dirty laundry and, when she stepped into the cold air, she turned towards the castle entrance. There was only one way in and out of the curtain wall that circled the castle. At the gate, a soldier and one of the earl's porters stood bantering. She passed through without either stopping her. But, as she began picking her way down the path, she heard them. 'Fine arse on that one,' said one.

'Not big enough for me,' laughed the porter.

Again, Amy wheeled. 'I have fine ears and a fine tongue too,' she hissed. 'And I'd be happy to use it to tell your wives what hungry eyes you have.'

The two men shrugged, folding their arms, and drawing their eyes off her. Perhaps she was a shrew, she thought, as she continued down. It was a long walk through woodland towards the little stream that had been siphoned off from the River Dove, but she wanted to be alone for a while.

Hearing that the maids disliked her had been an annoyance, but it was only the latest amongst many. Since coming to Tutbury everything had seemed off. It wasn't just that she rarely saw her husband – lots of women in service and out had to deal with that – but that when she did see him he seemed to have changed. That in itself was no great surprise. Jack was just like that, as she had known since she met him. It was how he had changed that bothered her. That strutting little peacock Heydon had put ideas in his head – and what they were she didn't even want to know. Probably, she thought, that he had the makings of a gentleman. Probably that he could better himself and improve his lot. Yet, if she were honest, it was plain and simple jealousy that was eating into her. Jack was hers, not some gentleman's toy. They were supposed to muddle through life together, doing their jobs but not liking them, and escaping at the end of each day into each other.

For a moment she hated everyone. She hated her fat little co-servants. She hated the Scottish queen and all the trouble she caused. She hated the earl of Shrewsbury and his castle full of leering men. She hated Philip Heydon. And she hated Jack most of all, because his distance from her was the betrayal that pinched the hardest.

She stepped over broken branches and the myriad half-frozen dead things that carpeted the floor of the parklands. The water would be freezing, but she would enjoy thrusting her arms into it, enjoy the shock. The musk of wet leaves and soil was a tonic. Then a sharper smell hit her. Something rotting. Some of the ground at her feet was stained – the waste parts of a hunted deer littered the ground and she drew carefully around it. She slowed her pace and paused, getting a better purchase on her armfuls of bedding.

It was then that she felt the iron band of an arm encircle her waist. She dropped her load and opened her mouth to scream. Before she could cry out, a brown-gloved hand clamed over her mouth.

'Peace, woman,' a metallic voice purred into her ear on a wave of heat. 'I don't want to hurt you. You've been watching me, haven't you?'

2

Jack looked out for Amy that evening but didn't find her. That was odd. Normally during the evening she would be holding court amongst the maidservants, and she would at the least give him a smiling nod. Instead, supper seemed to be an ad hoc affair as the process of installing Queen Mary's household separately from the earl's led to confusion and grumbling from everyone. Jack gave up wandering the halls and decided to make his way back to his sleeping corner. No one would want horses late on, and if he was with the male staff, they could reach him if he did.

Yet he found his feet taking him towards the rooms which had been allotted for the Scottish queen. He reasoned that perhaps Amy had been drafted in to sweeten the royal chambers, but he knew deep down that he wanted another glimpse of Mary Stuart. At the entrance to the apartments – or rather the small collection of rooms that had been given tapestries and furniture – he found a gaggle of boys arguing with a harassed-looking soldier. He brushed his fringe away and watched.

'You have no right to enter here. Orders are orders,' he snapped.

'The earl said the queen should be entertained in all majesty,' said one of the boys. Jack recognised them as the household musicians. Not one of them was near puberty.

'The earl,' repeated the soldier, as though the word tasted bad. Then he faltered, apparently unsure of who he was supposed to answer to. 'Go and fetch me one of the earl's men, then, and have him tell me that.'

'We are the earl's men,' piped one of the smaller boys.

'You are the earl's whelps! And I doubt the Scotch queen wants to hear a parcel of beardless lady-faced lads whine about their mistresses having no faith in them! Come back when you have some bollock hair and you've touched a bloody woman.'

Jack watched as the door opened behind the soldier and a woman stepped out, a halo of soft light framing her. She was handsome, in a way – or she would be if she didn't have such a haughty and arrogant air. 'Tush! Whit be the tulzie withoot?' she snapped.

'Pardon, my lady,' said the guard. 'Some lads here wanting to sing for the queen.'

'Then let them sing,' she said. Then her face softened. To Jack's surprise, she took the soldier's arm and began to walk with him – away from the door. 'Come noo, my man. If the earl's boys wish tae gie tae the queen's majesty a wee bit comfort, it's a hard heart should say no.'

The soldier evidently had little idea of what the woman was saying. In fact, she seemed to want it that way. He stepped around the massed boys willingly. 'And could ye no' mebbe go and find a man o' the earl tae make things smooth?'

'If … I … yes, my lady. I'll find a man at once.' He snapped a salute and moved away, passing Jack without a glance. When he had gone, the woman dropped her mask of civility and turned. Putting one hand to her chest, she snapped the fingers of the other. The boys took this as their cue to enter, the lead already starting to sing. As they slipped in, Philip Heydon stepped out.

'Thank you, Mistress Seton,' he said. She gave a stern smile and he made a sign of the cross before he spotted Jack. Annoyance crossed his face, replaced quickly with a smile. 'Be at peace, mistress – he is one of us,' he said. The woman, Seton, gave Jack a cold look before nodding and disappearing after the boys. The door to the royal rooms thudded behind her, robbing the outer hall of some of its light.

'You following me?' said Heydon. Then, before Jack could reply, 'come on, let's be away from here. Now, before that bloody soldier comes back.'

Heydon led them outside into the black, freezing evening. 'Too many will be about in the dorm,' he explained, his voice low.

'I wasn't following you, mate,' said Jack. No, he thought –

he still couldn't pull off the easy manner in which Heydon said it. It sounded forced and he cringed a little. 'I was just … I was looking for Amy.'

'Amy? She wasn't there.' Heydon barked a laugh. 'You know what they say about a man who loses control of his wife?'

'I was just – I haven't seen much of her. What were you doing in there?'

Heydon blew out an audible sigh, and then threw his head back. 'Ah, it was nothing. I …' He looked down towards his chest and then pinched at his forehead. 'To the devil with it. I reckon I've been honest enough with you, mate. The truth is … well, the truth is, I am not just a secretary. I'm not just a gentleman who was looking for a place. I'm … when I travelled abroad, I was ordained in Douai last year. Amongst the first. I'm a priest, Jack. I was going to tell you.'

'You're a Catholic priest,' said Jack, without expression.

'You're a sharp one, mate. Don't tell the world, will you? I was going to tell you when I was surer of you. I have to ask you now if you're in with us or not. There's no more time to think. Will you pledge yourself to the faith?'

'I … I mean I don't have to do anything, do I?'

'You just have to believe. You just have to accept that the heresies that you said your family loved were in error. That's all.'

'I suppose I have to call you priest, then. Or father?' God forbid, he thought.

'Nothing wrong with Philip.' Amusement played across his face. 'My son,' he added, before breaking into a grin.

Something flared in Jack. He had always despised what his father had stood for – everything about the man was to be scrubbed out. 'He was in error,' he said. He let his eyes wander up the castle walls. Few lights winked: the shutters were all closed against the cold. They might have been standing in the middle of nowhere. 'Yes, Philip. I'll join you, if that's what you want.'

'Bless you, Jack Cole.' Heydon reached up to his face and, very quickly, drew the sign of the cross on his forehead. 'Now you are truly in God's mercy, I can open your eyes to all number of truths and mysteries. But remember – you can't say a word to anyone, not until we have achieved what we must.'

Behind the dried-up well in the centre of the courtyard, though neither Jack nor Heydon could see her, Amy crouched. Tears in her eyes, she turned and crept off to pull down the still-wet bedclothes she had unsuccessfully tried to dry out in the old hunting lodge.

***

Jack found her a quarter of an hour later, crossing the courtyard towards him, her head bent low. 'Amy,' he said. 'Where have you been? I've been looking for you?' That, he supposed, wasn't a lie – he had been on the hunt for her, though for the last fifteen minutes he had been standing staring into space, wondering if he had done the right thing. Heydon had gone, but his parting words had been that soon Jack would feel the Holy Spirit rising within him. He had waited, figuring that it would find him more easily outside than in. Hardly anyone was about – just a disinterested gardener grunting as he took armfuls of dead shrubbery towards the middens. Jack ignored him and tried to focus his mind. Useless. He had felt nothing, although he would have to say otherwise if Heydon asked him.

'Good evening, husband,' she said. Her voice came out in a strangulated whelp.

'Hus – are you well? It's cold. Where have you been?'

'Laundry.'

He reached out a hand to her and she pulled away. 'What's wrong?'

'Nothing. Why should something be wrong?' She seemed to collect herself, shaking her head. 'I'm fine. I'm well. You?'

'I'm ... I'm very well, Amy.'

'Good. Been spending time with your friend?'

'I have. He is a good mate.'

Something tensed in her, and an odd look came over her face. He didn't like it. 'Why are you talking like that?' she asked.

'Like what?'

'Your accent. You're talking different. Can you not hear it? Talk right, won't you?'

'What? What do you mean?'

'Just there – you're sounding like him. Like Heydon.'

Jack bit down. Consciously, he made his voice what it always was. 'I sound the same as always, don't I?'

'If you say so,' she said, shuddering. 'You're right, it is cold. What did you want me for?'

'Just to talk. To see how you fared. That's all.'

'Right. Well, then, now you know. Jack, I ... you know, you can tell Mr Heydon that you're too busy for friendship. At the moment, I mean.'

'What? Why? I couldn't – I –'

'Life's full of folk doing things they say they won't or wouldn't or can't.'

'Your mam?' Jack raised an eyebrow, and Amy pulled a face.

He wanted to ask her why she was behaving oddly, but something in her manner stopped him. And he didn't care for her commenting on how he spoke. 'Well, anyway, good night to you then.' He considered whether he should kiss her or not. At length he did – a cursory peck on her cheek.

'Goodnight, Jack,' she said. Then, 'be careful. Please.'

'What do you mean?'

'You're getting yourself into something too big.'

Fear gripped at him. Had she been watching? For how long? 'What do you mean,' he repeated. 'What are you talking about?'

'Just what I say.'

Shrugging, he left her standing shivering in the cold as he made his way to down to the stables and his sleeping hole. Even if she had overheard him joining with Heydon, it shouldn't concern her. What did it matter what group of friends he had, so long as he went to the damned church every Sunday and listened to the sermons? He would prefer if she joined in, but he knew she did not care about religion either way. So what did it matter?

Yet one thing rankled. Catholics, the world knew – or said, at least – wanted to return England to the old faith. They wanted to force Queen Elizabeth down in London to accept them, to accept that her religion was a broken toy. But Heydon had said more than that. He had said that the year would see a Jezebel deprived of life. He hadn't given it much thought at the time, but if his friend was a priest, if he was part of a whole chain of priests, did that mean that they planned to kill the old girl?

He pushed the thought aside. Even if there was some dream of killing off the queen, it was just that. Dreams were things you hoped would happen, not things that did. And Heydon had said, after all, that he need do nothing more than believe.

3

As winter petered out, the news rippled throughout the household that Queen Mary had become ill. Precisely what the complaint was, no one knew, but Jack found himself less and less required to ready horses for her. Couriers would sometimes appear at the stables, nameless and badgeless, and sometimes pass him packets with dramatic flourishes. 'For the Scottish queen's eyes alone.' 'It is to be burnt after reading.' Some came from Norfolk, and he passed them to Heydon or others he trusted to have access to the royal apartments. But he didn't get to see her himself. Her escorted trips out into the parklands for exercise ceased entirely, and so he had to live on memories of her graceful hand slipping into his as she mounted and dismounted. He had no other touch of a woman, except for once, when, flushed after helping the queen to ride out, he had taken Amy into a rotting closet into the old hunting lodge. That hadn't been like him at all, and he had felt ashamed after it, but she had been curiously unprotesting. A man had conjugal rights, he supposed, but he didn't like to think of himself as one who would demand them.

As the weeks passed, he had spent a good deal of time with Heydon too. His friend had opened up his mind to the sheer number of men in the north who had embraced the Catholic faith – or who, rather, had never given it up. There were stacks of them in every household – the earl of Shrewsbury even had relatives who were willing to take up arms in defence of it. And wouldn't Jack like to count himself amongst such a noble number? He had said that he would. And wouldn't Jack like to be part of a great revival of a world before schism? Of course.

Jack knew he was a compliant man. He neither liked nor disliked it: it was just a fact of who he was. Trying to alter it would be like trying to fashion a whole new person out of nothing. In the past he had even reasoned that it was part of service to be an empty vessel in which a master could brew whatever he liked. That was better than thinking that he was tainted, touched by madness and inhumanity.

Even so, Heydon had a remarkable way of making him agree to anything. Perhaps, he supposed, that was the working of the Holy Spirit. At any rate, this faith – this ancient faith which men and women had died for – might finally be the making of him. Jack Cole, he thought: no longer a man who stands for anything and everything, but a man who stands for something. When people spoke of him in the future it wouldn't be as the weird, smiling mope who would agree with anyone, no matter the contradictions, but as a man who stood proudly up for what he believed in. The broken little shell of old had been traded in for steel. The only dark spot was his friend's insistence that their discussions be kept secret: that some spy in the household, more perceptive even than the stupid soldiers, was watching them. But probably that was just the natural fear of anyone who knows that their beliefs are persecuted by the ungodly.

With no horses to ready, he had nothing to do. The letters from Norfolk had dried up, the soldiers immediately arresting any man who appeared and searching him. If something had come in, it hadn't made it through Jack's hands. It was a Saturday – the day allotted for emptying the sewage pits, and men and women were grimly milling around the courtyard with muck-caked sacks tied around their feet. Swarms of flies buzzed around the yard in a cloud. There, thought Jack, was proof that winter had really gone. Thankfully joining in was now beneath him, but he watched the procession of people with buckets. The queen, he knew, hated Tutbury. Her two rooms – the rooms into which Heydon had gained access – were mean, the windows opening out only on to the curtain wall. When she wasn't able or permitted to ride, Mary was obliged to take her exercise walking around in circles in a potato patch. People had come and gone – an Irish gentleman in late February – to gawk at the captive queen, but her misery was infectious. Not only her own household but Shrewsbury's seemed to catch it. Amy certainly had it.

Across the courtyard, Jack spotted the earl emerge,

Woodward the steward at his heel. Shrewsbury looked more tired than ever. His usual stoop had deepened, and with each step he grimaced. From master to servant the unhappiness reflected. Shrewsbury took a few steps into the courtyard then, seeing the activity – the servants quickened their steps – he shook his head and went back inside. Woodward, however, paused. Catching Jack's eye, he beckoned with a finger.

'Mr Cole,' he said. 'The Scottish queen shall have her own master of horse shortly.' Jack felt his heart sink, his brief star as a royal servant falling into eclipse. 'I should think you will be relieved of the burden.' The sarcasm was heavy. 'For of this sort are they which creep into houses, and lead captive silly women laden with sins, led away with divers lusts.' Jack started. 'The second epistle to Timothy. Think on it.'

Inwardly, Jack smiled. Stupid, Bible-spouting heretic. How much better was Latin – a language that buried the irksome lessons of the words in music. 'Anyway, you should be free of that lady's influence by the time we reach Wingfield.' He mopped his forehead with his hand. 'Jesus, but it shall be a good thing to be quit of this evil place. The poor earl, too – the damp is doing nothing for his humours.'

'We're leaving?' asked Jack.

'Yes.' Woodward licked his lips and looked around with a frown. Then he shrugged. 'No secret to it. Not within the household. Still, if anything falls upon the Scotch queen on the road, I'll know who to blame, eh? Oh, good day, Mr Heydon.'

Heydon joined them, slightly out of breath. 'Good day, Mr Woodward. I understand we are to be on the move before long?'

'News travels fast. Yes, and may God be a light to our feet and a lamp to our paths.'

Heydon's mouth formed into the briefest of moues. 'Very good. Yet I understand the Scottish queen has a request.'

'A reque- what now?'

'Some items that are now in Scotland – she wishes them brought to her. Dresses, jewels, that manner of thing.'

'And how do you know this?' asked Woodward. Jack's eyes widened. The old man was sharper than he looked.

'I had it of Mr Morgan,' shrugged Heydon. 'He has traffic with the queen's train from time to time.' How easy he made lying look. Woodward peered at him down the length of his long nose for a time, as though hoping to detect something. 'The woman has only just dispatched a man to Scotland. Why has she not asked him to fetch her things back?'

'She forgot,' said Heydon, giving Woodward a wearied look. 'Women.'

'Forgot? Ha!' The steward looked up towards the castle and then back at Heydon. 'Don't think I am a fool, sir. Do I look like a fool? I think I begin to see exactly what is passing here.'

Jack sensed his seemingly unflappable friend stiffen. He did likewise, drawing in a sharp breath. 'That woman forgot nothing,' snapped Woodward, slamming a fist into his thigh. 'She dispatched her own man with no instructions hoping that the earl would have to shoulder the costs of her transport. That is her game – to spend nothing herself and spend our master into the almshouse.' Heydon and Jack relaxed.

'You have got the measure of her, sir,' said Heydon. Woodward looked triumphant, but it was a hollow kind of triumph. Eventually he sighed, his whole body seeming to crumple.

'And cannot these things be sent?'

'Apparently the queen wants them fetched. By reliable men of the earl's. Otherwise she fears they may be stolen and then she should charge them to our sovereign lady.'

'Of course she does,' murmured Woodward. 'And we must dance to her tune, eh? I tell you, I shall be glad when this queen is disposed of – ah,' he added quickly, 'when our lord is relieved of her.'

'You meet me in that, sir,' smiled Heydon. 'If you like I can fetch the things from Scotland.'

'You?' Woodward's face screwed up.

'Yes, sir. I don't mind. In truth if it means an escape from this castle ahead of our move, I should welcome it. If the earl can get me a safe conduct, I should be glad to go.'

'You cannot go alone.' He turned his attention to Jack. 'Take Cole with you. For the horses. He's still acting as that queen's imp, more's the pity, until her own master of horse arrives. I release him. Then you will go on your way in safety, and your foot will not stumble, eh?'

'Yes, sir.'

'Good, excellent. The earl shall have to write the secretary for that passport. Shan't be long. The road to London has never been so well stocked with messengers. Well then, get you gone. I've enough to do making good this move. Ah, but to be away from this damned place.' With a weary shake of his head, Woodward tramped in the direction Shrewsbury had gone.

'Fuck you,' mouthed Heydon after him. Then he turned to Jack. 'You see, mate. Told you that the true faith would grant you what you wish. Travel. I'm sorry it's only that heretic-riddled northern waste, but it's a start, right?'

'We're really going?' asked Jack in wonder. 'We're really going to travel?' Then he gave his own little look of distaste. 'To gather and bring back some dresses and jewels?'

'Haha! Not a bit of it. Oh, we're going, to be sure – right into the belly of the beast. The land of wild men in the mountains and fire-breathing preachers filled to the brim with heresy, eh? But,' he said, taking Jack's arm and moving him away from the stinking mass of servants, 'we need to get something out of that realm a damn sight worthier than some baubles and trinkets.'

***

Amy made her way down from the castle with her latest bundle of dirty laundry. This time the castle's guards ignored her entirely. She imagined that they thought her a vile shrew, neither worthy of speaking to or leering at. Good, she thought – let them think it.

She made her way into the parklands and sat down on a fallen log. Finally, winter seemed to have given up the ghost. She breathed deeply of the fresh air. One grew so used to the permanent stench of Tutbury that even on sweetening day the sewage didn't seem to bother you; but when you managed to get out into the open air it was like being given a fresh meal after starvation. She enjoyed a few lungfuls before she put her lips together and blew. A few bars of 'The Hunt is Up' were her signal. At intervals she whistled them.

For weeks now, she had been engaged in passing information to the mysterious man in brown. He had terrified her that first time, when he had grabbed her, and she thought she was about to be murdered or worse. Yet he had whispered in her ear, calming her. He was one of Queen Elizabeth's secretary's men – an agent working on behalf of Sir William Cecil. It was his job to discover what was really going on within the earl's household: whether anyone was too familiar with the Scottish queen, the earl and countess included; whether her confinement was too loose; whether the soldiers were reliable or lazy. It was a funny thing, that – Mr Brown, as Cecil's man called himself, had been encouraged to spy even on loyal English soldiers. A fake name, she guessed, or a convenient one.

She had acquiesced, because what else could she do? She considered feeding him only the weakest of information – saying that Mary Stuart's captivity was rock-hard, and that the earl's household disdained her entirely. But she didn't want to lie if the lies could be caught out. And Brown had caught her – quite literally – on a day when she had been eager to spit hatred at everything within Tutbury's walls.

Her husband, she suspected, had developed some fascination with the damned Scottish queen, as ridiculous as that was. She had felt it – known it – when he had come in from one of her hunting expeditions. His eyes had been bright and wild, and he had kissed her with an unusual force. Then he had half-carried her into the crumbling lodge – the place used now for drying sheets whilst workmen fitted it out as a servants' dormitory – and made love to her. It was quite unlike the sticky fumbling that had characterised their relations in their old chambers – the ones which were over as quickly as she suspected all lovemaking was the world over. It was wild and, in other circumstances, might have been exciting. Afterwards, she had felt cheap. It was no better than whoredom making love to someone who was thinking about someone else.

Worse, she suspected Mary of encouraging Jack's lusts, casting her smiles around at everyone to win friends. But more than anything she wanted the traitorous little priest Heydon to be carried off, preferably by an armed troop. But how to engineer that without compromising Jack? At all costs she had to protect him. He was being an idiot and worse, but he was her husband. He needed her protection.

At length Brown appeared through the undergrowth. As always, he made no sound, alerted her in no way to his coming. As always, she started.

'Good day to you, Mrs Cole,' he said. 'What have you got for me?'

'They're moving her to Wingfield,' she said. She liked that he went straight to business.

'When?'

'I don't know. Before April is out.'

'I see. I suppose the earl has already sought permission for that, then. I shall find some lodging nearby there – do not try and reach me. I will reach you if I can.'

Not for the first time, Amy wondered how on earth Cecil and his men operated. From Brown's example, it seemed they gathered information that was freely given by honest means. It almost seemed like they distrusted one another – the great secretary his men, and probably the men each other. 'The priest Heydon,' she said. 'He is still overfamiliar with the Scottish queen's folk.'

Brown spat at the ground. It was rare for him to show emotion but mention of priests always brought it out. 'Damned rat.'

'Have you discovered anything about him?' she asked, genuinely interested in the man who had stolen her husband from her.

'No. I have passed his name on.' That was disappointing. 'He will be one of many. We had out of one that there is something planned on the true queen's life.'

'What?' She stood up. 'Queen Elizabeth?' A clever woman,

people said. Dressed extravagantly. Amy's mother used to say of her 'she's her mother all over again, that one' – whatever that meant.

'It is the wish of all that rabble, whatever they say, to make an end of our sovereign lady. Their foul religion – these are the corruptions it breeds in the mind and body. Others like me have heard similar across the north, as I understand. Though what they are plotting we cannot see. Nothing has come from Norfolk? The soldiers haven't been turned to Mary and brought her letters?'

'No, sir.' Amy had always tried to dance around the issue of Norfolk. Jack was too involved in that, she suspected. How could he not be? But Brown's piercing blue eyes held hers.

'Your husband is in no danger from that quarter. Mr Secretary knows all about my lord of Norfolk. He is willing to let the farce play out. It may stop that damned Scotch whore from applying her mind to bloodier designs.'

'You mean Queen Mary knows nothing of any plot to kill Queen Elizabeth?' At this, Brown gave her an appraising look. She thought she saw something like grudging respect in his eyes. But he only shrugged.

'Who knows with the papists? They have their hands in many evil enterprises. Did you know there was a man killed near here last year?'

'Yes,' said Amy, thinking of the countess's enquiries at the town's tavern. 'I heard something about that.'

'One of our own – one of the queen's secretary's men. Stuck like a pig and left on the highway, as though some thief had robbed him.'

'How do you know it was a Catholic who got him?'

'Because,' snapped Brown, looking at her as though she were stupid, 'a gentleman in the service of my master and our queen does not give way to thievery. No, he was butchered by one of these papist animals, God rest him. But ...' He took off his cap and ran a hand through silvery-white hair. 'You understand what should happen if our queen is taken off suddenly?' Amy shook her head, her eyes wide. 'A whole army of northern men will come down and carry that whore out of here – out of any place she rests her wicked head – and proclaim her queen. A Catholic queen. And then there will be bloody civil war. And it will be the full fury of Catholic Europe unleashed against good Englishmen.'

'Oh,' said Amy. The Catholic faith meant little to her. It was simply the smell of her childhood. Her mother, God rest her, had burned candles, and invoked saints when she lost things. She had had nothing against it, but no strong feeling for it, either. That was, until she had heard Heydon converting her husband to it.

'Oh? Oh? I don't think you understand the horror, woman. Do you know what the Catholics will do? Babes shall be roasted alive on spits. Women and boys shall be raped by pock-marked priests, and good men torn asunder. Unless ...' She let his silence draw out, looking past him into the horrors of war. 'Unless,' he added, 'you have the courage to use this.'

From a pocket hanging from his belt, Brown withdrew a tiny stoppered bottle. 'What is it?' she asked. But she already knew.

'A few drops of this will see that accursed whore in her grave and this realm secure.'

'You ... you want me to murder Queen Mary?' gasped Amy. She had stood, and she began backing away. Through the canopy of leaves a spear of sunlight hit the bottle, making it twinkle.

'No,' said Brown solemnly. 'Not unless you have word – unassailable word from every mouth from here to London – that our sovereign lady lies dead and Mary Stuart still lives. Then, and only then, to save the lives of every loyal subject of Elizabeth, should you ensure that the Scot drinks of what she has brewed herself for many men. A few drops alone will do it.'

She stood transfixed by the little vial, slowly shaking her head. 'I ... I can't. I couldn't.'

'You have no choice,' snapped Brown. 'I may be in London – I may be anywhere – when the Catholics strike. Master Secretary must know that should our queen fall, there will be no false papist usurper to take her place.'

Brown moved towards her and grabbed her wrist, forcing her hand open and jamming the vial against her palm. It was cold, but her fingers closed over it. 'There,' he said. 'And pray God you never have to use it, for if you do, it means that our sovereign lady has been slain. Lock it up somewhere safe. Under a loose board, or some such secure place.' Amy was still shaking her head, but her eyes had fallen on Brown's, hazel green lost in the glare of crystal blue. 'Of course,' he said, his voice turning smooth, 'you can prevent all that.'

'How?'

'You help me stop any Catholic plotters dead.'

'But … but the Scotch queen will have someone to taste her food. Before she eats it. Surely she will?'

'Bah! A nonsense job of work. No good poison goes to work immediately. This one will take some hours, long after the queen has judged her meat tasty and fair. If she eats it at noon, by the time the sun falls she will have given up the ghost. First her insides will churn, and then her innards will revolt. I …' He paused, watching Amy's face. She had felt the colour drain from it. 'Never mind tasters, girl. This must be used to stop any plotters in their tracks, to rob them of their false idolatrous queen. No matter who they are, do you understand me?' His tone thickened with meaning. 'If your husband falls in with these evil brutes, I will do what I can to save him. If you tell me all that you see, tell me all that they do, open up their hearts to Secretary Cecil.'

'Yes,' said Amy. 'Yes. I will.' He nodded once and then turned, marching deeper into the woodlands. She fell to her knees and buried her face in the sodden laundry. After a while, she stood, her legs wobbling, and tucked the vial into her bosom.

4

Letters and documents had never greatly interested Jack. They were the stuff of lawyers, of masters, of nobles. But the document Heydon had spoken of – the one locked in a casket deep in the private home of Queen Mary's bastard brother – that was different. It was exciting. It was a dusty thing – probably, Heydon said, a forgery – but something necessary to a far greater scheme. It purported to be a charter written by the ancient Scots acknowledging England's suzerainty over them. Who had really written it, and when, and why – none of that mattered. If it could be pried from the earl of Moray's secret coffer and brought to England, it would kill off any of the stuffy old lawyers' claims that Scotland's kings – that Scotland's queen – were foreigners and unfit to inherit the English throne. If Elizabeth died suddenly, and proof were discovered that Scotland was a mere vassal of England, its people not foreign but English subjects, then Queen Mary would be the rightful heir.

And Queen Elizabeth would die suddenly. Of that Jack felt quite confident.

He had balked when Heydon had suggested it, but his friend had quickly pointed out that the English queen was older than Queen Mary. She led a single life, which everyone knew dried out the body. She had had smallpox before and nearly died – the next illness would carry her off for sure. And then there would be men who would say, 'we cannot have the Scotch queen be our mistress – she is a foreigner and the laws of the land decry it'. Those men, Heydon had explained, had to be shut up. If it took a dodgy document filched from the servile earl of Moray, so be it.

As April marched on the household at Tutbury – now a sprawling confusion of arriving Scots and French and the Shrewsburys' English staff and hangers-on – began to pack up for the move to Wingfield. The day before he and Heydon were due to leave for Scotland, Jack sought out Amy.

He took a gift – a little package of honeyed pastry he had begged from the kitchen – and found her carrying some folded napkins in from the courtyard. It was almost exactly a year since they had been married; it seemed the thing to do. She gave him a wan smile, looked down at the bundle of soiled rags in her hands and then at the package he carried. 'Your thing looks more interesting,' she said.

Jack smiled and took her by the elbow, stepping to the side with her to allow some men carrying a table board to pass outside. 'I wanted to see you,' he said. 'I've missed you.' That was true. He had been sleeping poorly at nights. He had grown used to the sound of her light breathing near him, lulling him off. Sleeping in a corner of the stables at Tutbury, the night was punctuated by farting, snoring, and often mumbling. Worse than that was the intermittent sound of marching feet as soldiers patrolled the castle grounds above. Lights burned incessantly too. It was difficult to sleep in a place that never slept itself.

'I thought you had plenty of company with your new friend,' she said, before biting her lip. 'Sorry.'

'I've been busy is all. But now that Queen Mary has her own man to look after her horses and grooms things will go back as they were. I think. I just have to do one thing first.'

'Oh? What's that?'

'I have to go with Philip up to Scotland.'

'Scotland?' she said. He noticed it came with mingled scorn and disbelief. He tossed his head, his fringe flying. It was something to do to avoid her eyes. 'Why?'

'Just to fetch some things down from … there.' He realised he had no idea whereabouts in Scotland Heydon was taking him.

'So you're going up through the north?'

'That is the way to Scotland,' he smiled. 'Yes.' She didn't smile back. Instead, she seemed to be frowning, a little line creeping across her smooth forehead. It wasn't like her to ask stupid questions – that, he suspected, was more like him. 'Why?'

'No reason. And why does high and mighty Sir Philip want to go?'

'He doesn't.' Irritation flared and, without realising it, Jack felt his hand tighten on the package of pastry, crushing it. 'I mean, why shouldn't he? The earl has custody of the queen and Philip works for him, so he goes where he's sent. And he can hardly go alone.'

'Can he not find someone else to go with him?'

'No,' said Jack. He was bored of the conversation now. 'It won't be for long. We just have to go there and back.'

'I see. Well thank you for telling me. When are you off?'

'Tomorrow.'

'Be careful, Jack. Please. You don't have to do anything you don't want to – remember that. And remember that there are folk who'll probably be watching the road up there and back.'

He leant in and kissed her, meaning it. 'I'll be fine.'

'Just ... just mind how you go. And mind who you talk to.'

He watched her scurry away, wondering what on earth she meant. Amy was a sharp girl – he suspected she already knew that he had turned his mind towards the old faith. If that was all that was worrying her, she had no need. Philip was an ordained priest. He travelled with the protection of God. No, if Amy was worried for anyone, it should be for herself, stuck in a moving prison full of heretical soldiers.

It was only when she had gone that he looked down and realised he was still holding the little napkin of sweets. Somehow, he had crushed it. He cursed silently, regretting his temper. Still, he supposed it would still be edible. It would do him and Heydon on the road north.

***

They left early the next morning. Amy watched them go from a window in the castle. When they were out of sight, she pulled the shutter closed. It didn't fit all the way and she gave up trying to force it.

The whole household was already up and about and, as

Amy considered what she would have to get counted and packed, her mind turned to Brown. It wasn't a day on which she could see him. He was always strict about that. If she had information, she had to wait until a Saturday. Even then, she must whistle the correct tune if she had something to impart. If he heard anything else, he would stay away. It was, he said, of critical importance that no one know of their meetings. If word got out that Cecil had men spying on the household, it might destroy the honest channels of communication between the Shrewsburys and the government. Amy liked the countess – Bess was a big, capable woman – but Brown was quick to tell her that as long as what she told him tallied with what the earl and his wife told Cecil, all would be quite well.

What her meetings meant, though, was more than just a furtive excitement. It was more too than a desire to protect Jack from himself and Heydon. In truth, she had begun to grow lonely. Her fellow maidservants barely spoke to her now – and then tersely, with the weight of their words and hers hanging between them. Brown was strange, even spooky, but he was someone to talk to – and not about linens and cloths.

Grudgingly, she began to tramp through the hall, now spartan and barely furnished. Her eyes were on the ground and she jolted when she felt a large mass loom up in front of her.

'You, girl – what are you about?' She looked up into the narrowed eyes of the countess.

'Sorry, my lady,' said Amy, dropping a curtsey.

'Haven't you got something to do?' Bess folded her arms. She looked like she had had little sleep. Amy supposed that the role of a gaoler's wife must be a tiresome one. Neither Bess nor Shrewsbury liked the place, but Queen Elizabeth had forbidden the earl from leaving their new charge even for a day.

'Yes, my lady.' Amy began to back away and to the side.

'Wait. You are still newly come into our household. How do you find it? Are you liking your time here?'

'No, my lady.' The words were out before Amy thought better. Bess frowned and then a smile split her broad face.

'Ah, I remember you now. The honest chit. It's this castle I fancy you dislike. Well, I can't blame you for that. You joined our household at a hard time.'

'Yes, my lady. Only ...'

'Well? Speak your piece.'

'I find the other servants here don't take to me. They don't take to my tongue.'

'Then you had best see that you stop it up when you're around them, my girl. You've made some enemies, is that it?'

'Something like that.'

'Then unmake them. Make unfriends into friends. And then if they still don't like you, they can go to the devil, can't they?'

'Yes, my lady,' said Amy, smiling despite herself.

'You take it from me – sometimes you have to feign a little to make life a little less to bear. If ever I have cause or let to get away from the place, though, remind me to watch out for you.' Bess looked down. Clutched against her chest was a collection of spooled coloured threads. Amy looked at them longingly as the image of a little shop drifted into her mind – she in the back sewing and Jack at the front, smiling at every customer. The countess shattered the image, looking back at Amy and winking. 'Now, be off with you and don't let me find you moping again. I have enough to do keeping my guest entertained.' Then her voice took on a wistful tone. 'Enough colours here to make her another new periwig. Ach, shall today's conversation be France or Scotland or what'll it be at all...'

Bess seemed to have forgotten Amy entirely. She stomped off towards Mary's apartments, muttering darkly to herself. As she disappeared, a goose walked over Amy's grave. There, she thought. That is the woman you are betraying. That is the mistress to whom you owe loyalty, and about whom you've just been looking forward to whispering about in the shelter of her own parklands.

Her hand wandered to her bosom. She had kept the vial on her, shuttling it between clothes, sleeping with it secreted under her bodice where it could jab at her ribs. Maybe it would be best if she just swallowed it all herself and there made an end to a world full of secrecy and deceit. The thought, depressing and grim, had no time to fester. Besides, it was only the weak, evanescent feeling that she imagined everyone might have when they realise that they've involved themselves in something that might overwhelm them. Before it could grow, Queen Mary herself appeared, a harried-looking Bess behind her.

'We think not to be confined. Your chamber is finer, and I would that we work our needle there,' she was saying.

'As you like, your Majesty.'

Amy flattened herself against the wall and Mary sailed past. As she did, she smiled down, a tired 'isn't this all a dreadful to-do' smile. Her hair today was blonde, looped up under a cap studded with pearls. Amy had heard that she had had to crop her hair close during her flight out of Scotland and that was why she had taken to a variety of wigs. Cattily, she wished silently that it would never grow back straight or fair.

Queen and countess passed out of her sight when a thought struck her. Hitherto she informed Brown only of pointless things – things that should confirm what the Shrewsburys would likely be telling Cecil and Queen Elizabeth anyway. Yet, as she thought of Mary Stuart and her little pearls and her little smiles, another thought occurred to her.

Men had been coming and going from the Scottish queen, her husband and Heydon included. But more importantly, they had been having private talks with her. When it was her turn to gather the royal party's bedsheets and take them for cleaning, she had always waited at the door until one of the queen's minions had delivered them. Yet no one would pay any attention if she went right in and took what she was there for. In fact, it would probably be welcomed by Mary's servants. On the heels of the thought came the realisation that if Brown wanted information – not warmed-over stuff, but the Scottish queen's private whispers – she could seek them out. No one would bother about a lowly maidservant bustling about with bedclothes. She could move like a wraith. And if Mary Queen of Scots was up to something under the earl of Shrewsbury's nose, then Brown could tell Cecil, and Cecil could have that great lady taken away and locked up in the Tower of London. Let's see her, thought Amy, turn the keeper of the Tower into a Catholic slave.

5

Travelling meant taverns. It meant an endless parade of inns, each operated by the same band of ostlers, suspicious tavern keepers, and the occasional pretty barmaid who indicated by her manner whether she was as available as the place's rooms. It meant, too, backside-numbing riding and the itch of sweat as it gathered under the armpits and down the back of shirts. Jack loved it. At each stop, he tried to memorise the layout of the town and the inside of each tavern. The whole world seemed to change: the flat lands of the midlands had turned bumpy, and then hilly, and then opened into yawning valleys misted with curtains of cool, refreshing rain. This was making memories. It was being a new person in every new place.

They had stabled their horses and took benches in the wood-beamed hall of an inn somewhere on the north road. Jack didn't know the name of the town, but the building called itself The Red Lion. Jack sat down and waited whilst Heydon got them some ale. He swept over when he had been served. He seemed to sweep everywhere, Jack thought, walking across every room as though he was its master. A knight in a tale of chivalry. 'The finest south of the Tweed,' he announced, setting the wooden mugs down before them. Heydon looked excited, as though lit from within. He was wearing all black – priestly clothes, he had joked – but with a rich furred vest over his doublet. He had stopped hiding his cross and it sat between the bushy lapels.

'You were a time,' said Jack.

'I was asking after the village. I know Darlington.'

'Where are you from? I mean, before you travelled.'

Heydon looked around the tavern. Apart from a couple of young boys playing dice across the room they were alone. 'The north.'

'You sure seem to know a lot of folks up the north road.' Since they had left the midlands and entered the north of

England, Heydon had enquired after a plethora of names Jack didn't know. Rolleston; Dacre; Norton; Hall; Stanley. And then there were the names he did know: Northumberland; Westmorland; Norfolk. He kept quiet when Heydon spoke with his succession of grave and stony-faced associates.

Sipping at his ale, Heydon looked at him over the rim. He licked the foam from his upper lip and then waved an arm about the room. 'The north, mate. This fine land. It's the backbone of England. And what does that woman in London think of it?' He snapped his fingers. 'That's what. Oh, she expects – demands – loyalty but she wouldn't set foot up here. Knows what would come of her if she did. So she sends up new men – rats, men of no family – and has them tell good honest northern folk what she wants doing. We're oppressed, Jack, held down. You, me, all of the north.

'They won't stand for it. They're not standing for it. But,' he added, lowering his voice, 'they're like lambs without a shepherd. Too many ideas, too little ... too little knowledge. They're all at sixes and sevens – in pursuit of their own designs, not trusting to one another. A mass of sheep in need of someone to bring them together. More like herding cats.'

'Mass,' said Jack, laughing awkwardly. 'Well that suits you then.'

Heydon appraised him for a moment. 'Not word games, mate. Nobody likes jests with words.' Jack felt colour creep up his neck and he bent his head to his mug.

The door to the tavern banged open and both their heads turned. A man Jack didn't recognise came in, swaggering. He was well dressed, his furs outstripping Heydon's. He nodded at them, before making his way over to the bar. Jack was about to take another drink when he saw Heydon staring at the man's back through narrowed eyes. 'One of your friends?'

'No. Have you seen him before?'

'No.' Jack looked at the slim back again. 'I don't think so. Have I?'

'You should have. I reckon he was in Topcliffe.' Jack cast his mind back. He couldn't remember which place Topcliffe was.

'He's following us, do you think?'

'It wouldn't surprise me.'

'But who is he?'

'I don't know. One of Cecil's men, maybe.'

A chill ran through Jack. He had never seen Secretary Cecil, but he had heard rumours about him. A rich old knight of gentleman stock. The kind of man you would bend your knee to even though he wasn't noble. It was his job to keep eyes on every corner of the kingdom. On every corner of the world, some people said. Was that the kind of man that becoming a Catholic made an enemy of? How easy would it be to bring such a man down – especially for a horse keeper?

'Stay here,' said Heydon, drumming his fingers briefly on the table.

'What – where are you going?'

'I'm going to lock our things up in our room. The tapster has given us lodging upstairs. I'll be right back. Keep an eye on our friend over there.'

Heydon disappeared up a narrow wooden staircase beside the bar, their packs tucked under his arms. Jack did as he was bid. The man who might have been from Cecil took his own mug of ale and seated himself on a bench on the opposite side of the room. He dabbed delicately at his mouth with a silky napkin after every sip, but his eyes never left Jack. Irritation and then anger replaced fear. Who was this fool anyway – this fool who didn't even bother to hide that he was watching him?

As Jack felt truculence rise like a cork, Heydon reappeared. He let it go. 'All done?'

'All done. Any word from him?'

'Not one. He's just sitting there watching me.' Jack let his voice rise on the last two words.

'Easy there, mate. No need to fire him up. I'll find out later if the tapster has seen him before. Let's not let him spoil our ale.'

They drank awhile in silence. The appearance of the watcher seemed to call for it, and Jack was glad. If they talked, he didn't yet trust himself not to let something slip about what they were doing. The tavern began to fill up, men pouring in from the fields and the shops. Heydon didn't speak to any of them, and Jack thought he sensed a nervous kind of energy building in him.

'It's getting late now, don't you think?' said Jack, when the place had begun to rock with drunken singing and laughter and profanity. 'I mean, if we're to make a good start in the morning. Down south.' He had decided that lying loudly might be a good way to throw anyone listening off their scent. Heydon laughed. Again he drummed his fingers on the table, stood up and turned. He peered through the close pack of bodies.

'Shit,' he said.

'What is it?'

'He's gone.'

'I didn't see him leave.'

'He didn't go upstairs, did he?'

'No – I'd have seen that, wouldn't I? He must have crept out when someone came in. Is that bad?'

Heydon took a deep breath. 'No. No, I suppose not. He's fishing – casting out lures. Whoever he is he can't know anything or he'd not be here. He'd be flying south looking for reward. There are knaves like him up and down the country. They creep about and if they see anything or anyone they suspect of something, they follow. Hoping to hook a great sturgeon to slice up and serve to Cecil and the London masters. Idlers. Come on.'

They pressed through the crowd and up the stairs, Heydon in the lead. He opened the door to their chamber and entered. There, bent over their bed, rifling through their packs, stood the spy. Heydon threw himself into the room. 'Jack, close the door,' he hissed.

'I've got you fellows to rights,' smiled the stranger. He had Heydon's rosary beads looped through his fingers and he raised them up. His smile disappeared. Heydon launched himself over the bed, his fist flying out. It caught him in the stomach and the man doubled over in shock.

'Knave,' cried Heydon. 'Jack, help!'

Jack stood irresolute. The stranger recovered, his eyes

lighting up with fury. He bared teeth, some of them missing and threw himself forward. His hands came up, the beads held taut between them. 'Jack!' The man pushed Heydon back onto the bed, bringing the rosary up to his throat. He pressed down, his hands on either side of his neck. Heydon bucked, his knee shooting into his attacker's groin, making him moan.

With the stranger yelping, reaching between his legs, Heydon rolled sideways off the bed. He got to his feet and squatted, his hands twisted into fists. 'Come on then, you stinking prick,' he hissed. 'Come on then.' The rosary fell to the floor, the string snapped. The beads flew in all directions. Jack took another few steps forward, his drawn dagger at his hip.

As Jack watched, mouth agape, Heydon and the spy flung themselves at one another. They had hold of each other's shoulders, their fingernails singing into the clothing, knuckles turning white. For a few seconds they seemed to hold in that absurd position. It was like a strange tribal dance. They fought for dominance, circling on the spot. As they twisted, the man's back appeared before Jack. He looked down at his dagger. He moved it up, as though to sink it in. Before he could move, Heydon sank low, catching the man under his centre of gravity. He gave him one hard push, and the spy fell backwards. He almost seemed to totter on to the blade. Jack felt the clothing resist it. He felt his wrist weaken. And then Heydon pushed again. His tightened his grip on the dagger, holding it steady as Heydon pushed the shocked man onto it.

Still, he fought back. He tried to twist as the steel sought his kidneys. And then a slow scream burst from his lips. Before it could reach a great pitch, Heydon punched him hard in the throat. Their victim flopped. Still he was skewered on the point of Jack's dagger. 'Twist it, Jack. Finish him!'

Instead, Jack's hand dropped away, leaving it sticking out of the man's lower back.

It made no difference. The body on the floor continued to wheeze in shallow, stuttering gasps. It made no other sound. 'He's still alive,' said Jack, his voice expressionless. Heydon slid out the blade. Blood had begun to leak onto the wooden floor. It wasn't the gush he had imagined – like a bladder full of it being punctured – but rather a slow, remorseless dribble. His mind had turned backwards, back to another day in another year, and he stood dumb and horror-struck.

'We have to make an end of him,' gasped Heydon. He was fighting to get his breath back, and had leant over the bed, his balled fists down on it. 'We have to get rid of him.' When Jack said nothing, he looked up. 'You … you haven't killed before?'

As though from some distance away, Jack said, 'Yes, Philip. Yes. I murdered my father.'

***

Amy had been gathering all that she felt she needed to impress Brown. Like a bee collecting nectar, she had busied herself listening in on information from the Scottish queen. As she had suspected, no one paid any attention to her. Only the queen's gentlewoman, the haughty dame called Seton who did up her wigs, seemed suspicious, and that too had faded when Amy had gone out of her way to find pins and little ribbons of cloth that made her job easier.

They were at Wingfield – a manor house rather than a crumbling castle. But still there was a hard press of people. The tiresome old steward, Woodward, had been wandering the place top to bottom, creating a list of names. Apparently, there were more than two hundred folks crammed into the place, spilling out into the town. It would, the steward kept lamenting, take several weeks to get an accurate number – 'Were I to count them, they would outnumber the grains of sand – Psalms'. It made moving about unnoticed easier rather than harder. There was such a press, such a crush of people around, that no one looked twice at anyone else.

'No, no. It is no' true.' The sound of Queen Mary's voice drifted from her bedchamber.

'It is that, Majesty,' returned her visitor. Amy had watched him go in when she gathered up the linens, before she dropped a curtsey and backed out of the chamber. But she did not go too far. 'The whole damned pack o' them are in airms and the honest, loyal men o' your party are beaten back and harried wi'oot let or mercy. And ... and I'll no' be sugarin' it, Majesty. The common tongue aboot Edinburgh cries you for a whore, a common jade. And a murderess.'

Silence spun out, followed by a sob. Amy used the moment of quiet to try and make sense of the man's language. If only he would speak more slowly, the translation would be easier. 'Aw, now, come now, please. It's that br'er o' yours.'

'I have no brother,' snapped Mary.

'Moray. It's Moray. You ask me he's paid off traitors in the city to slander your name.'

'Where is he? Did you set eyes on him?'

'He's going north, as I heard. To the wild lands, to subdue the heathens in those parts. Better they should slay him, you ask me.'

'Faithful Sandy,' said Mary. Her voice still carried the ragged edge of tears. 'Oh, what is to become of me, shut up like a common thief.'

'You'll be freed, Majesty.'

'My loyal subjects – they are planning my return?' Silence drew out, followed by the man's awkward coughing. 'Then there is nothing. Nothing to hope for. I have nothing but fair words from this country's mistress.'

'This country's mistress ... you leave matters in the hands of the bishop. Dinnae cry, sweet lady. Leave all to your faithful men.'

There were sounds of movement; Amy suspected that the interview was drawing to a close. In response she began to walk away, humming to herself. She slowed her pace as the man emerged from Mary's chamber and swept past her, intent on fixing his hat back on his head. His name, she knew, was Alexander Bogg or Bock – a Scottish servant the queen had dispatched north for news before Jack and Heydon. Possibly he had met them somewhere on the road.

'Leave matters to faithful men,' she thought. She let it unroll in her mind. Was there some whiff of trickery or treason in it? That would be for Mr Brown to decide. 'The bishop' was the bishop of Ross, Mary's ambassador to the English Court. Yes, it might be a plot. She left the tower rooms and went out into one of the house's two courtyards. The ground was rutted and mutilated. A short distance away two workmen were prying at a cartwheel that had come loose and become wedged in the ground. They were too intent on grunting and heaving to bother with her, and the soldiers at the gate were themselves muttering darkly about their pay when she slipped out.

Like Tutbury, Wingfield stood on a hill. Like the castle, it also had parklands, although they lay at the back of the house sloping downwards towards rangy and uncultivated ponds. Amy had no idea as she quickened her pace whether Brown had reached Wingfield. She reasoned, though, that if he did, he would keep to the usual time and a similar place. The pond itself would be too visible from the house's tower rooms, so she wandered into the parklands.

It was a strange feeling, seeing everything so spongy and budding and green. She looked down at her greying, patched dress as she crunched through the undergrowth. It had been white once. As the world turned green, she remained a drab. Funny; she had never cared about appearances, beyond neatness. In the past she had always relied on her mother's constant, 'don't fuss – no one's looking at you' to excuse her poor dresses. Suddenly it felt a little hollow. Someone was going to be looking at her.

So much for a new start with Jack. A pair of oddballs they were now. In her mind, her mother wagged a finger at her. What would you think of me now? she wondered. Telling tales for … not even for a reward. For a husband who seemed to get further away from her with each passing day.

She began whistling her tune. Time passed, and her cheeks grew tired. She switched instead to the lyrics and began singing in her wobbly contralto.

Behold the skies with golden dyes
Are glowing all around;
The grass is green, and so are the treen,
All laughing with the sound.

'The wrong verse, woman,' snapped Brown. She didn't jump. She had begun to expect his sudden appearances. Relief washed over her.

'Yet the same tune.'

'And you – are you still playing the same tune, or have you turned up something of use?'

'She has had a visitor,' said Amy. She leant against a tree with one arm. Under the other she had bundled the bedlinen. 'The man she sent north. Sandy, she called him. Bogg. Or Bock.'

'And?' Brown was wearing his usual brown suit. She noticed that it always looked neat and pressed, the brass buttons always shining. Even his boots looked fairly well polished despite the fact he must skirt around undergrowth from wherever he lodged.

'And he made her cry. Melancholic knave. Made her weep with tales of how her city slanders her.'

'Good. A broken woman is the best type of woman.' Amy opened her mouth to speak and then closed it. Something in his expression told her he would not stand for a rejoinder. 'It is right that the whore weeps, for the sake of the world that weeps that a woman such as she has brought such destruction on good men. Does she plot with him? Has she spoken treason out of her own mouth?'

Amy wished that she could say yes. But simple honesty prevented that. 'No. No, she sits daily and plies her needle. It's … it's the men around her, the men of her household – them who whisper in corners and plot. I think she knows nothing save a desire to marry with the duke and be delivered up to him.'

Brown folded his arms and gave her a hard look, his grey eyebrows knitting. Not for the first time she wondered what age he was. Somewhere near forty, she guessed. His face was smooth and unlined – a young man's face with a young man's eyes – but the frosted hair made him look older. 'Has she turned you?' he asked without expression. 'Has that witch charmed you?'

'No! Of course not. I ... but I can't lie. I can't invent treasons where I hear none.'

'Hmph.'

'It is ... well, she is in the dumps all the time.'

'Does she speak treason out of her own lips?'

'No!' Brown seemed infuriatingly unable – or unwilling – to understand the emotion in her speech. 'Just ... she's given to crying and fits of weeping. The earl and the countess, they can't long endure her for it. Would a woman who has schemes of freedom and liberty be in the dumps so? Would she weep at the thought of getting herself free?'

'A wicked woman would,' he said. 'A woman who can murder her husband and marry her fellow murderer can play at whatever she likes.'

'Oh,' said Amy. 'That. I hear she hopes to be divorced from her husband.'

Incongruously, a grin spread across Brown's face. 'Ha. The Scots will keep her chained to Bothwell until time runs out. They will recognise no divorce. If her hopes of Norfolk hang on that she is deceived. What else?'

'She complains often of the draughts. And the smell of the privies.' Brown rolled his eyes. 'And ... well, that man, Sandy. I heard him say that she should leave matters to faithful men. That was when she mentioned Queen Elizabeth. There was ... it was the way he said it. I didn't like the sound of it.'

Brown nodded slowly, approvingly. 'It's as I thought. It's as I've said. I've taken lodging in the town and since that wench's coming hither her people have flooded it. Some of them speak openly of her being the rightful English queen.'

'What does that mean?'

'It means,' he said, slamming a fist into his other palm, 'that their design is to murder our sovereign lady. You must keep your ears open for whispers of that. If any plot can be proven it can be stopped. And if that whore knows of it, approves it, then, by God, we shall have the wolf by the ears.'

6

'Murder? By Christ's codpiece, I … Jack!' Heydon snapped his fingers before his eyes. 'Jack Cole. Listen to me now. You can tell me later. You understand that by the Holy Father I can hear your confession and grant you penance. For this and … for anything you care to confess. But not now.'

Dazedly, Jack's eyes came into focus. Heydon was still speaking. 'Right now, we have to figure out what to do about this.'

'Is he dead?' Jack heard his own voice. It was flat, detached, as though the bleeding man in front of him was a swatted fly.

'Not yet. No.' Heydon threw his hat on the bed and ran a hand through his hair. 'We need to get him out of here. Away.'

'Wait. We should wait until everyone's gone away.'

'Until the tapster has locked the front doors? Think, mate. Think!'

Jack began to move. His legs were surprisingly steady. He stepped over to the man he had stabbed. 'He's bleeding.' The blood, brown in the candlelight, was running over the floorboards. As it reached the edges it sank down between them and he imagined it dropping through the ceiling below.

Heydon reached into the mess of stuff the dying man had upended from his pack and withdrew a shirt. 'Jesus, but it kills me to do this,' he said, before tearing off a strip. He dropped and walked on his knees over to the prone form. Then, biting his bottom lip, he pulled up the man's doublet and shirt, revealing the wound. 'Small. Deep.'

'Ugghhahhh….'

Both men flinched. Heydon set to work tying the strip of linen around the wound, knotting it above the hip. When it was tight, he took the rest of the shirt and mopped up the blood. Wadding it into a ball, he stuffed it down the man's waistband, rifling through pockets. He produced some papers and skimmed them. 'No name on these. But notes. On us, where we've been. Who we've spoken to. These will do him no good.' He stuffed the papers under his own shirt. Then he eased off the man's furred vest. 'Better than mine,' he said. 'Do you want this?'

'What? No, I ... I couldn't.' Jack whitened, bringing a hand to his mouth.

'Then I'll have it. We should have been changing apparel now and again anyway.' He pulled the man's doublet back down where it had hiked up and then strode over to the open window, leaning out and down. 'Right,' he said. 'Bastard climbed in from the yard. On a barrel. Here, help me get him on his feet.'

Jack stood irresolute for a few seconds before getting down on one knee and looping an arm under his left armpit. Heydon did the same on his right side, flinging the arm over his shoulder. 'What are we doing, Philip?'

'We have to walk him out. Downstairs. Make it look like we're just a band of drunken friends.'

'Through all them folk?'

'Do you have a better way? Just ... just let me take the lead.'

Heydon nudged open the door and peeked out. Turning, he looked past the unconscious man between them and gave Jack a grim smile and a brief nod. 'Let's go.'

The staircase could not fit three men abreast. They went down sideways, holding their victim up, his feet bobbing and scraping. Near the bottom, Heydon began laughing shrilly, punctuating the sound with snatches of song. Jack kept his head down. The crowd at the bottom barely parted and so he nudged through them. Occasional glances were thrown, not curious but annoyed. Still, Jack flinched under them and turned his eyes to the floor, where the man's feet continued to sway and catch.

'Your friend has a bit too much?' said a middle-aged man, amusement on his features. 'Get the bugger home before he pukes.' Jack said nothing, but Heydon mumbled, 's'a just-a bit too much ta drink.' He continued through the throng until he reached the door, throwing it wide and letting in a stiff breeze.

Together they half-dragged the dying man out into the night. Using his foot, Jack hooked the door and pulled it closed, muffling the sounds of conversation and bawdry.

'Stop,' said Heydon, all trace of drunkenness gone. 'I need a rest. Just a moment.'

'What next?' said Jack. 'We can leave him here, can't we? And just say he was killed by strangers?'

'No. We've been seen together. Don't want any watchmen with sharp eyes asking questions. We need to get him far away. But I can't see how.'

'The barrel,' said Jack.

'What?'

'You said he climbed into our chamber on a barrel.'

'Yes.'

'Well if it was sitting in the yard it should be empty. The tapster wouldn't leave a full barrel sitting in the yard. I've seen how they do it in the duke's household – and the earl's. They lock up the full ones and leave out the empties and work them round.'

A smile split Heydon's features, barely visible in the moonlight and the ambience drifting from poorly-shuttered houses. 'So we can get him in the barrel. Yes, and then we can roll it into the river. The Skerne isn't far from here – just beyond the village.'

'Will it take him away?'

'I don't know. Far enough away, I hope.'

'But ... is he dead yet?'

'Who cares? We'll leave the bunghole of the barrel open. If he's not, he soon will be.' Jack clenched his jaw and swallowed. 'Better that than he lives to tell his tale. Do you want to hang, Jack Cole? Do you want to leave your wife widow to a murderer? A Catholic murderer?'

'I'll get the barrel,' said Jack. 'Here, let's get him in there.'

They dragged the body under the short archway that led into the tavern's yard. Across the way were the shuttered stables. To Jack's left stood a number of barrels. He spotted one under the window that he supposed was theirs. It was too dark to see, but he could feel the depressions in the mud where it had been moved. He tensed before easing it onto its side, knowing how deceptively heavy they were. Thankfully the lid came off with a couple of kicks – only a few nails secured it.

Rolling it under the archway, Heydon and Jack folded the man up on his side, his knees to his chest, and forced him head-first inside. An arm flopped out and Heydon stamped on it. A crack rang out like a thunderclap. Jack closed his eyes briefly and shook his head, trying to chase the sound away. 'There,' said Heydon, nudging the broken limb inside with the tip of his boot. 'Get the lid on. Doesn't need to be on tight.'

Working together, they secured the lid so that it fit snugly, but they made no attempt to nail it shut. 'Now, the river.' Heydon stood up straight and looked around, as though getting his bearings. 'Right. We can't keep to the streets. It's over that way.' He pointed behind the stables. We'll have to go out and find a lane.'

Taking an end of the barrel each, they began rolling it out onto the high street. Its new load made no noise other than soft bumps at it shifted. 'This way,' said Heydon, indicating towards their left. They moved off. It was slow going, slower than Jack had imagined rolling a barrel would be. Past the tavern, a number of timber buildings – part-shops, part-houses – were closely packed. Past them, on the left side of the street, they broke before the residential houses began. Between the two collections of buildings ran a little alleyway, bushes lining it on either side. They passed into it.

'Who's there?' snapped a creaky voice. 'Is someone there?'

Both men froze. The voice – an old man's – came from beyond the bushes to their right. A little light wobbled, moving from side to side. 'I'll call the watch.' Jack looked at Heydon, his eyes wide. His friend raised a finger to his lips. After a while, a young female voice drifted over them.

'What is it, dad?'

'I thought I heard someone. After the chickens.'

'It'll be a fox. It won't get them.'

'Strange sounds for a fox.'

'I can't hear nothing. You've scared it off. Come inside, it's still getting bitter at night. Look, you're not even in your coat.'

'Eeh, you're right there, girl.' The old man raised the light high again. 'You hear that, foxy? The chickens are well tended here.'

The light disappeared, followed by the soft click of a door. Still, Jack and Heydon waited, as though not wanting to tempt fate. Eventually Heydon whispered, 'get moving'. Jack did.

The lane did not last long, the muddy track giving way to patches of grass. Heydon veered them to the left, but before long Jack needed no guidance. The soft burble of the river announced its presence, and the vegetation underfoot grew thicker and reedier. It was interspersed by flat stones.

The river itself was a thick black viper cutting through the darkness of the night. They stopped alongside it. 'Watch yourself, mate,' said Heydon. Jack moved away from the barrel. Pulling open the lid, Heydon threw in a couple of large stones he pried out of the wet ground. Then he worked loose the barrel's bunghole before replacing the lid. 'Right, help me give it a heave.'

The barrel rolled down the slight incline towards the river. It slowed near the bottom and for a moment Jack suspected it would stop there, become stuck, a mute witness to their crime. But Heydon skipped through the reeds, his arms out for balance, and gave it a kick. It landed in the water with a soft splash and bobbed there, moonlight glinting on the metal bands that circled it. Then it spun on the spot. Water must have found the bunghole, and it submerged without a sound, before bobbing again just a little, further along. Heydon reached into his shirt and pulled out the man's papers, tearing them up and throwing them into the water too. They flashed grey in the moonlight before the water claimed them.

Jack thought of the man he had stabbed. He imagined him coming to at that second, trapped in a rapidly filling black chamber, throwing his hands out and looking for escape as his world was cut off. Heydon interrupted him. 'He's gone. We have to get back.'

They walked back to the tavern. Before opening the door, Heydon clapped his arm. 'You well, mate?' Jack said nothing but attempted a nod. 'Good man. You have to be. We'll talk upstairs.'

They re-entered the merrymaking chaos and made their way back through the crowd, heads bowed. Before they could reach the stairs, a man stepped into their path. 'Good evening to you, lads,' said the stout thirty-something.

'Mr Wytham,' said Heydon. 'Jack, this is my good friend Mr Wytham.' Then, with meaning, 'one of this good town's constables.' Jack looked the man in the eyes briefly, before returning his glance to the floor. The constable looked harmless enough, sheep-faced but sharp-eyed.

'Did your friend get to his lodging?' asked Wytham, hooking his thumbs into his belt and letting his stomach protrude.

'He did that, sir,' said Heydon. 'Although he spoke of riding for the south with speed.'

'In that state? He'll not be fit for a ride in the morning.'

Heydon shrugged in response. Then he said, 'this is my man, Jack Cole.' He dropped his voice. 'He's the faithfullest and more fire-filled man of the faith.' Jack's heart leapt. But Wytham only gave him a hard look, followed by a smile, his eyes moistening.

'Good man, Jack,' he said. 'Pray God you can prove that before long.'

They exchanged little half-bows all round and Jack and Heydon went upstairs, closing the door of their room. Heydon flopped down on the bed, lying right back and gazing at the ceiling. 'Done,' he said.

'But what have I done?' asked Jack. He remained by the door. Now his legs seemed to wobble, and he slid down, letting them splay out in front of him. His head fell into his hands.

'What needed doing.'

'They'll be after us now though, won't they? Cecil's men? Cecil himself? I mean, I've killed one his men. He'll want – what do you call it? Retribution! He sees everything. He'll send people.'

'Calm yourself, mate.' Heydon's tone was business-like. 'There's no one going to come. Not for him.'

'How not? Won't –'

'Hush. Do you think that Cecil or his queen give a merry fuck about the men they employ?' His brow darkened – in anger, it seemed to Jack. 'They hate them. They hate their informers. Think they're dirty and shameful. Men like Cecil – his mistress too – they are ashamed that they must trade in secrets with grubby little men like that. They would deny them in an instant. If any are killed or disappear, they will shrug. "One less grasping urchin – let us find a cheaper one," they'll say.' He mimicked a high-born London accent. 'No, old England's rulers have no loyalty, no more than creatures like yonder drowned fellow have loyalty to them. They are just useful cutpurses, to be used and then discarded. No one will come. Even if his body washed up on the shore at Cecil's house, he would betray no knowledge of the man and have his corpse cast into a midden. His death will mean nothing, not even a trail of papers. He is trash.'

'But it was wicked, wasn't it? I killed a man.'

Heydon sat up, swinging his legs off the bed. 'It's a war, Jack. We're at war. They understand this up here. Men die in war. Woman too. Especially if they're their generals.' At the word 'women', Jack spluttered.

'What will Amy say? What will she think of me?'

'She won't know. A soldier doesn't trouble his wife with tales of his doings. I wasn't speaking of your goodwife, mate.'

Jack looked up. 'You said that a man might be forgiven his sins in the faith, didn't you?'

'I did. Provided he confesses them fully to a priest, in the expectance of God's mercy. And provided he does his penance.'

'Then … I suppose … then I could confess to you, Philip? As a priest? And I could be forgiven for all that I've done, couldn't I?'

'Of course, my son. Would you like to make your confession now, in God's presence?'

'Yes. Yes, if I could?'

***

Amy dreamed that she had poisoned Queen Mary. She had dropped the vial of poison into the broth that was nightly carried from the kitchen for the woman's supper, and throughout the night Wingfield Manor had rocked with cries and shouts of horror and relief and fear. And then, in the dream, she had turned into a bird and flown out one of the windows. She had found Heydon and pecked him to death too, and then she had landed next to Jack and transformed back into herself. Then they had been old people together, working away in a little timber-framed shop, and people had come by so that he could smile his old crazy smile at them and she could be safe in the back, plying her needle. And no one would ever know that she had killed an anointed queen.

What had woken her? The other female servants snored and rolled in their sleep. Lights still burned all around the dormitory and she could hear voices drifting in from outside. They were too low and indistinct to make out what was being said. She rolled onto her side, the blankets tangling between her legs. Next to her bed – not that it was really a bed, with neither mattress nor pillows – was a little book. Taking the countess's advice, she had decided to try and mend fences with the other servants. Amongst the crates and carts full of stuff still being trundled from Tutbury she had found it, lying dejected in the courtyard. Its cover was mud-splattered, but the thing was still quite readable, though she knew that she could never hope to understand many of the words inside. Its title page proclaimed it as *The Tragical History of Romeus and Juliet*, by a man called Arthur Brooke. Few of her peers could read at all, but all of them liked being read to, and so she had offered to read the book to them during their evenings. At first, they had rolled their eyes, but when she had begun to read it, they fell under the spell. Finally, she had thought, her busy tongue might work in her favour. She could do as her mother used to do – read and tell stories and make people smile. Her mother had not had the luxury of a book, though, reciting her rhymes and tales from memory. So, Amy thought, she was in an even luckier position. It would be a crime not to use your gifts to make the world more liveable, anyway.

How they had giggled when she had warned them, using a deep, manly voice, to avoid the fate of a couple of unfortunate lovers, giving in to dishonest desire; neglecting authority and advice; listening to drunken gossips and superstitious friars, attempting all adventures of peril to meet their lusts; using confession to further their wicked designs. The girls' giggles had given way to something like serious contemplation when she had warned them of dishonest living hastening unhappy death, just as it did for Romeus and Juliet. She had felt her own throat prickle with fear when she had recited lines which read:

What if with friendly speech the traitor lie in wait,
As oft the poisoned hook is hid, wrapt in the pleasant bait?
Oft under cloak of truth hath Falsehood served her lust;
And turned their honour into shame, that did so slightly trust.
What, was not Dido so, a crowned queen, defamed?

Then she had affected a yawn and insisted that she would finish the story on another night. But the words haunted her, though she had no idea who Dido was. It was the word 'poison', she guessed, which had spurred on her nightmares.

If it came to it, could she kill Queen Mary? And what would happen to her if she did? Surely there would be someone to taste her food – to prevent it from happening? Or perhaps, as Brown had said, the poison was too slow for a taster to be of any use. Then she'd kill two people, unless she found some subtle means of getting into only Mary's mouth. Could she? She wasn't worried for her soul. She believed in God, but beyond that she had never cared for forms of worship. Church was somewhere you went to gossip, to hear about what was happening and to speak to people you never otherwise had a chance to. It was only the old and the eccentric who took it seriously. Faith, though – that was different. That was what you were when you were alone. It was your beliefs. It was what helped you when you were facing death or loss or cruelty. It was not what you performed on the stage of the world, and it was not what the men and women of politics burned and maimed and killed for.

And Jack. She thought she knew why he would care about worship and forgiveness and could see how easy it would be for a man like Philip Heydon to spot that and recruit him.

Yes, although he did not know it, she had worked hard in uncovering Jack Cole's secrets before she had agreed to be his wife. Some of what she heard was rumour, no doubt embroidered, but she felt she had sifted enough wheat from chaff to understand a good deal about him. And what she had learnt did not disgust her or even frighten her. It had moved her to pity.

She rolled over again, so that she faced away from the book. But still the image of dead lovers, doomed before the story had even unfolded, lodged in her mind.

7

'My mother died when I was born. I mean, that's usual, isn't it? For mothers to die abed in childbirth.' Heydon nodded encouragement. Still he sat on the bed; still Jack sat on the floor. 'I came out wrong, he said. My father.' He held up his hand and twisted his knuckles, the joints shifting and bending even at the wrist. 'Said it was a mark of the devil, that I was ill-formed and wicked. Said that I'd killed my mother coming out like that.

'Then since I could remember he would beat me. Beat the devil out of me, he always said. It got worse when he drank. Then he would whip the devil out, all over my back. The marks are still there. I can feel them when I reach round. When I was old enough to walk and talk, that's when I learnt to be silent. I tried to please him, to show him I wasn't touched by the devil. But he didn't want me speaking.' Jack shrugged, his eyes on the floor. He thought he could still see the blood stains. 'I suppose he thought if I was talking, then I could complain of him. And he was an important man. Always seemed so anyway. He was in the duke's household. He preached reform – not as a minister or anything, but to the other servants. He got a name for it, Henry Cole. The Godly man. I suppose I reminded him of ungodliness. His own ungodliness. So I learnt to keep quiet, not to speak loudly.

'I think I tried to be good. I tried to make him stop. But as I got bigger, he got worse. His drinking got worse, though he still was able to see to his work, I suppose, or we'd have been thrown into the gutter. But then he looked at me differently. I think I must have been about six or seven. He had never taken a new wife. I heard him speak about it often enough. To the other servants, to his friends who came to listen to thoughts on reform and religion.

'He beat me more and more, for shame, I think. He … I can't right remember all that happened. I suppose I went quiet.
106

Quieter than ever. And I just let him. I just let him hold me down and hurt me, whipping, beating. It was for discipline, he said. A good father disciplined his son, even if it was really a devil's son. Nobody said nothing. Nobody would see anything wrong in a Godly man giving his son right good discipline. But I decided I would make it stop. I tried once asking one of the women servants for help. She could see there was something wrong. Said I was too quiet for a little lad. I showed her the marks on my legs. Most folk never saw anything. He never beat me anywhere you could see unless I was unclothed.

'She was a good woman. Older – a mistress of the old duchess's wardrobe. Kind too. Told me stories of chivalry and knights and escapes and all of that stuff. She said she would help me get away – maybe get to sea and start a new life there. I don't know what happened, really. I was supposed to meet her one night outside the house and she said she would have a friend ready to take me away. I went.' Jack gave a humourless smile. 'But no one came. I never saw the woman again. I heard she had been sent away for stealing. My dad told me that. He was smiling when he told me. He said, "I know all that passes in my house." He didn't hurt me that night, I don't think. I suppose killing my escape was hurting enough. I never tried again. I didn't want to hope. I didn't want to get anyone else into trouble.

'His drinking got worse though. They say that about men who drink. They can start by hiding it, but one day they can't anymore. One day it masters them, and then their work starts to fall off. His friends stopped coming by our chambers. He ranted about God forsaking him. That was my fault, I suppose. He didn't say that, though. He just laid into me. But I was getting bigger by then. I must have been … I don't know – I think about thirteen maybe. By then I'd taken to keeping away. I didn't try and be good for him anymore. Knew it didn't work. So I would go and try and make myself useful to other people. Helping move hay for the horses. Listening to what other people said. Trying to show them all that I wasn't a devil, that I didn't need disciplined because I was a good boy.

'I found him at the foot of the stairs by our chamber. It was summer, I remember, because I could hear birds singing early in the morning. He had been drinking all night, I thought. He must have fallen on the stairs. He was getting pretty bad by then at hiding it – did I say that? There was some blood coming from his head. But he wasn't dead. I went down and checked. I could hear him breathing. It was a strange sort of breathing. As though every breath was like a little thunder. Rattling like that, rumbling. His eyes were open but not all the way. He saw me. I could see that he saw me. And he mumbled something. I don't know what. I knew that I should fetch someone, get his head all tied up to stop the blood. But I didn't. I just stood and watched him a while. And then…' Jack swallowed. 'And then I leant down and pinched his nose tight. I put my other hand over his mouth. And I waited. Just waited. I don't know how long. Too long; I remember that my legs started to hurt. When I let go his eyes were still open, but he didn't make that sound anymore. He didn't breathe. And then I ran away to fetch help.

'I pretended to cry. Maybe I did cry a little. It didn't seem like I'd done anything right away, you know? It seemed just a small thing, like a dream. And then after that I went quiet for a long time. I tried not to think about anything. I know that people came and went, wondering what to do about me. Maybe some of them thought it was odd, what had happened. I think they did. I mean, he must have been looked at by someone, a physician or someone, mustn't he?

'But no one ever said anything about me. I wasn't sent away, as I'd hoped. I just stayed on, in the same rooms. I was put to work in the stables. Because my father had been a loyal man, they all said. And that was all good. But … Philip, I never felt a great guilt. You know if you've done something wicked – something you know is wicked – they say you feel it in your soul? I didn't. Never. I was just scared that one day I might say something. Or that maybe I was mad, a broken person. That people would find out what I did and then the whole world would cry devil at me. So I tried to be good. I tried to be just as good as I could be. I smiled upon everyone. I tried to be friends with everyone. But that only made them distrust me. Call me names. So I just hoped to be ignored. Maybe one day to get a wife and make a new start somewhere. I feared it – do you know that? I feared leaving the duke, even though that's what I wanted more than anything, to go out into the world. I don't know why. I think – I reckon like I've been cursed. Like everything will turn out bad that I do. I have such a mad temper sometimes, I do foolish things in a trice, in heat, and think I might be tainted. In the blood. So I was afraid.

'And that's it. That's what I did. I ... If I could be forgiven, if I could get God's mercy ... is that something you can even get after you've ... done something like that?'

'Jack ...' said Heydon. He was staring at him intently, with soft brown eyes similar to Jack's own. He made the sign of the cross, and then chanted, 'indulgentiam, absolutionem, et remissionem peccatorum tuorum tribuat tibi omnipotens, et misericors Dominus. Amen.'

Jack gave a solemn nod at the words. They were beautiful, ancient, mysterious sounding. As though just saying and hearing them made some change in the world: in him. 'Thank you,' he said, not knowing if that was appropriate.

'I can grant you forgiveness. I can offer you the chance for penance. But this is a great crime. Though God knows you had faced a brutish man. If you had had the strength to speak against him. If that ... But yes, I think God in his mercy can receive you. Even after such a sin. If you truly repent. Do you?'

'I ... yes,' said Jack. In truth he did not know if he did. Still, he did not regret killing his father. Oh, he wished that he had not done it, not had to do it, if that was what repentance was. But he had, and he had never once wished the man was alive again. 'Yes.'

'Your wife – does she know what you did?'

'No,' said Jack, panic rising. 'She doesn't. She can't – I don't want her to know. You won't tell her, will you?'

'Of course not. You have confessed freely. I am God's ambassador here. I intercede only with him. If I opened my mouth to anyone else, it would be me sinning.' Jack relaxed. It hadn't felt quite as freeing to reveal his past to someone as he'd hoped, but it was something. 'But this matter of your penance.'

'I'll do anything,' said Jack, nodding the truth of it. 'Anything you like.'

'It will be a great thing, mate. For something as large as this matter. And the other – the work you have done tonight.' He paused, putting a hand up to knuckle his temple. 'I told you we're at war. I meant that. I said sometimes women are killed in war.' Jack felt his stomach clench as Amy popped into his mind, her impish smile on her face. 'The thing is this. There are great plans in train at this moment. Plans to free Queen Mary. You should like to free the queen, would you not?'

'I would. She is a sweet lady.' Jack let modesty turn his eyes to the floor again. He was sure that lust was a sin – and one he did not want to confess to. 'It's not right that she is kept a prisoner. She should be sent home.'

'She should be given this realm,' said Heydon. 'It is her birth-right as much as Scotland. The heretic Elizabeth is a bastard, as everyone knows. She sits on England's throne by trickery – by the false will of her father, who took a sword to law and custom to let his bastard child take his throne. The Holy Father would be rid of her. The kings of France and Spain, of every Catholic country, would be rid of her. All would have Queen Mary given her place. All would have her most Catholic Majesty restore this poor realm to the Pope's obedience. Only Elizabeth stands in the way. I … I regret I cannot get rid of her myself, being a priest. Not until the Pope gives holy sanction to such an act.

'But you, Jack. If you wish to be truly shriven – if you want your soul cleansed by a Godly act, then you might turn your hand to it.' Heydon's voice had shifted from the joviality he usually employed to the stirring eloquence he adopted when he got onto religious matters. 'Perhaps that's what this has all been about – your father and this night. God has shown you that you can turn your hand to cleansing the world of wicked folk. I must ask, then, that you make your penance by getting rid of another such one. Kill Elizabeth.'

Part Three: A Summer Storm

1

The walls of Berwick stabbed at the sky. They paused at the sight before Heydon led them in a trot across the bridge that spanned the churning Tweed. Jack kept his eyes fixed ahead, refusing to look down. He knew it was stupid – no barrel was going to bob along with a greying hand jutting from its lid, but still…

As they drew closer, the mass of grey resolved itself into neat grey blocks, dressed and fitted together. But as they approached one of the gatehouses, the shabbiness of the new-built defences became clearer. The walls stood unfinished, some sections dressed and smooth, rearing twenty-odd feet into the air, and others a jumble of giant dice. Queen Elizabeth, Heydon had told him, had been having them constructed since her reign began. Only this year had she abandoned the effort, leaving her northern subjects to the Scots. All about money, he had said. Money was raised in the north but spent in the south.

It had been days since they had gained the last hundred miles from Darlington; Heydon seemed in no hurry. He had wanted, he told Jack, to get the mood of the whole north. Jack had been happy enough at that. Privately, he wanted to spin time out, to make it last. It was not that he was enjoying the journey – not after what had happened at Darlington – but rather that if time slowed, he might not have to do what he had promised. What, he reminded himself, the Holy Father and his brotherhood were now relying on him to do.

Who was Queen Elizabeth anyway? He had asked himself that often during the previous days. A woman he had never seen – a bastard, whatever you believed. Her father had seen to that, divorcing and killing her mother. Yet she had been his sovereign lady since he was a child. He had heard his father talk about her in the old days – about how she would take the throne when the old queen finally went to hell, and thereafter confirm England as a reformed realm. Then he had imagined her as a rampaging monster. That was the only kind of woman he could see his father approving of. As he had grown, though, he had heard little about her. She never came into the duke's lands, and when the duke went south, he visited her only in her private chambers. Whatever it was that she did – make laws, make friends and enemies with the rest of the world, gather in money – none of that had ever touched him. Would that make it easier or harder to kill her?

'Remember, mate – you're my man. The passport allows me one man.'

Jack shook away the cobwebs as they approached the gatehouse. Two soldiers stood sentry, both of them old and scrawny, in a parody of military bearing. 'Good day,' saluted Heydon. 'My man and I are going north into Scotland.'

'Are you now? Your name? You got your papers?'

Heydon handed them down. 'I'm Heydon. This is my man, Jack Cole, of the earl of Shrewsbury's household.' The first man passed them to the second without a glance. 'On the secretary's authority?' asked the more interested of the two.

'We are that.'

'Not too many of you going north. Most've been flying south. To the Scotch queen.'

'We're not most,' said Heydon, waving a hand in the air.

'Is it the Scotch regent you're up for?'

'No,' said Heydon. Then, 'yes. Look, it is private business with the queen's license. Allow us passage, will you?'

The sentry's bottom lip jutted, and he seemed to weigh up whether to be difficult or not. Eventually his face smoothed. 'Aye, well, go on then.' He held out the paper. Heydon gripped it, and then the man's own grip tightened. 'Remember,' he said, 'to keep this close. If ye're attacked in that land, it'll cause us all aches, so keep yer heads down and yer wits sharp.'

They passed through the gatehouse and into the town. Before them lay a green, houses bordering it. The road stretched off to their right and Heydon led them. He seemed, thought Jack, to know the way. Not for the first time, he wondered where exactly in the north his friend hailed from. He seemed to know a good many people, all of them secretive and shady, but had never spoken of his family, who they were or what they did. They passed what looked like a communal altar with a stone cross surmounting it. Here and there wives walked with baskets on their arms, marking out the buildings on either side of the road as shops. The smell of fish was strong in the air, a salty nip that forced its way down the back of the throat. But it was a clean, fresh smell. Aided by strong sea air, it washed away the usual stink of middens and outhouses.

'This way,' said Heydon, drawing short. Two women separated and skirted them, throwing up aggrieved looks as they had to walk closer to the sewage ditches. 'I know the tapster.' Of course you do, thought Jack.

When their horses were stabled, and they had been shown to their chamber, Heydon collapsed on a crate that served as the room's chair. He let one arm dangle languidly and the other wandered to the crucifix he had taken to wearing on the outside of his clothing. 'We could probably make Fife in a day or two if we ride hard and don't stop. Depends on the weather. We'd have a job doing any more today. Don't like the look of that sky.'

'Where's Fife?' asked Jack. He put his pack down and sat cross-legged on the floor. It was a stupid question, probably, but he didn't know Scotland. He pictured it only as a land of jagged mountains and people living in caves.

'Up the coast.'

'Is that in Edinburgh? Is that where Queen Mary lived?'

'Mate, you don't know your maps,' smiled Heydon. 'No, Edinburgh is the town. We'll go around that. It's reformer country now. But we'll have to cross the Forth to get where we're going.'

'Where's that?'

'The good regent's house. Queen Mary's brother. The rumour is that he has that proof of England's governance of Scotland locked up tight there.'

Jack shifted position. The bones of his backside were

already starting to ache, and he switched to kneeling. A little twinge of disappointment passed through him. He had wanted to see where Mary had lain her head – the palaces and the chambers. He had assumed that her brother had taken them all over. 'And then what? Do we … do we have to fight our way in?'

'No, mate, no. The earl of Moray is in the north – the wild country. Trying to break the wild men to his will, probably. His house will be empty enough. Just his wife and her attendants.'

Jack paled. 'We don't have to hurt anyone do we? Won't he have taken the thing with him?'

'No,' said Heydon. His face hardened, and Jack felt it better not to ask any more stupid questions. 'Calm yourself down. We won't hurt women. The papers will be there. They're in his own private possession, not state papers. Not to be carried about and stolen or lost. We'll just scurry in like mice, as fine as you like, and scurry back out and away.' He had been idling with the crucifix, and he lifted it and touched it to his lips. 'Do you speak their language?'

'Scots? No. Will I need to?'

'Not a word. I get by in it. Latin, French, Italian – I have a bit of it all. You just keep your mouth shut and let me speak for you. Come, sit by me, mate.'

Jack shuffled on his knees over to Heydon. His friend reached down and took his hand. 'You're not worried about the task God's given you, are you?'

'No.'

'Don't lie,' smiled Heydon. 'It's a good thing to worry. Keeps a man sharp. On his toes. You'll be known to all history. The man who brought a cursed realm back to its proper obedience.' Jack swallowed.

'When?'

'When things are all in good order. Haste makes waste, and all that. When the north is ready to rise up and free Queen Mary. This year, though. Winter would be good.'

'Why winter?'

Heydon stood up and turned his back on Jack. He leant

against the plastered wall and began to trace a crack with his finger. 'We have in mind already a course for ridding the world of that woman. But only at the right time. See this wall? I could chip away a little bit and it would still stand. But if I just waited until lightning struck the building, I could find the right place – downstairs – and tear out a keystone. The whole place would fall in fire and smoke. And I could rebuild it. Better, new. You see what I mean?' Jack didn't. He nodded. 'There'll come a time when the men of the north stop fighting with themselves. Stop arguing about what's to be done. Stop seeing no further than the end of their noses. When it comes, they'll need a little push. They want the queen gone, of course they do, but they're frightened folk. And that's when we'll be ready to strike.'

'Strike,' murmured Jack. He pictured himself stabbing at the queen. He had seen her image on coins, and the duke of Norfolk had a miniature portrait he had treated like a shrine when people visited. In the one she looked like a hawk with swirls at her neck and head. In the other, she looked cold and mannish, overdressed.

'She travels by boat often. From one of her stolen palaces to another. You can't get at her directly, not without being caught.' The word 'caught' made Jack's eyes widen. He had tried not to think about the actual doing of the act, still less what might happen afterwards. Did men ever kill great people and get away with it? Yes, he thought. Whoever had murdered Queen Mary's last husband had done that, blaming her. 'Don't worry. You won't get caught. Not if you follow my direction. We should rent some chamber looking over the river. A lodging house, something like that. That's easy enough in London. They don't ask questions. Probably think we're lovers at some game. But I'll have got us a gun, mate. A firearm. And you'll just poke it through a window and when the Welsh harridan's barge gets close by, you will blow her into hell.'

Jack could see it. The flash of a gun – not that he knew how to use one – the explosion and smoke and confusion. The boat would rock as men and women jumped from their seats. The queen would collapse, maybe not realising what had happened at first, before she looked down and saw blood spreading on her bodice. They would then carry her ashore, all in a tumult, and she would bleed to death. Men would search the chamber, but all they would find was a spent gun.

A jolt of reality intervened. 'But barges – I've seen them – they have glass windows. She'll be inside the little chamber.'

'Bah,' said Heydon. He had turned, and his back was against the wall, arms folded. 'A cannon can blast through glass. It'll be moving slowly. You'll have time to aim it.'

'But I don't know how to shoot,' said Jack, holding up his hands. He realised that he must seemed to be making excuse after excuse. It was cowardly talk – not at all what the Holy Father or the Church would want to hear.

'So? If you miss, you miss. You'll strike the barge then. A good gun will hit a mark. If it bites into her foolish boat, it will tear a hole in it. The whole thing will sink. If we do it near London bridge, the oarsmen won't have a chance. Water will pour in and the whole thing will sink into the waves. Freezing waves in winter, mate. And the whole pack of them will be dragged down. You can't swim when you're trapped in a cabin and weighted down with stolen jewels. You'll have her in hell without the bullet touching her.'

'And then what happens?' Jack wanted to move past the images of death and murder – assassination, he quickly corrected – as fast as possible.

'And then her whole rotten government tumbles. The heretics. The men who've tortured the realm to line their own pockets. Cecil and his new men. All of them will stumble around like rats in a sack. Whilst the faithful will free Queen Mary and carry her south. And who'll there be to resist her? No one. They'll all be looking to their own heads and their own purses.

'Man alive, it will be beautiful. A realm in chaos. Needing order – crying out for it.'

'Will – will people know it was me? That I did it?'

'Only those you want to know. I can inform the Holy Father and the whole college of cardinals, or no one at all if you like.

God will know you did your duty, though. You'll get your reward for that.'

Silence fell between them. Jack screwed his eyes shut, trying to make sense of the world. Here he was in an inn he didn't know in a town on the edge of the world with a priest he had only met months before, plotting to kill England's queen. Heydon had made everything sound so right – so achievable – so desirable. He wanted to be back in Howard House or Arundel or anywhere where he had his own chamber. A place he could lie with Amy and listen to her talk about her day whilst he stared placidly, his stupid old smile plastered on his face.

As he opened his eyes, he found Heydon staring into them.

No, he thought. He was being weak, as weak as he had been as a child. He had killed two men now, and God wanted him to do this … this other thing. It was only his faith that had wobbled for a second, caught in the wind of cowardice.

He wouldn't waver again.

2

It seemed for a while that Amy wouldn't need to use the mysterious little vial. Queen Mary appeared to be doing everyone a favour and dying of her own accord.

Since the messenger had arrived from Scotland and told her she was railed upon as a whore and a murderess, the Scottish queen had seemed to wilt. Each day news came that some old illness had returned. A physician was in constant attendance, and she gave up leaving her chamber entirely. When Amy went in to remove the bedding and bring fresh stuff, the room was shrouded in darkness. On the occasions Mary went out to walk on the roof leads, she was half-carried, flashing pained smiles at those who held her under her arms. Player, thought Amy: the woman was a stage player. If that were true, though, she had to admit that Mary was a good one.

What seemed to Amy to have happened was that the Scottish queen had given up on life. That was a thing that suited her well enough. It wasn't her day to carry out the linens from the royal apartments, but she hovered outside anyway, hoping to see something.

When the time for morning dinner arrived, she watched, pretending to wipe the dust from a window frame, as a team of the queen's servants marched in procession past her. Each of them carried wooden trays covered with cloths. At the head of the troupe one had under each arm a series of wooden boards. He placed them by the door before rapping with a gloved hand. After a short time, the door was opened and the whole group went in. What had caught Amy's attention, though, was the man carrying a silver salt urn. She considered the poison tucked away again in her bodice. If she could somehow get it into the urn, which would be kept locked somewhere in the kitchens, and swirl it around, that might work. It would also mean that the queen's taster would not be affected; he or she would taste the food, find it uncompromised, and then pass it to Mary. Mary would then feel quite safe salting her own food.

There were many things wrong with such a plan. Amy knew nothing about the poison. Did salt counteract it? Absorb it? Surely not – or else salt itself would prove a wonderful antidote. At any rate, it did not matter. She had time to refine the idea. No word had come, and none had been whispered, about Elizabeth being attacked. It might be that she would never have to act at all. It was her job now to watch, to listen, and to wait.

She walked away from the royal apartments, steeling herself for another round of gathering in the servants' soiled clothes and bedding. It was time for a proper hot wash with soap for the sheets, and a stiff brushing of garments. She looked down at her hands. The pads of her palms were calloused and rough, as they always were. The skin on the back of each was red. Only her nails looked to be in rude health, long and sharp. As sharp as needles, she thought, and for a moment she allowed herself to imagine a life free of queens and earls and countesses – a life in a quiet place where her hands would be soft and the most work she would have to do would be plying a needle when she chose to.

The fragility of her dream was shattered by the sight of Bess, standing in the corridor, and speaking in low tones with a gentlewoman. Whatever she was saying, she cut it short and sent the woman off towards Mary's rooms. The countess made to move away, as though intending to ignore Amy entirely. Then she seemed to think better of it.

'Good morrow, my girl.'

'And you, my lady.'

'You're kept busy? What were you doing?'

'I ... I saw a soiled window.' She held up a finger that still had a streak of grime on it.

Bess raised an eyebrow. 'Good girl. You ... you have been laundering the Scottish queen's bedclothes, haven't you?'

'Not today, my lady.'

'No, but it is your duty?' A note of irritation crept into Bess's voice, making her sound like a parent addressing a stupid child.

'Yes, it is.'

Bess inhaled deeply. From her waist hung a scented pomander, and with one hand she began swinging it slowly from side to side like a censer. Occasionally she batted it hard into the palm of her other hand. 'What do you hear in there, girl?'

'Hear?'

'Come now, you're not stupid. You have ears and no end of a mouth. What does she talk about with her folk when I'm not there and she's not squawking in my chambers?'

'I don't know, my lady – I...' Amy read the mounting anger on Bess's face. 'She talks of the duke of Norfolk,' she shrugged. 'She and her ladies used to whisper and gossip about him, before she fell into sickness.'

'I see. What else?'

'I can't say, my lady. They often speak in French and Scots. Very fast. I can't understand.' Bess sighed and let the pomander fall. Amy chanced her luck. 'Will it be much longer that she is with us?'

'Ha! A fair question. I can't say. I wish I could. My lord ... the earl ... he is not a well man himself. These last months ...' Amy thought that tears might be starting in Bess's eyes. The catch in her throat betrayed them. 'All my business, my work ... and my husband...' She trailed off, and then coughed hard, shaking her head a little. 'Not long, let's hope, eh? It's a stout courage that can stand some mishaps and hard times.'

'Yes, my lady.'

'And ... if you should hear anything of interest in your duties. In there, I mean,' said Bess, nudging her chin in the direction from which Amy had come, 'you know what you must do?'

'Tell the earl,' said Amy.

'Tell me, lass, tell *me*.'

As Bess walked away, only knuckling her eyes when she had turned her back, Amy felt a ripple of pity for Queen Mary. No doubt the gentlewoman had been given a similar task: watch, spy, inform. Even in her own bedroom the Scottish queen would never be alone.

***

Moonlight wobbled on a coastal inlet where the River Eden rushed to meet the North Sea. They had come into parklands, somewhere further up the coast than the old cathedral town of St Andrews. The trip from Berwick had taken days, despite the outbreak of good weather. It was not that Heydon had had a multitude of friends to swap plans with – they had been left behind in the north of England – rather, the simple fact of their horses' exhaustion had required frequent stops. They entered in between the sculpted trees and bushes where the stars couldn't reach, the warm wind whipping at their coats.

Jack had been surprised to find that Scotland didn't look all that different to northern England. He had heard somewhere that the air changed north of the border – that it was coarser and bred hardier people. That had made him imagine small, gnarled, hairy men and large, thickset women. But in the town and villages they had stayed in as he and Heydon made their way up the coast and around Edinburgh, he found that all that had really changed was the language. Still there were the ubiquitous taverns, the towns with broad main streets, the wives and their friends gossiping over baskets.

It was when they were in an inn earlier in the evening of their planned raid that another difference struck him. Although he could barely understand what was being said, he realised that the same attitude had been prevalent in almost every stop in Scotland. The people, quite simply, had no respect for their authorities. Occasionally Heydon would translate a joke or a comment. The Scots language, he said, was really just a cross between good English and the sound of someone buggering a mastiff. When a burgess or a baillie – apparently their words for alderman and justices – entered a tavern, he would be met with catcalls and men shouting, 'chase yersel' and 'away ye go an' shite.' For their part, the town authorities seemed to be in on the jesting, returning insults with vigour.

More strangely, the places seemed abuzz with political conversation. Men were arguing over the war between the queen's supporters (whoremasters, apparently, followin' a daft French murderess) and those calling themselves the king's party (treacherous basturts who wahnt tae suckle fae England's teats). Town men seemed to be abreast of what was happening – probably, said Heydon, because that part of the country was so small and its leaders within spitting distance. In London one heard similar discussion – in occasional country inns too – but it was always secretive, furtive. All it took in England was one man to inform that you were speaking sedition and you might find yourself before the queen's justices.

In every man's mouth had been the news that the Scottish regent, Mary's brother Moray, was in the highlands, as Heydon had predicted. Yet still it was well known that Queen Elizabeth had only just threatened him with the return of his sister. Depending on the speaker, it was either a good thing – she could then be executed for murder – or a bad thing – she would breathe life into her harried supporters. Of course, others seemed to say it was a good thing because she could rid the land of her bastard brother, or a bad thing because she would harm the new faith. About the only the leader the men – and often women – seemed to be unanimous in their liking for was their prince-cum-king, James. And that was because he was not yet two years old.

Jack took Heydon's advice: ignore the ranting Scots. They simply enjoyed arguing amongst themselves.

'We should be near,' said Heydon, his voice low. Jack trusted his knowledge. It had, after all, been gleaned from Queen Mary's inner circle.

The park gave way to a gravelled path, and they rode to one side of it. It wound through the trees in a series of twists and turns. Then, all at once, it gave out onto a wide expanse of gardens. Beyond them, black against the stars, was a stone lodge, a turreted tower on the right and a thatched roof on the lower building to the left. No lights burned; if there were windows, they were shuttered. 'Right,' said Heydon. 'Tie up the horses, mate.' He slipped down easily, Jack following.

'Do we go in through the back?'

124

'No, we do not.' Heydon did not trouble to lower his voice. It bounced around between the trees and the house, making Jack shudder. 'Up there,' he said, jabbing a finger towards the tower. 'That's where the earl will keep office.' Jack opened his mouth to ask how he could be sure, and Heydon pre-empted him. 'This place was the old king's hunting lodge. Claimed by his bastard. He used to use the towers of his houses for secret chambers.' With that he began crunching over towards the place. Jack went after him, stepping more lightly, aware of every footstep.

The tower was not tall. Now that his eyes had grown used to the light in the clearing, he could see up to the first floor. Its window was made of horn, dyed grey by the darkness. 'Can you lift me, mate? I'll stand on your hands and get onto your shoulders.'

Jack nodded, locked his fingers, and leant down, making a hoist for Heydon's foot. His friend put one foot in and Jack lifted. Thankfully Heydon weighed little, and Jack was able to rise, grunting as quietly as he could. When he was standing, he launched him upwards and, wobbling a little, transferred the foot to his shoulder. Heydon managed to find his other one, knocking his ear as he did. A smooth operation, Jack thought, brushing the caked dirt of his palms and onto the cool stones of the tower. He could do nothing but stare ahead, trying not to move, as the vibrations of Heydon's movements juddered through him. Several hard thumps above threatened to dislodge him. Heydon stilled. 'I've got it,' he hissed down. 'Get my feet again, mate. Push me up.'

Jack did, and this time he looked up to see Heydon's body disappear into the small aperture. His legs followed, jerking madly, a deformed snake in its death throes. Then he was gone. A moment of panic descended, as Jack realised was alone and exposed in front of the Scottish regent's private home. He looked around, as though expecting to see an army of iron-faced Scotsmen emerging from between the trees. Was Heydon, he wondered, really going to have the nerve to wander through the house and open the front door for him?

'Here!' Jack looked up. A rope fell down by his head. It was no makeshift thing, no bedsheet twined up, but a real rope. 'I've got you. Come up.'

Jack grabbed it, glad of his gloves, and planted one foot on the tower. A pain ran through his thigh, the numbness from the ride already wearing off. Gingerly he raised his other foot and hung like a monkey. He started to walk up the building but found he could not bear to move his hands up the rope. Letting go, even for an instant, seemed like an invitation to land on his backside.

He was still screwing up his courage when his whole body shot up a foot, and then another, and the momentum got him moving. Between his tepid climbing and Heydon's yanking, he reached the height of the window. With one hand still on the rope he reached out, his insides tumbling, and Heydon grasped at his arm. He missed. Grasped again, swearing. And then Jack had gained it; he half-threw himself into it and let Heydon do the rest.

He landed on the floor, his upper body and arms first. 'That was graceful, mate.' Heydon's disembodied voice was close. Jack gathered himself up and stood, wearing his old lopsided grin. It was a good cover, he thought, for nerves.

'What do we do now?'

'What's that?'

'Where do we look?' In response, Heydon struck at a tinderbox and, after a few tries, a small pool of light spread around them. He held it high, making the shadows quiver.

The room they were in was part office and part storeroom. A bare desk still stood, though the other furnishings must have been carried elsewhere. Some barrels stood against one wall, making him shiver. Ropes were still tied around the lower halves. Jack guessed his means of ascent must have been one of the liberated upper ones. Heydon moved slowly around, his light moving in arcs. 'Here,' he said.

The wall opposite the barrels was dominated by criss-crosses of shelving. It created dozens of small square openings, most of them stuffed with rolled up papers. Some were simply black, and Heydon poked his free hand in, cursing when he found nothing. 'You could help,' he said.

Jack moved immediately, bumping the desk. 'Yes, sorry. It's – what is it we're looking for?'

'A casket – a small coffer. Wood, silver, I don't know.'

Jack joined him in the search. He noticed that Heydon was pulling out papers and either cramming them back in or tossing them to the floor. For his part, Jack carefully put everything back as he found it. After sliding a roll tied up with ribbon back into its slot, he moved to the next. It looked empty, but when he put his hand in, he stubbed a finger on something hard. He tutted and, more slowly, reached in again. His fingers closed around something hard. Something square. His heart leapt as he slid it out. 'Is this – this isn't it, is it?'

Heydon drew closer and held the light over the box. 'Could be. Well done, mate. Open it.'

The box was made of dark wood. It felt thick. On the front was a little metal catch. 'It's locked.'

'Give it here.'

Heydon took it, shook it, and then handed his tinderbox to Jack. He then tried to prise it open between his fingers. 'Damn it. Here, you try.'

They reversed their swap, and Jack tried the box. It was locked, but it was so small he felt it shouldn't hold its secrets for too long. He squatted, putting all his strength into it. A gap opened between the coffer and lid. And then his fingers slipped, and the thing closed tight – tighter, it felt, than it had been at first. 'So close, *fuck it*,' Jack hissed. Before he knew what he was doing he had lost control and smashed the thing off the desk. It fell to the floor, the lid cracking off. 'Stupid thing – I'm sorry, I'm sorry!'

'Jesus, Jack,' said Heydon. 'That mad temper of yours has just proved its worth.'

On the floor at their feet was a brown, folded square of paper.

Heydon leant down and scooped it up. As he unfolded it, his lips began moving in silent prayer. It was surprisingly large when unfolded. 'By God,' whispered Heydon, as though he had uncovered a holy relic. 'This is it. Here is the proof that Scotland's kings might rule England.'

'Or queens,' said Jack.

'This is from a time before queens,' snapped Heydon, making Jack take a step back.

'Is it real?'

'Real? Who cares if it's real? It ...' Heydon seemed to weigh something up. He averted his eyes to the paper and began folding it up. When it was small enough again, he slid it into the lining of his doublet. 'No. It's not real. But no less powerful for that. It ... it was drawn up at the time of James IV, when he married Margaret Tudor.'

'Why? Why lie and say that your kingdom is ... is not a sovereign land? That its owned by another?'

'Why?' spat Heydon. 'This is why.' He gestured at the office. 'This day is why, and tomorrow, and tomorrow. Even Henry VII knew that the Scottish marriage might one day provide an heir to England's throne. They say Margaret was a clever woman. Well, they say that about all royals, don't they? Well she knew well enough that if her brother's line failed, her own children might gain the throne. Or grandchildren. But the English wouldn't like that. Not being taken over by a foreigner. So this,' he added, patting his breast, 'makes the Scottish sovereigns no foreigners, but English subjects. And all looks very ancient.'

'I see,' said Jack, his face blank. 'Why would Moray want it?'

'He's the regent,' shrugged Heydon. 'And he won't want Queen Mary to have it. It makes her path to Elizabeth's throne that *wee bit* clearer. We should –'

A soft thump.

'Did you hear –' began Jack.

A door on the far side of the room opened, a black silhouette framed by the light of the hall behind it. 'Whit be this, then, a parcel o' sleekit knaves at thievery?' said a cool, high woman's voice. The silhouette stepped forward into the light. In the woman's hand was a large empty candlestick, held aloft, as though it were a club.

3

Heydon moved towards her, and for a moment Jack feared that he was going to attack. So, it seemed, did the male servant who had followed the woman, lighting her way with a torch. But then something odd happened. Heydon began speaking to her in rapid Scots. It made no sense to Jack, but he thought he heard the word 'wean' or 'wee ane' several times.

Eventually, Heydon stood back from her, and Jack got a good look. 'Mr Cole,' he said, 'this is the countess of Moray. Lady Agnes Keith.'

She was petite, and pretty in a severe kind of way – but it was her eyes that caught Jack's attention. They were enormous and dark, two glittering coals. When she spoke, she had dropped the Scots, and spoke in English with a clipped Scottish accent. 'My husband has taught me your native tongue,' she said. 'A good and faithful servant to England, my husband.' Jack thought he detected an edge of irony in her tone. Humour, at least.

She crossed to the desk and put down the candlestick. Jack noticed her casting curious glances at the shelves, before dropping her gaze to the floor, littered with papers. She said nothing, but tutted.

'And so,' Heydon said, 'the regent will have us on our way, then.'

'Such a fine man, not wishing me disturbed.' Again, that note of cynicism. 'Good of you to let yourselves in.' Jack cleared his throat.

'And you'll give him my regards when he returns?'

'Of course. What faithful wife could do otherwise.' She wheeled back to them and leant her back against the desk. She was wearing a thick nightdress, all in the black that Jack had seen on wealthy reformist women throughout the country. But Lady Agnes had had some silver and white threads and loops sewn into hers. Jack liked it. It was like one small rebellion against the austerity. 'I suppose you have your papers?'

Heydon stepped towards her and dropped to a knee, fishing in his coat. He brought forth his passport, though for one terrible second Jack thought he would somehow accidentally free the stolen document. She raised a hand and beckoned at the doorway. Her man came in with his torch and stood by her as she made a show of reading. 'Well this all seems in order,' she said at last.

Jack relaxed, before making a bow. Heydon did likewise, and they began backing towards the door. 'Wait!' she snapped. Both froze. 'Do you not wish to take what it is that you have come here for?' Neither spoke. 'The dresses. My – the queen's – jewels.' She eased herself off the desk and began to move around them, making for the door. 'And I must bid you the welcome of my house. You are welcome to lodge here for the night. If you wish?'

'No, ma'am. I mean – thank you, my lady. But we are already so late in our business, we have not a moment to lose,' said Heydon.

'I see. Well, I am sorry you have given me so little warning of your coming. I will get what I can for you. Yet we might have to see more of each other hereafter. Wait here and I will have my man send you on your way with ... something.' She gave them both a strange smile and left the room, her servant scurrying after her.

They were left in silence. 'What was that?' whispered Jack. 'She didn't believe us, did she?'

'Not a word,' replied Heydon. 'That lady knows exactly what's what.'

'You mean ... you don't mean she knows what we're stealing? What did you say to her?'

'Not exactly. Don't worry, mate. The good countess has a mind of her own.'

'I heard you see wean. That's child, isn't it, in that tongue?'

'Sharp lad,' said Heydon raising an eyebrow. 'What else did you hear?'

'Nothing. What's it all about a child?'

'I simply pointed out that when the little laddie they call

their king grows older, he might not take to kindly to the folk – even an auntie and uncle – who let his mother suffer in a dank cell in a foreign land. Religion aside, that boy will grow up. A woman like the good countess can see that he'll one day ask "what of my mama?". And she'll want to be able to say that she did what she could for his mother's restoration. Not that she and her husband left her in a pit.'

'She's not one of us, is she?' The silver and white decorations laced through Jack's thoughts. 'A Catholic?'

'You ask too many questions, mate. Trust me. That lady is … she's … a woman of practical good sense. Like her husband. No Catholic, but – well, you've heard what's said abroad in Scotland? That Elizabeth will restore Mary?' He lowered his voice to a whisper and let his light die. 'I've let that lady think that all we've sought is means to stop that. More proof of her sister-in-law's troublesome spirit and dark nature. But that it won't be seen to come from her man, and so the little boy will never have cause to think dear uncle defamed his mama.'

'And she believed that?' Jack wasted a look of disbelief on a dark room.

'Probably not. But what has she got to lose? If the queen was to be restored, she can say that she helped on behalf of her husband. And when Elizabeth's dead, she can do the same. When the boy king grows up he will have no cause to punish dear auntie and uncle for ignoring his mother's plight. Yet if Queen Mary is further defamed, she thinks she will be kept in England, and the world will think the proofs were not given by her husband's hand. Either way, she can see herself and the regent winning. That is a rare woman, the countess – for a heretic, anyway. A woman who can see farther in time and clearer than her husband. She'll smooth that old traitor down, I'm sure.' Heydon threw his head back and let out a short cackle. 'This is living, isn't it, mate?' A feverish excitement had crept into his voice. 'You feel it, don't you? Locking wits with people. Secret knowledge and secret places.'

Jack nodded, still not understanding exactly what was going on, what had passed between Heydon and the countess. It seemed to him that the lady could only get in trouble if she let something important be stolen. But then, he realised, looking at the candlestick, Lady Agnes Keith was probably more than a match for any man's anger.

***

At Thirsk, the news Jack had dreaded reached them.

They had made slow progress south. It would not have been fair to say that they were laden with dresses and jewels. On the contrary, the countess of Moray seemed to have gone out of her way to provide them with only bits of clothing – odd sleeves, out-of-fashion kirtles – and unashamedly cheap trinkets. Some of them Heydon had tossed in the River Eden as not fit for a laundress. Jack had balked at that but said nothing. Besides, the items were only a cover for their real mission.

An unsettling feeling had come upon him that he was a pawn in some greater game, but what it was he couldn't quite understand. His part in it, though, was key. That, he suspected, was what was really worrying him. The journey south meant time passing. Each day meant he was another day closer to having to do what Heydon had commanded of him: what God had commanded of him. To take his mind off of it, he had begun to worry about everything else that might be wrong in the world. Chief amongst those things was the death of the spy at Darlington. He hadn't insisted on much – on anything, really – except that they took some other route south, staying at other towns and cities. Heydon had agreed, claiming it would let him grope at the minds of other northern men.

Thirsk's main street was a welter of people, mainly women. Heydon had called down to one of them, asking what news there was. 'A corpse found up near Darlington. Murdered, they say. And they'll be hanging the man what did it!'

Jack's stomach had flopped, and a lightness caught hold of his head, making his vision swim. The woman had wriggled into the crowd, sharing the news. 'Well,' said Heydon. 'That's the end of that.' But it hadn't been. Jack had refused to go on, unable to stand the idea that someone would be hanged for what he had done. Heydon had tutted, cursed, and cajoled, but on this he was immovable.

'What you said – about secret knowledge. About living. The things we've done. The things I have to do. I … well, we can do something about this.' He was about to add 'can't we?' but was sick of turning everything into a question. That was a mark of weakness, and on this he was determined to be strong.

And so they rode back towards Darlington.

Several constables were keeping order in the town, one of them the man, Wytham, that Heydon knew. Several young boys were jeering outside the town's guildhall. They drew in at the inn and dismounted, passing the horses to an ostler before returning to the high street. 'What's all this, Mr Wytham?' asked Heydon.

'A murder,' the constable replied. His eyes were clouded, and he had a strange half-smirk on his face. 'Feller was found in a barrel by some lads picking through the reeds.'

'Do you know him?'

'Can't say as I do. A stranger to these parts.' He gave Heydon a meaningful look. 'But the barrel was stolen alright. From yonder inn – the one you know well enough, my friend. We've got the feller who did it. Been done for stealing before. Knew another theft would be the end of him but thought he could get away with murder too.' His thumbs went into his belt and he gave a sombre head shake. 'From the south originally, as I hear. What else can you be expecting, eh?'

'How do you know it was him, though?' asked Jack. Heydon silenced him with an angry look. Then his face softened.

'Let me speak to the constable, mate.' He then took Wytham by the arm and walked with him towards the other constables. The group of men then moved towards the Guildhall, some of them appearing to argue, shaking their heads and waving their arms. They disappeared inside, leaving Jack standing in the street biting his nails. It had been raining in this part of England, and the ground had turned sludgy. He moved off to stand under the overhanging wooden awning of a shopfront, where he could better see the Guildhall.

After a while, Heydon emerged, this time leading a painfully-thin old man in rags by the arm. The old fellow appeared frightened, and when the boys outside saw him, they began throwing handfuls of wet mud. When one splattered Heydon, he moved towards them menacingly and they scattered, sliding through the muck.

'Well, mate, he's out. For now. They'll get him again for something else if they really want him.'

'That old man was the thief? How did you get him free? You were only away ten minutes.'

'I've told you, mate. I'm a gentleman of the north. There's nothing a gentleman's name can't buy. Justice included. That's Elizabeth's England for you. That's the old boot's justice. They'd hang a man just to be rid of him and free him for fatter purses.' He patted at his purse. Jack had wondered about that. Heydon seemed to have an inexhaustible supply of money, carried in various purses at his belt. He had even had some Scottish coins, got out of Queen Mary's growing flock of followers. Evidence of the Vatican's infamous riches. He had heard that the streets of Rome were paved with marble and gold.

'Thank you, Philip.' Heydon wafted his hand through the air. 'But won't they be after someone else now?'

'I doubt it. The folk around here will still blame that poor old bastard. They'll feel cheated of a hanging. It's not often folk are found in barrels. But the law won't touch him. Not for that, anyway.'

'I suppose that just leaves … you know – well, the body.' Jack wondered if that too was in the Guildhall. Probably not. Probably it was festering in an outhouse somewhere, smelling of the river. Fish would have taken its eyes. 'That'll fetch up in a ditch, I suppose.'

'Not at all,' said Heydon. 'I've even left enough for a proper Catholic burial. Whoever he is, I doubt he's a Catholic, but I think God will accept him. His death was part of the design plan for us all.'

'You didn't give him the last rites.' Jack hadn't thought

134

about it at the time. Heydon's face hardened, and he wondered if he had said the wrong thing.

'The last rites are for those who confess and leave this world with their consciences clear. Not for thieves working in the service of devil's minions and usurpers.' Jack didn't know how else to express his thanks and deflate Heydon's show of fervour, so he gave him a wry smile. 'Jesus, look at you, mate.'

'What?'

'You look like you've been dragged through a hedge.' Jack looked down at himself. His clothes were grimy, but he had not given much thought to his appearance. Being stained and soiled was part of travelling, as much as it was part of working with horses. 'Can't have a gentleman's man looking like that. What would Queen Mary say, having such an ill-kempt ruffian in her service? Let's get you to the barber. Don't want you looking like a beast if you're to be a hero either, do we?'

Jack felt his heart sink again. He had managed, in the sudden reverse ride to Darlington, to forget about that.

Heydon had his way, and Jack was barbered and shaved in a shop not far from the inn. The barber even had the luxury of a small, chipped looking glass. When he held it up, Jack drew his breath. The fellow had cropped his hair as short as Heydon's. His fringe – the floppy, disobedient fringe he had always had – had been shorn. What, he wondered, would Amy have to say about that?

4

Amy had lost track of how long Jack had been gone. After all, it seemed as though he had been drifting away from her even before he had been sent on his foolish little trip to Scotland. His absence had been made even more keen by the fact that she was at Chatsworth again. It was here that they had had their separate berths in a private chamber, before Mary Stuart had walked, legs-shackled, in her mind at least, into their lives, prancing little priest waiting. If she wanted to smile at the image of the queen in chains, the realisation that she thought now of their lives rather than their life prevented her.

They had not been at Chatsworth for long. The countess had insisted they go to let her husband recuperate from an attack of gout, which the nearby Buxton baths would help with. In reality Amy suspected that the mistress of the house was simply fed up of Wingfield and eager to see if the workmen were lazing on the scaffolding at Chatsworth or not. But they couldn't remain for long. Wingfield was where Queen Elizabeth apparently wanted them. Where there were lots of workmen and walls of scaffolding, after all, there were lots of opportunities for escape.

The moves between houses had taken on a different complexion. Amy rode in the phalanx of women near the back, with only some carthorses dragging luggage behind. Ahead were some soldiers, with Queen Mary's retinue ahead of them. Near the front was the queen herself, still milking her illness in a litter, the countess at her side. An armed troop formed the vanguard. All were assembled and ready to return to Wingfield, except the earl.

The chatter that always accompanies large groups gave way to grumbling as the morning wore on, and still there was no sign of Shrewsbury. Eventually Woodward appeared out of the door to the house's great hall. He held open the door and the earl hobbled out on a stick. He nodded thanks to his steward and then took a few faltering steps forwards. He smiled up at the assembled staff, and some of his household gentlemen broke away and moved towards him, offering arms. He waved them off and then winced. The wince turned into a grimace, and the grimace turned into a fall. As he went to his knees, his male servants all fell to the dust beside him, and a chorus of cries rose from the waiting servants.

Shrewsbury was carried back into Chatsworth, leaving confusion behind. The countess went after him, but no one seemed to think of the servants, still in their riding garb. Without orders to disband, they could do nothing but wait. Amy turned to the girl riding beside her – Alice, one of the girls she had caught talking about her and insulted in turn. They were not quite friends yet, though finishing *The Tragical History of Romeus and Juliet* had thawed things somewhat. 'What should we do?' asked Amy. She knew it was a stupid question. Alice would have no idea. But she felt the need to say something. 'It's going to be too hot to stay out here for long.'

It was true. Already the sun was riding high. It beat down on the courtyard, turning the mud to dust, and reflected heat off dozens of windows. The smell of sweat had already begun to make its presence known, moving amongst the densely packed people in noxious waves. Flies were swatted, and horses fidgeted. The servants had gone quiet, all eyes fixed nervously on the house. Their silence eventually became an uncomfortable noise unto itself, punctuated by occasional jangles and the odd impatient whinny.

Eventually, the earl's usher appeared, crying out, 'make way, make way'. He led the liveried gentlemen, who between them carried a litter similar to the one in which Queen Mary was still lying shielded from the sun. Amy craned her neck for a look and saw Shrewsbury, a look of abject humiliation twisting his already pain-contorted face. Bess and Woodward followed, the countess with her arms folded.

At Amy's side, Alice whispered, 'he's not been poisoned, do you think?' Instantly, Amy regretted reading the story to her. Stories filled people's heads with foolish ideas about what might really go on in the world.

'It's just gout,' snapped Amy. Then, remembering she was supposed to be mending fences, she added, 'he'll be well enough, Alice.' Privately, she thought that the decline in the earl of Shrewsbury had begun with the arrival of the crying and demanding Scottish queen. If this was the state he had reached in – what was it? – about six months, who knew where he would be before the year was out.

***

Jack and Heydon rode into one of the two courtyards at Wingfield Manor. A porter made a desultory attempt to salute them, but there was no kind of security. It was clear to Jack that the household was not in residence; only a small crew of those needed to stop the place crumbling would be about. He wondered if Amy would have been left behind and suspected not. Sheets didn't need laundered in empty houses.

'Well this is a fine welcome,' said Heydon. 'You might do one last duty as my man, mate. Stable these poor brutes. They must feel that like they've been to hell and back.'

Jack thought, but didn't say, 'I know I do.'

They parted, Jack leading the horses down to the stables. For reasons he couldn't explain, he was glad to be away from Heydon. It was a good thing having a friend, and better still one who knew your secrets and had the power to forgive them. But there was something tiring about living cheek to cheek with the same person. With a wife it was different. With Amy he could meet her at night when their sleeping arrangements allowed and be off at their own business during the day. Not only that, but there was something frightening about Philip Heydon. It lay in his intensity. In his ability to court danger and encourage others to do the same.

Jack was enjoying breathing private air when the sound of an approaching cavalcade drew him out of his own thoughts. He left the stables and watched as the riot of banners and noise picked its way uphill, like a giant, colourful centipede. Behind the soldiers at the front he saw two horse-drawn litters, the unmistakable figures of the countess of Shrewsbury riding between them.

He watched as the soldiers escorted the queen indoors, wondering at what plagued her. The earl's gentleman followed, his wife barking orders at them. It was only when Mary's retinue began to break up, some entering the house and others leaving for lodgings in the village, that the servants began to disperse. Jack considered helping with the horses, but the team of grooms who had travelled with the troupe was already about its business. Instead, he passed the lines of dismounting people and reached the laundresses.

'Amy,' he said, unable to contain his grin. 'I'm back.'

'Jesus,' she said, her eyes wide. She had been bent forward, brushing down the front of her old grey dress. As she rose, she seemed to look at him as though he were a monster. His smile died on his lips. 'What have you done to yourself?'

Jack ran a hand ruefully over his cropped head. 'Don't you like it?'

'No! I mean … no. You look like Heydon.'

'Do I? I suppose I do a bit. Well it's only hair.'

'But it was your hair, Jack. Yours.' He frowned at her, not sure what she was getting at. It was, as he said, only hair. She had never said she even liked his old brown mop. She shook her head slowly. 'Never mind. How was your journey? Did you get what you went for?'

'Yes,' Jack nodded. 'Oh yes, the dresses and jewels. We got them.'

'Well that will make your little friend happy, then. And your little royal one too.'

Jack crossed his arms. He had wanted a happy reunion, but something seemed to have put her out of sorts, making her tiresome. Making her forget her place and run at the mouth. He tossed his head in irritation, forgetting that he no longer had a lock of hair to flick away. For some reason that seemed to get a faint smile out of her. 'We should speak somewhere, Amy. I have something to tell you.' He cast an eye around. The other servants were busy unloading their mounts and carrying bits and pieces of household stuff towards the buildings. No one took any notice of a husband and wife greeting one another. Still, what he wanted to say required privacy.

'Where?' she asked. 'I have things to do.'

'It shan't take long. I …' He paused, thinking. 'Let's take a walk. I'll take your horse away. Wait here.' He led the beast to the stables and returned to a tutting Amy stamping the dust free from her boots. 'Whilst folk are still all at sixes and sevens finding their lodgings. Come on, let's walk in the park. It's so hot today.' This seemed to draw a look of alarm. He bit on the inside of his cheek. 'Or the garden.' He gestured beyond the courtyard. 'Come on, do you want to speak or not?'

'Yes,' she said in a mild voice. 'I think we should.'

The gardens at Wingfield were emerald in the summer heat. They had been only indifferently kept up, but the countess had set the gardener to begin something that Queen Mary could take pleasure in. Jack knew that he and Amy had no business being there but hoped that no one would care with the earl apparently sick and the household busy reclaiming the building.

After they had walked a while in silence, the bulk of the house bathing them in pleasant shadow, Jack blurted, 'I'm Catholic.' Immediately after, his nervous smile twisted his face. It was not how he had wanted to announce his conversion, but he had never seen anyone make such an announcement. He had no reference point, no model to follow.

'I know,' said Amy. It was her turn to cross her arms. 'I suppose you're telling me that I'm Catholic too?'

'No, not if you don't want to be. I mean, I'd like you to be, but…'

'And we have your Mr Heydon to thank for this, do we? He's the man who's pricked your conscience? I must say I wonder if you'd be so hot on that old faith if the Scotch queen was ninety-five with crooked teeth and one eye.'

'Mr Heydon is …'

'He's a priest,' she snapped. 'I'm no idiot, Jack. I've been watching what's been going on.'

Fear coursed through him. If Amy had seen through him, who else might? 'But … I …'

'And why are you telling me this now, husband?'

'I thought it your right to know.'

'Just now? Not weeks ago – not before you risked your life on the road?' They had passed out of the shadow, further away from the house. Without realising it, they had begun going in a big circle, all the way around the house. Amy paused mid-step, drawing a finger to the bridge of her nose. Sweat stood in tiny pearls on her forehead. 'Are you in love with him?'

'What?' spluttered Jack. 'What the hell, Amy?'

'It's a fair question. This man – this priest – appears and all of a sudden you are dancing to his tune. You're speaking like him – you're even making yourself look like him. It's a fair question.' Challenge rose in her voice as she repeated her question.

'It's a damned stupid question from a foolish woman,' he snapped. 'I see how it is. You don't like me having friends. Because then you can't see everything. That's exactly what you've always been like, Amy Wylmott. In love with your own opinions. The sound of your own voice.'

'Go to the devil, Jack,' she said, her voice rising. 'Do you know, I don't even know who you are. Do you?'

'I'm a gentleman's man,' said Jack, tossing his head.

'Pfft, a gent – you're a nobody, Jack Cole. You're nobody, just like me. Nothing.'

Anger rose in him, flaring up his throat and into his cheeks. He fought the urge to shout, to strike out at her. He clenched his jaw, letting it pass, and instead he said, 'I don't think that's a good thing to say. I …' he raised his finger and pointed at the Shrewsbury badge sewn onto his livery. 'This, this says that I'm somebody. The passport Heydon got – it said that I was somebody. I don't think that's a good thing to say at all.'

'Oh, quit trying to be so damn chivalrous. Be angry, if you're angry. Be *something*, Jack. That's it with you, isn't it? You're never anything unless someone tells you to be. Weak. A man who stands for nothing – he falls for anything. And you have, haven't you? You've been ripe to be plucked by that

141

poxy priest!'

'Shut up,' he snapped. 'You shut up. You're my wife, not some shrew.'

'Wife? Pah! You've become wife to the Catholics. Wife to Heydon. I suppose you know your new friend is leading you straight to the gallows.'

'What do you know? I'm going to be a hero, Amy, and then you'll be sorry.'

'No, Jack. It's you who'll be sorry. You think you're the only one who has made new friends? No, sirrah. I have a friend myself and he's no Catholic! You've been watched right from the beginning – so has he. We all have! So you're not so damned clever as you think.'

'He? What do you mean? What have you been doing?'

Amy tilted her chin to him and smiled. 'You would like to know that, wouldn't you? You'd like to know so you can run to your little priest and tell him. Well it's none of your business. But you have a care, Jack. Believe whatever you want in your heart. The likes of him aren't as safe as they think, whether they hide under the skirts of that Scotch strumpet or not.'

With that, she turned on her heel and strode away, wiping her brow with an already-stained sleeve. Jack remained in the garden. His heart was racing with the fury of an unexpected confrontation. She had been up to something. He looked beyond the gardens, to the fringe of trees that marked the park boundary. Why had she been so reluctant to talk there? And what did she mean 'right from the beginning'? He cast his mind back, galloping past all that had happened since he left for Scotland. When they had first joined the earl's household, when they had arrived at Chatsworth – that was the beginning. Then, she had made some comments about a man watching them. A man in a brown suit with silvery hair.

He shrugged it off. His heart had begun to slow. She would just bear watching, that was all. In the meantime, he would have to behave as normally as possible. The duke of Norfolk would be sending letters, and now he would be here to read and pass them on. Tedious work, but it would take his mind off what Heydon had in store for him later in the year, when the baking days of summer passed into autumn and winter.

5

Amy regretted fighting with Jack almost instantly, but pride rose up in her, refusing to admit it. She took herself to the servants' dormitory and tore off her sleeves, casting them to the ground. Then she sat, her head in her hands and her knees bunched up. What had he said? Something about being a 'hero'. That was bad. It might mean anything. She had to calm down, to think rationally. It would have to be passed on to Brown, but not until she had decided what it might mean. A rush of angry love welled up, unbidden. Never before had she wanted to hug her husband to her and rip the hair from his scalp more strongly. He had even denied her that possibility.

She began to sort through what she knew and what she could safely reveal. Heydon had spirited her husband north. He had converted him to Catholicism, presumably after noting what an easy target he was. And he had promised him something – that he would be a hero. What made the Catholics heroes? Working for the pope, certainly. Doing things – things against the English faith. Burning down churches? Leading armies?

Killing Elizabeth?

Her mind shied away from that possibility. Yet it was the one that Brown had warned her about. The queen's death was the one thing every man in Elizabeth's government feared, for it was the one thing that would make an end of their faith and probably their lives. But would her husband really be seduced into an act so wild? She bit her lip, knowing the answer. And how much should she tell Brown? It was his job to ferret things out, and she didn't trust herself enough to reveal only enough to serve as a warning. Angry as she might be at Jack, she did not want to get him into real trouble. The trick would be getting Heydon and Mary Stuart cast away. Perhaps she could cut some deal – arrange for Jack to be left alone in exchange for information. Yes, that was fair enough. Hitherto she had given up information freely, hoping to protect him. She had even agreed in principle to rid the world of Queen Mary if the unthinkable did happen. The least Brown could do would be to have her husband's life spared in the event of some plot coming to light.

That was, of course, if the English government gave a damn about honouring deals with laundresses.

There was another possibility, and she grasped for it like a blind woman. She could confront Philip Heydon. She had to know if she was in the right and Jack in the wrong, or if somehow it was the other way around. But how? If she went in with her tongue unsheathed, she might spur him into ever greater secrecy. No, she would have to play the aggrieved wife and hope that she could warn him away from whatever he was planning for Jack by more subtle means.

She drew herself up. There were other servants in the dormitory, but they had been absorbed in making up their own beds, and were now covertly bent over, hiding their few personal possessions amid the folds. She passed them, nodding greetings without interest. Sunlight slanted in on her, a woman with a mission she neither understood nor felt ready to undertake.

She asked after Heydon, finding him unpacking books in a small chamber underneath the earl's rooms. 'Mrs Cole,' he said, smiling. Then he looked down at the coffer before him. 'Every time this household moves, I reckon that fewer books survive.'

'Is that so?'

'Such an icy stare from those emerald eyes,' he said, putting one down. 'A fair thing on such a hot day.'

'Forgive me for not getting down on bended knee, Mr Heydon. My back's a little sore today.' No, she thought. She could not afford to let her tongue run on. She lowered her eyes. 'I understand that you've made certain promises to my husband.' Pretending to know more than she did might be worth trying.

'Promises?'

'You know what I mean, I think.'

145

'You intrigue me, mistress, and that's the truth. I understand he's told you of his faith?'

'That he is now a Catholic? Oh yes, I know that.'

'As well you should, being his wife. It is your duty to support him. You can't do any less now, can you?'

'I ... I respect my husband's conscience.' Heydon smiled indulgently. It made the hairs on the back of her neck stand up. 'Yet I would not have him in any trouble.'

'What trouble are you talking about?'

'You know what I mean.'

'I'm not sure that I do. Your husband doesn't have to do anything he doesn't want to do. If you'll forgive me, I think it's no place for a wife to grow jealous. To try and control her man's actions.'

'Ohhh,' said Amy, her temper flaring. 'And what would you know about that, *father*? You fellows aren't allowed wives, are you? That's why you steal women's husbands to your band.' Already she felt control of the situation fleeing her, the cool attitude she had wanted to convey melting.

Heydon held up his palms. 'I don't know what you mean. I hope you're not planning to make trouble, Mrs Cole. Jack and I are friends. We sink or swim together, as true brothers of the faith.'

'I ...' Brown sneaked into her mind, as stealthily as he sneaked into the parklands. She could see him, jaw clenched, warning her against what she was about to say. 'You're being watched, sir. By great men. Have a care how you proceed.' She gave a sarcastic bow and turned.

'What?' he called after her. She paused in the doorway and half-turned back.

'I can say no more. Only that your actions are not as privy as you might think. You'd be a fool to try anything – to make Jack try anything – because ... because you will be stopped.'

A nasty snarl twisted Heydon's features. 'Then,' he said, 'we'll just have to make sure that those who try and stop us are carried out of this world, shan't we?'

Amy left the chamber, slamming the door and hurriedly moving away from it. His meaning was not hard to discern.

She might well have just put Brown's life in danger. And her own.

***

She walked down to the village, not even bothering to make some show of household business. If anyone tried to stop her, they'd get the rough edge of her tongue. The sentries seemed to sense this and averted their eyes when she passed out of the grounds of Wingfield Manor and marched, her fists balled, downhill. She was almost disappointed. A tongue lashing would have been welcome. One she could dole out and then walk away from, with no consequences. Not like the fight she had had with Jack. That would always be there now.

She was breaking the rules, she knew. Brown had told her that she must never seek him out. It would be too great a risk. If they were seen together, it might compromise him. After her discussion with Heydon, she had taken herself off to the privy and sat, simply as an excuse to be alone, to formulate a plan. It was there that she had decided to find Mr Brown. A veiled threat on both their lives surely warranted it.

She had no idea if he would be in the village, but she knew he took lodgings nearest wherever Mary Stuart was being kept. She had not seen him during the brief week at Chatsworth, but that had not bothered her. Nothing of importance had come up during the queen's sickness anyway. Plus, she surmised, it would make sense for him to make sure of a chamber in the village inn ahead of the plague of Mary's extended household.

The village of South Wingfield wasn't far, but the heat-hazed path to it felt longer. On a horse, one didn't notice, but walking it was tortuous. When she reached the place that wags in the household were calling Petty Scotland after the influx of Mary's people, she looked around for an inn. Eventually she gave up, asking an old woman.

She strode into the sprawling wooden building and made for the bar, elbowing her way through a gaggle of French-speaking men and women in rich clothing. The innkeeper was arguing with a woman who seemed to be speaking rapidly in French.

'No. More. Rooms. No. More.'

'Vous avez dit que vous nous réserveriez une chamber!'

'Excuse me,' said Amy. Then, louder, 'excuse me.'

'An English girl? What can I do for you, girl?'

'Nous étions ici les premiers,' cut in the Frenchwoman. Amy and the innkeeper ignored her.

'I'm looking for a Mr Brown.'

'Brown? He's upstairs.' The man gestured towards a steep flight of steps. 'Last room on the right. But he's with a guest at the moment. Won't want disturbed.'

'A guest?' said Amy, frowning. She had to shout it over the mounting protests of the courtly lady.

'Yep,' said the innkeeper, also raising his voice. Then he gave her an amused look. 'He's right well loved by folk from the big house, is Mr Brown. You can wait down here if those pretty ears of yours can stand a bit o' noise.' He turned his attention back to the lady, raising placatory hands.

Amy looked around the room and then over to the staircase. It was absurd, but a little stab of disappointment prodded at her heart. Brown had other informers in the household. That was probably to be expected. After all, he only saw her once a week, if that. But these other folks were invited to his private lodging. They must be more trusted than she, or privy to better information. It made her feel somehow less special. Just one voice amid a chorus. She made up her mind and made for the stairs.

She found the last room on the right and put her ear to the thick wooden door. Murmuring came from within, but it was too indistinct to make anything out. All that marked it as conversation was the cadence of speech. Suddenly it ceased. Footsteps. Something bumped at the door, making the handle on her side beat a brief tattoo.

Panic rose in her breast and she wheeled, almost tumbling over her skirts as she made for the first door across the way. She grasped at the iron ring and threw herself in, slamming it behind her and putting her back to it. Why she did it she wasn't sure, but she knew that Brown would be furious if she made trouble with his little network of informers.

'Whit's aw this?' screeched a man. 'Christine, get yersel' cover't up. There's some lassie stolen in oan us.'

'I'm sorry,' said Amy. 'I'm sorry. I … the wrong room.'

Before her a man and woman were in a state of undress, the woman in her shift and the man in breeches, his bare chest soapy. She raised a hand over her eyes and then, unable to contain herself, began to laugh. 'Whit are ye, a maidservant or the like?'

'I'm sorry,' said Amy again, bending double. 'I'm gathering the bedsheets. I … the wrong room.'

'Ye should be chappin' afore ye intrude oan good honest wights,' said the man, wagging a finger. But her fit of giggles seemed to have burst his shock and stalled any anger.

'Go out now, would ye?' said the woman.

'Yes, yes. Sorry. I'm so sorry.'

Amy drew herself up, shaking her head to chase away the laughter. She took as much time as she dared making her way out of the room and closing the door on a waft of olive oil scent. The passage was empty, the rise and fall of arguments floating up from downstairs the only sound. She crept along to Brown's door and listened. Silence.

She knocked once. Twice.

'Who is there? What have you forgotten?'

'It's me, sir,' she cried into the wood, as loudly as she dared. 'Amy. I must speak with you.'

Brown opened the door, his face a mask of shock, fury, and, she thought, worry.

6

'What the devil do you mean by coming here, you stupid girl?' he hissed, grabbing her by shoulder and yanking her into the room. 'When did you get here?'

'I just did,' she protested. 'I … I went into the wrong room.'

Brown's eyes roved over her, his face like thunder. 'You saw nothing?'

'No,' she said, shaking her head. 'The man downstairs, he said you were with someone. But I didn't see who.'

Brown folded his arms across his chest, still staring her in the eyes. She met his gaze and held it until he relaxed. 'I have others who wish to speak with me,' was all he gave her. A rising urge to know who, though, gnawed.

'I thought so,' she said. 'I … I know I'm not supposed to know who the others are, but…'

'Some are too grand to meet in mud and mire,' he shrugged. 'I thought she might have forgotten a glove, I …' Colour rose in his cheeks. Amy's jaw jerked in an involuntary half-smile. 'Why have you come here? You little fool. If you were seen coming hither then you're known. You're no good to me. And I – I am known too.'

'It couldn't wait, sir, I promise you.' She waited for him to invite her further into the room. He had slammed the door behind her as soon as she'd entered. He did not. Instead he walked over to the closed window and stood with his back to it. She looked around. The chamber was spartan, devoid of any personal effects. It suited him.

'Well?'

'It's Heydon, sir. The priest. He … he has turned my husband. I suspect he had drawn him into some plot. Some foul deed. He has promised him that he will become a hero for the Catholics.'

'You have proof of this?'

'Out of both their mouths. Heydon, he said that anyone who

151

tries to stop him will be in danger. I supposed that meant us.'

'Us? There is no us. What have you told him?'

'Nothing. I only warned him to leave my husband be. But … only, he said that he knows he's being watched.' That was gilding the truth a little, but only a little. 'And I thought that … when he said he would make my husband a hero, I thought that it might be some design upon the queen's life. You said it's what they aimed at, that lot.'

Brown's brow knitted. It was the first time she had seem him look flummoxed. 'The priest has returned from Scotland then,' he said, almost to himself. 'And is making converts.'

'Yes, and I –'

'Silence.' Amy closed her mouth. 'It might be the case. Yes, the rumbling in the north. The discontent. It might also be part of some grander stratagem. Destroy the sovereign, raise the north, and free the Scotch viper. All threads in a great tapestry.' He turned a sardonic smile on Amy. 'You realise that if you speak truly you have hanged that pretty husband of yours?'

An icy hand descended on Amy, despite the heat of the room. 'No,' she whispered. 'I thought … I only thought that if I brought you this, you could stop it. Jack – well, Jack isn't anybody really. But that priest is a gentleman. He's to blame. You could … I suppose you could forget about Jack. I promise to you that if Heydon is gone he'll never be any trouble. He just … he falls under spells.'

Brown seemed to consider this. 'I promise you nothing, woman.' Before she could reply, he said, 'but that I can try.'

'It is all Heydon. Get rid of the priest and all will be well. The queen will be safe.'

'No. The other queen will attract new priests. New popish plots. Oh, we know something of your husband's friend.'

'What?' asked Amy, her eyes widening in anticipation.

'Philip Heydon. He comes from an old family in Newcastle. Wandered from them all, a disgrace to them. Learnt a rough and uncivil tongue in the stews of God-knows-where. We have traced his movements from up there to the continent. Throughout the last years he has travelled backwards and forwards, consorting with papists at Rheims and in Paris. We lost him a while ago. Until he turned up begging service with the earl of Shrewsbury, affecting kinship to some other northern Heydons. Oh, we'll take him up, to be sure. He'll swing. But not quite yet. Not until his whole design is revealed to us, his entire chain of Catholic filth.' Brown drifted off, before appearing to remember that she was there. 'As you are here, have you any other news?'

'Only that the Scottish queen is still ill.'

'Not been testing that vial I gave you on her, have you, girl?' he said, giving something close to a smile. She ignored it.

'And the earl too. His gout. The countess, she still spends time with Queen Mary. Sewing and that. I don't think she enjoys it, poor lady.'

'Forget the countess,' said Brown, his voice sharp. 'And Shrewsbury. There has been a sight too much familiarity between the whole pack of them, then.'

'Give over – it's not their fault. It is her – her presence. It … wears them down.'

'Forget them, I said.'

'Yes, sir. But … will you do something? About Heydon?'

'Something will be done.' That was not quite an answer, she thought. Then he put a hand up to his chin, where some silver whiskers sprouted. 'Do you trust me, Mrs Cole?'

'I … yes, sir.' She thought, one always trusts someone until they ask that question.

'I wouldn't be surprised if there are changes afoot in yonder household. Soon. Queen Elizabeth cannot fail to hear that your old master is in correspondence with that Scottish strumpet. And when Master Secretary decides it is time she should know – then … then, the Catholics' house of cards will tumble.

'Now, get yourself away from here, woman. Make sure you are unseen. If you come here again our meetings will be at an end. And then,' he added, 'I shall not only leave your husband to his fate; I shall see to it that he swings as high as the filthy rabble he has taken up arms with.'

Amy left, walking dejectedly back up to the manor. She did

not trust Brown, not when it came to saving Jack. In fact, she had the distinct and uncomfortable feeling that the man would let any plot unfold, even until Queen Elizabeth was in real danger, just to scoop up as many conspirators as possible and have them gutted on the scaffold.

***

Jack turned the gemstone in his fingers. It caught the light, reflecting a rainbow. It was real – not one of the cheap pieces the countess of Moray had foisted on him and Heydon. It came with a gold ring and, more extraordinarily, a promise of money. Vast sums of money – thousands. It came from the duke of Norfolk and was addressed to his beloved, Queen Mary. Finally, too, there was a small package of money designated 'for the faithful servant.' Jack slid that into the pocket hanging from his own belt. He had worked enough for it.

Jack dutifully secreted the items and letters on his person, before setting off to find Heydon. Letters and presents for Mary had mounted up and he had had a lot to sort through. He was quite willing to pass the things on, to do his part in encouraging the marriage. But it seemed a fruitless thing. He had heard in Scotland that the Scots would keep Mary wedded to her brutal, rapist husband, Bothwell. More than that, the thought of shifty-eyed Norfolk, small and scrawny, taking a beautiful woman like Mary Stuart to his bed filled Jack with something like revulsion. She had never even seen him and would be unimpressed when she did. The only reason for the marriage would be to free her from captivity, and Jack knew that there were surer means of doing that. It was none of his business, really, but he would raise it with Heydon.

With the packet secure under his coat, he went out into the courtyard. He had thought to find his friend somewhere inside and was relieved to hear his voice coming from the manor's guardhouse. Heydon was playing dice with a soldier, laughing at how poor the man's game was.

Jack stuck his head into the small room and nodded. He had

grown adept at those little upwards nods, the kinds that signalled, man-to-man, that there was something to discuss. Heydon smiled. 'Well, lads, I've relieved you of enough cash for one day. You can owe me your losses. But I don't mean to wait around forever.'

He followed Jack outside on a wave of good-natured grumbling. 'I have letters and gifts for the queen.'.

'What's that?' Jack patted his chest in response and jutted his chin up towards the house.

'Can we speak?'

'Yes, Jack. Follow me.'

Heydon led them up into the house, to the small chamber used for books and accounts. When they were inside, he shut the door before taking a seat on a book chest. He left Jack standing. 'What's on your mind, mate?'

'I have this all for Queen Mary. From Norfolk. Gifts and letters. The usual stuff.' He produced the leather packet and handed it over. Heydon emptied it out on the desk in front of him – a wooden board supported by other book chests.

'Money, too? The good duke is an earnest suitor. Is this all you wanted? I'll pass it to her Majesty.'

'No, Philip. I was thinking.' Heydon cocked an eyebrow. 'About this Norfolk business. What is the point in it?'

'It's what the queen wants. It's what the men of the north want, or some of them.'

'But surely … I mean, if our plans are to happen, then all of this – it's all bootless. It's not the queen's marriage to Norfolk that'll free her, nor get the north up in arms. It's that other thing.'

'Ah, Jack. Yes, of course, you're quite right. But Queen Mary knows nothing of … that other thing. This,' he waved an arm over the jewels and letters, 'is where she places her faith. A belief that marriage to old Norfolk will remove her from prison.'

'Then we're acting with her knowledge. Without her…' he scrabbled for the word. 'Approval.'

'And?'

Jack took a deep breath. 'And I think we should lay our plan before her and see if she says yea or nay.'

Heydon stood up and came around the desk. He put a hand on Jack's shoulder. 'You're thinking, Jack. Thinking for yourself. That's a good thing.

'But no. No, mate, we have to let this nonsense, this marriage, I mean, proceed. Don't worry, if you fear for the good lady being wed to that old trout. It'll never come to pass. But she would not approve anything else. I mean, for all she's a discreet and gracious lady, she is a still a woman. She will take fright if she knows what we have put in train. No, let her fuss and pine about the release marriage might bring. It will be the usurper who puts an end to that, when she discovers it. Then – then Queen Mary might be told of our plans. Then she might be willing to put her faith in our design. But for now, no. We encourage this marriage. You just keep passing these letters – no need even to hide them.' He winked. 'Trust me that all will proceed. This marriage foolery buys us time for the men of the north to talk to one another. To trust to one another. The only thing that will bring us down is to mistime our adventure. Only that might lose us the game.'

As Heydon spoke, he steered Jack in a circle by the shoulder, leading him out. 'Now off you go, mate. Don't worry. Oh,' he added. 'I had another guest in this room earlier.'

'Who?'

'Your wife.'

'What? Why? What did she want?'

'Nothing much. I regret to say this, Jack, but … I don't trust her. She has some strange ideas in her head. Thinks I'm leading you astray, I reckon.'

'You didn't tell her anything?'

'No, no, no. She tried to trick it out of me. Dissembling, you know – making out she knew something. She means to protect you, mate. It's no bad thing. It's what a good wife ought to do. But if she gets it in her head to talk to anyone else … the earl, the countess, a soldier, even. Well then, you realise that she will have to be kept quiet.'

Heydon closed the door, leaving Jack in the corridor. A

warm breeze blew in from somewhere, making a man further down the hall curse as he perched on a box and tried to fix a tapestry to the wood panelled wall. Jack walked away, wondering how on earth one could keep a woman like Amy quiet if she chose not to be.

And as much as he loved her, and despite her stinging words, he knew that she often chose not to be.

Part Four: The Fall of Leaves

1

Queen Mary leant forward. She was sitting on her gilded wooden chair underneath a canopy bearing the arms of Scotland and France. She reached out an arm clad in white silk and raised him from his knees with a flick of her hand.

'I have missed you, Jack. You hear, my English is now not so bad as it since was.' He looked up and found her smiling at him. The dark smudges under her amber eyes only made her look more enchanting. She lowered her voice to a conspiratorial whisper. 'My own master of horse, he is not so very good as you were, my faithful friend.'

Jack beamed. He was in her bedchamber. The windows were shuttered against the autumn air. Heydon had brought him in, he said, at the queen's request. For the remainder of the summer he had been doing as he was bidden – passing letters and gifts along, keeping the fantasy of a marriage between the queen and the duke alive. It was now well into September. The weather had turned rainy and chilly, but the queen's health and spirits seemed to have returned.

'Thank you, your Majesty.'

'It is I who should thank you, Jack.' He liked hearing her say his first name. It had more music to it than when others used it. 'It is men like you who make this life easier to bear. I hope that one day I might be in a better place.' She struggled for meaning, frowning, and slowing to a more deliberate register. 'That I should have a means to do some favour for you.' When she had got it all out, she smiled again, seemingly with a little glow of pride. 'You understand this?'

'Yes, your Majesty. And there is no need.' She gave him such a look of warmth that he crimsoned.

'There is need. When I am free of this place – when I am in a better one – you might join my household then. If you wish. You and your wife. This is her, is it not?'

Jack's spine stiffened. He twisted his neck to see where

159

Mary was looking. In a far corner of the room, half-hidden in shadow, Amy was bent, folding up some cloths from a prie-dieu. She must have been there the whole time, watching and listening. Heat scratched itchy fingers up his neck, under his collar. 'Mrs Cole,' said Mary. 'Please come and stand by your husband.'

Amy dragged her feet towards him, refusing to meet his gaze. 'A fine pair you are, a most handsome pair. But …' She trailed off, seeming to read something between them. 'You should have a care for one another. It makes me sad, in my heart, to see people look so unhappy. Be kind to one another. God has put you together, yes?'

'Yes, your Majesty,' they both droned, he with enthusiasm and she with barely-concealed dislike. They both knelt before backing out of her chamber, through her anteroom, and out into the hall.

Jack felt that he hadn't exchanged more than a dozen words with his wife for months. He had, however, tried to watch her. At first it was because he had worried that something bad might happen. He did not think Heydon would hurt her to keep her quiet, but others might; and a number of Catholic gentlemen had been coming and going from the manor over the late summer. But he had begun to be intrigued by her movements also due to her strange claims about a friend. If she had one, he did not come to Wingfield. She took her meals with the laundresses, she slept in the female servants' dormitory, she bustled about with her linens and her napkins and her clothes, out to the woods and back with sodden bundles. He began to suspect she had made the whole thing up. Perhaps it was she who was jealous of his having a friend, and she had hoped to excite the like emotion in him. That was something people did, after all.

'Are you well, Jack?' she asked when they were alone.

'Yes. Yes, Amy, I am. And you?'

'Quite well.'

How strange it was. Only a year before, they would have had an open conversation – quiet on his side, yes, but frank and laughter-filled on hers. Now there was a coldness between them, a distance. He bowed his head, realising it could never go away. If he followed through on the plan Heydon had given him, Amy might never forgive him. She would certainly never trust him. Unless she converted to the true faith herself, she might even be disgusted by him. He felt a little dirty himself.

'I have to go and –'

'It's my day to –'

They cut one another off and, almost managing smiles, they went in different directions.

Jack had not made it to the stables when a rider cantered in, dropping from his horse almost before it had stopped. 'What news?' he called up to the messenger.

'Urgent business for the earl of Shrewsbury,' the man cried in a clipped accent. 'For them alone.' The man half-ran into the courtyard and called out for assistance. Before long the usher appeared and showed him inside. As always happened when someone arrived with 'urgent business' on their lips, a crowd began to gather in the courtyard, sharing theories on what it was all about. Jack found Amy amongst them.

'It looks,' she said to him, 'like something is happening at last.'

'What do you mean "at last"?' She shrugged. 'Oh look. Here's your friend. Like a fly smelling …' Heydon pushed through the milling throng and took Jack by the arm, shooting a hard look at Amy. Loudly, she said, 'well I can see I'm not wanted, husband. You fellows enjoy your talk.'

'What is it?' asked Jack, as Heydon drew him into a shadowy corner.

'It's Norfolk. The bastard Elizabeth has discovered his plan to wed Queen Mary.' Something like excitement twinkled in Heydon's eyes. 'It seems the old earl of Moray told her. You remember, you met that charming wife of his in Scotland?'

'I remember,' said Jack, picturing the huge, dark eyes. 'He wrote to her, I suppose. He must know that the paper was stolen by now then.'

'I'm sure of it, mate. He must have known for a while. I wouldn't be at all surprised if he thinks his sister has it somewhere here. Less surprised if this place is now searched.

Tutbury is probably being torn apart right now. Moray has put fire into the bastard, all right; she'll want Mary's rooms taken to pieces to uncover any secret papers she might have. She wants Norfolk locked up. She wants the queen back in Tutbury, in a cell if possible. She blames the earl and countess for their lax guardianship. You know what it all means?'

'I...' began Jack. Then more firmly, 'Yes. This whole marriage thing is over. We have to – I have to – look towards the other plan.'

'Quite right. The time is now. If Norfolk is locked away the northern counties will rise in anger. And all they will need to give them a winning hand is ... well, you know what, mate.'

Jack did know. But to hear Heydon talk of it as though it was all a grand game – a game at dice or cards – was troubling. 'When do we move?'

'To Tutbury?' asked Heydon. Jack actually meant to London, but he shrugged, happier with the misunderstanding. 'Up to the earl. I'd hoped not to have to see that place again, but it can't be helped. It's close enough to the north to be useful too, I suppose.

'Your wife – what was she saying to you there? And when you left Queen Mary's chamber?'

'Only that she thought something was happening. At last, she said.'

'What did she mean by that?'

'I don't know.'

'And still she's met with no one – you've found her sharing news with no man?'

'No. She speaks only with her fellow maids. Sometimes with the countess – the old woman seems to have taken a shine to her.'

'I see,' said Heydon. 'Well, you're forewarned. I expect Woodward will be along soon to give you a bellyful of the Bible and get you moving. Get a start now and avoid him.'

***

Amy felt no sense of elation. She had hoped that when

Queen Elizabeth found out about all the back and forth of letters between Mary and Norfolk, the Scottish queen would be sent out of the Shrewsburys' care and into the Tower of London. Yet all that seemed to be happening was a move back to draughty and smelly old Tutbury. If Brown had a hand in any of it, he was not the most effective agent in the world.

As the preparations to remove the queen back to the crumbling castle were begun, Amy went out of her way to consult with the countess – ostensibly on the trifling matter of which bedlinens should be packed. In truth, she suspected that Bess herself was working with Brown. Only she would warrant entry to his private lodgings. She had, too, tried to recruit Amy as a spy, and sent other gentlewomen into Mary's chambers as watchers. It might be her.

Armed with her cover story, Amy made her way to the countess's private office. Before she could reach it, she heard raised voices. Bess's Derbyshire drawl was the loudest. As Amy listened, she felt her heart flutter – if only a little.

'It's a matter of trust, my lord, trust. The queen don't trust us, that's all there is to it.'

'Yes, my love. But what can we do?'

'You leave that to me, husband. I know Elizabeth well enough. And this man, this Huntingdon, what is he like? You know him?' Shrewsbury's response was too muffled to discern. Bess's next words drowned him out anyway. 'It's a punishment, too. She blames us for this Norfolk foolery. Cecil knew – they all knew, all about it. Yet she calls us ... I can't even say it. She blames us because she can't blame them for their deceit, simple as that.'

Amy had no idea who 'Huntingdon' was.

'We didn't ask for this,' said Bess, 'not none of it.' Her voice lost a little of its heat. 'And yet we have the expense of it. And the blame when the queen's ministers keep secrets from her. I don't know why we bother, sometimes, really I don't.'

'But what to do, sweetheart?' asked Shrewsbury. His voice was still weak. He had never really recovered from the illness that had plagued him early in the summer.

'Put up with him, I suppose. Put up with him spying and informing Elizabeth that we're soft and weak and in thrall to the prisoner she thrust upon us.' The earl made a weak little noise. 'Yet we needn't put up with it quietly. No, my lord, not all. If Huntingdon is going to lord it over us in our own house, poke his nose into the way we keep custody of this queen, then he'll hear our complaints too.'

'We should then write her Majesty?'

'Write, fie! I shall go to her.'

'But you cannot – we cannot leave our guest.'

'We can't – I can!'

Amy eased her ear away from the door. So someone called Huntingdon had been drafted in to keep a closer eye on Queen Mary than the Shrewsburys had been doing. Perhaps Brown had come through after all.

The door flew open.

'What the devil?' asked Bess. 'You girl, what do you mean creeping along corridors?'

'I need to find out about the linens, my lady. Mr Woodward says we're all to be moving soon.'

'Does he indeed?' Bess stepped out and closed the door on her husband. 'I want only the cheapest and the meanest linens brought out of this place,' she said, her voice low. 'See to that. I want no more good things spoilt by rot and damp. And...' she trailed off, as though deciding how much to say. 'Well, you'll all have to know soon enough. Her Majesty Queen Elizabeth has ordered that a new man be sent up to us. To help us keep custody of the Scottish queen. The earl of Huntingdon. A good man. I don't want him thinking that we keep the lady in luxury, coddling her and letting her scheme and plot. You understand me?'

'Yes, my lady.'

'You recall I said that I might go up to London some time, to court?' Amy nodded her head. 'Yes, I said I might bring you along, girl. I don't forget a promise, not to one of my girls. Should you still like that? A visit to London?'

'Yes, my lady. Very much.' Changed times, she thought, to be saying that. London was a pit. But anywhere was better than a prison.

'I'll remember that. Do you sew?'

'Yes,' said Amy, delight streaking across her face. It felt a long time since she had really smiled. 'My mother was a seamstress. It's what I want, to ply –'

'Good. I mean, I couldn't take a laundress to court. Might as well say I find the queen's servants poor – that I think the queen sleeps in her own filth.' Bess seemed to find this hilarious, and she barked laughter. Amy smiled politely. 'Right. Away with you, girl. Remember what I said about the linens. Be sure that only the meanest are packed. We'll show this Huntingdon that we're no slaves to the queen of Scots.'

She gave Amy a little push to get her moving and then returned to her husband. Amy kept her smile. Huntingdon, she was sure, would be the answer to her prayers. He would be the man to take Mary Stuart and her minions away. He would be the one to free Jack from their rotten influence.

2

Jack had his shirtsleeves rolled up. He had finished brushing down the stallion that Norfolk had sent with him – the stallion that had never seen any hard riding. It seemed that Norfolk would never send anything else. The rumours were that he was under house arrest – probably bound for the Tower. No one seemed to know exactly what was happening, but there were no more letters, no more trinkets or pledges of love and money sent to Queen Mary.

The quality of light changed in the stable and Jack turned. In the doorway stood a tall man. Even with the light at his back, Jack could tell who it was. The earl of Huntingdon had been awaiting them when they arrived at Tutbury, a tall, austere man with a neat blonde beard, waxed to a fine point. He remained in the doorway for a few seconds, saying nothing. Then he raised a hand, clicked a finger, and pointed to the side. From behind him a soldier appeared and took up his station where Huntingdon had indicated. The earl then strode in. In his wake hobbled Shrewsbury, leaning on a cane and looking very small.

'So this is where her couriers arrive?' asked Huntingdon. His voice was high-pitched, making it sound like everything he saw and spoke of was beneath him. He did not wait for Shrewsbury's response. Instead he strode forwards, towards Jack.

Heydon had warned him about the new earl. He was apparently related to Queen Elizabeth – he stood somewhere in the royal succession, though he showed no particular interest in the throne. Instead, his interest was in ferreting out Catholics and seeing them to the gallows. As they stood toe to toe, Jack could almost imagine the man sniffing at him, detecting his change in faith. 'Name?'

'Cole, my lord.'

'This is the fellow sent from Norfolk with the horse?' asked

Huntingdon, not taking his eyes from Jack.

'It is,' wheezed Shrewsbury. 'He is a well trusted young fellow.'

'By you, perhaps. We all know what trust reposes in you.' Shrewsbury said nothing, but Jack coloured. Huntingdon was of Shrewsbury's rank. He owed the old man respect. Instead he was belittling him in front of a servant. 'I don't trust you, Cole. I don't trust any of you who've been working in this tainted place.' He stepped backwards, and brushed down his doublet, swishing his half-cloak back. Jack realised he wanted to give the impression that proximity had soiled him. 'I have no doubt you, boy, have been passing that woman's disgusting letters to her. Under your nose,' he spat at Shrewsbury. Jack kept his eyes ahead, staring at nothing.

Huntingdon clicked his fingers again, and another soldier came into the stable. 'I want this place taken apart. Look under hay. Look in any barrels of feed – empty everything. The slaves here can put it together again. If you find anything – anything – bring it to me immediately. Come, my lord of Shrewsbury. Where do the servants sleep?'

'We have had the old hunting lodge made up into sleeping chambers. As at Wingfield, male and females separate. To stop them having to leave the castle.' Shrewsbury sounded like he was making a bid to be helpful.

'Hmph. Some sense, then. Yet a place for them to gather and plot together. We will see what the kitchens and the laundry have to offer first.' He turned to look again around the stables, where already a soldier had begun kicking at bales of hay. 'Yes, you've all had rather a high old time of it here. That is all over, I assure you.'

Huntingdon swept from the room. Shrewsbury gave Jack an apologetic look. He did not look at the soldiers but began limping after his departing new tormentor.

When they had gone, Jack left the ongoing destruction. The soldier at the door did not try and stop him – in fact, he had joined his fellow and was using his sword to stab at haystacks. He caught sight of Huntingdon's tall, straight back as he went up the hill to the castle proper. He did not pause, letting his half-crippled old peer totter after him. For a man in his early forties, Shrewsbury had aged in the past year to something nearer sixty.

If Huntingdon was intent on finding something – proof of Mary resistance to Elizabeth, or the resistance of her servants – that meant the possibility of the stolen Scottish document being found. He began walking uphill himself, hoping to find Heydon and discover where exactly he had hidden it.

***

Within days of Huntingdon's arrival, Amy had begun to wonder at what she had unleashed on the household. She stood in the laundry as men tipped over coffers of sheets, thrusting their hands in and pulling them out. 'Here, hold on,' she cried. 'You'll rip them.' She and her fellow maids were lined up against the wall of the room.

The soldier gave her a crooked smile, held up a sheet, and tore it down the middle. Huntingdon looked on, his face impassive. 'What have you found? I tell you, lads, it will be these women who fall under that wretched Scottish queen's spell. Fools – addle-pated fools.'

'There's nowt here, my lord.'

'Nothing? Well, they have just gained wit in hiding their crimes. How now, girls, have you passed your secret notes and papers into the Scottish queen's own hands?'

No one spoke.

'Very well. Hold your peace, then. We shall take the queen's rooms apart. But know this: if anything is found there, we know that it did not walk in by itself. We know that some crooked members of this household have given the woman succour. Come, lads.'

She watched the earl and his men go, leaving behind their whirlwind of destruction. No, this was not what she had wanted at all. She would have to find Brown and let him know that the new man was overzealous. In truth, she had begun to wonder just how a lowly figure had managed to get an earl sent down. That is, if he had had a hand in it. She had no idea how the structures of power worked. Perhaps Brown reported to someone, who reported to someone, who eventually reported to Cecil and the queen. Probably Mr Brown had no real influence as to who was sent or recalled, or what they did when they arrived. Still, she would have to try. If Huntingdon was going to rip apart the castle every time the whim struck him, then she was responsible for everyone's misery and fear. What would suit everyone, then, was if the high-toned bastard found something – some proof of treachery and took Mary away.

She thought of the Scottish queen. She had hated her, wanted her gone, imprisoned somewhere dark and forgotten. But the woman had tried to build bridges between her and Jack. What was more, she felt that Jack might actually have listened to her. Was that artifice? Was the woman exercising the charm that men always spoke of? Or … or could it be that she was simply a sad, pleasant woman who had fallen victim to the men around her?

It did not matter. What mattered was getting Mary taken off the Shrewsburys' hands and making sure Jack didn't suffer for falling under the spell of a priest. Something, though, drew her feet up towards the royal apartments. She crept along the wall of the corridor, the sound of angry sobs drifting towards her.

'Where is it? Where are your letters, woman, where are your secrets? We know you have them.'

'You are speaking to a queen,' said Shrewsbury, his voice small but steel-edged.

'I know to whom I'm speaking, thank you, my lord – and she is now a queen without a kingdom. She is nothing but a papist scourge on this land. Well, where are your letters, your *Majesty*?'

The sound of Mary's sobbing rose in pitch, and Amy heard Bess. 'That's enough, my lord. The queen is … she's distraught.'

'My lord of Shrewsbury, if you would control your wife.'

'I can speak for myself,' Bess growled. Good for you, thought Amy.

'Control your wife, my lord,' Huntingdon repeated, no trace

169

of emotion in his voice. Shrewsbury made inarticulate little noises. 'But see that she is not so familiar with this woman in future.'

'Come, your Majesty,' said Bess, her voice suddenly all honey. 'I'm sure my lord of Huntingdon is just being a mite cautious. Won't you sit?' Amy couldn't see what was happening, but when Huntingdon spoke, she could hear that Bess's attempts to needle and undermine him worked. He positively squeaked in rage.

'You see! You see! You see, Shrewsbury, what stuff there is between women? Your wife has become a ... a *friend* to this woman. A friend to a prisoner of the queen of England.'

'It's no crime to pass the time of day with a woman. We've had no commands to lock this lady in a dungeon,' said Bess. Her voice had turned calm, making Huntingdon sound crazy.

'Your wife has been turned,' he shrieked. 'I shall have to tell the queen of this. Tell her that her prisoner is being cosseted and preened by her gaoler's wife.'

'My lord, please, I think there's no need for –'

'I understand you have even allowed her visitors.' Huntingdon all but spat the word. 'VIS-I-TORS!'

'Some gentlemen have come, it is true,' said Shrewsbury. 'To pay their respects to her Majesty.'

'To pay – to gape like landed fish at a caged lioness, a caged viper. And to plot with her, I'll be bound, to wink at her escape from this place. I see what goes on, oh yes. You and your wife – you've been enjoying the fame of this enterprise. Showing her off to the local gentry, eh? Your captive que–'

'Nothing, my lord,' said a new voice. Amy recognised it as one of the soldiers who had helped destroy the laundry.

'Nothing in the bedchamber? You checked under the bed? I heard that this queen once hid a lover under her bed and killed him when her brother discovered it.'

'Nothing. Just papist toys and books.'

'What books?' The soldier did not response; Amy supposed that he must have shrugged or shook his head. Perhaps he could not read. There was some more stomping and crashing, but no voices spoke for a while. She started to wander away,

170

when she heard Mary speak.

'You are a cruel man,' she said, dignity giving weight to a sob-ravaged voice. 'I can see that. Yet your cruelty shall not get you anything. There is nothing to get. I have done nothing.'

'Nothing, eh? I have heard the rumours from our eyes in the north, madam. If there is discontent there it is you have sewn it. And these people who have let you. All of them, the whole pack, top to bottom. No more. If those fools up there raise arms and die for it, it is all of you who will have the blame.'

Amy walked away from royal apartments. She paused at an open shutter downstairs and let the breeze wash over her. It was rancid, heavy with the smell of sewers, as all breezes seemed to be at Tutbury, but she welcomed the sting. She deserved it. It carried the sounds of hammering, sawing, kicking, tearing, and crying.

*****

Heydon was in the little office room. 'Jack,' he said, rising. 'What's the face for?'

'That man, Huntingdon. He's tearing apart the stables. He's looking for anything he can to hurt Queen Mary. I ...' Jack let his eyes wander over the room. Books and papers were all laid out neatly for inspection.

'He's yet to get here. I won't have him tearing anything apart.'

'But ... the paper we took from Scotland!'

Heydon chanced a look at the closed door behind Jack, before he removed his hat and set it on an empty space on the table. Then he turned it over. 'A fine lining, isn't it?' With a deft movement, he pulled the lining out of the hat, revealing the square of paper. Then he replaced it, pressing it in tight with the tips of his fingers. He put it back on his head and bowed.

'I still don't think it's safe enough on your person. I should bury it somewhere. In a box. In the woods.'

'Oh no. The queen's bastard brother thought that leaving it

off his person would keep it safe. And here it is, hundreds of miles away, in a foreign land in a man's hat. I won't be making that mistake.'

'Hmph,' said Jack. Again he tossed his head, forgetting about the missing lock. Worse, he reminded himself that his head had begun to itch interminably as the hair grew back. 'If you say so, Philip. But this Huntingdon – he's a monster.'

'He's a reformer. One of the hottest of them, thinks the queen hasn't gone far enough.'

'You said he was the queen's cousin.'

'No, I said his mother was a Pole. An ancient family of noble blood. He has a claim to the throne, but not the vigour to pursue it. And Elizabeth ignores it. A man with no sense of his entitlement. Forget him. He'll discover nothing.'

Jack went silent. Heydon had the upper hand when it came to the politics of the world. It was, after all, his world, not Jack's. Still, something rankled. Something that had dug its way in when they were in Scotland and not quite left him.

'He has gone up to abuse the queen.'

'Fuck him. He's a weakling. A big mouth and heavy boots, but no heart. No ambition. He won't be around forever. It might steel her to realise what manner of man she can expect to govern her under Elizabeth. She's been lucky, the good queen – we all have – to have had such a soft gaoler for this long.'

Jack left, the thought of what might be happening up in Mary's rooms jabbing at him. Heydon seemed unaffected – even disinterested. He began to wonder if his friend was working in her interests or in his own. Queen Mary seemed almost a simple means to an end, rather than a woman of feeling and passions. At the moment Heydon's interest, the restoration of Catholicism, might dovetail with the Scottish queen's interests, but who knew how long that would last.

3

'A fine man, the earl,' said Brown. 'A fine, fine fellow. A scourge upon the papist hordes. And the papist whore.'

Amy had slid out of Tutbury and down to the woods. She hadn't seen Brown since she had intruded on his lodgings in South Wingfield, but he had arrived almost immediately she had begun whistling her call sign. 'I'm glad to see that you can follow instructions,' had been his only greeting, before he launched into a paean of praise for the man she had come to complain about.

'He is a brute,' she said, kicking at the carpet of burnished leaves.

'It takes a brute to get things done. What has he found?'

'Nothing.'

Brown tutted, before moving around a fallen trunk. For a moment she thought he was going to sit – something he never did – but then he beckoned her to. She kneaded the small of her back before easing herself down.

'He's making it impossible for us – for any of us – to live our lives. We never know when he'll descend on us, tearing things up. And his men all digging into our private things. They even came into the women servants sleeping chamber. Kicked up all the blankets, ripped open the pillows. Alice said she's finding feathers in places she didn't know she had.'

'Who the devil is Alice?'

'One of my friends,' she said, a little hesitantly. 'And they tore up my book.'

'You had a book?'

'Well it was one of the earl's books. A tragedy about Rom – '

'I don't care,' he said, rising a silencing hand, 'about your petty thievery.'

'I didn't steal it – it had fallen –'

'I don't care. Ye Gods, there is little more tiresome than a woman who thinks her opinions and her petty acts matter. Why did you call for me – what news?'

'I want you to relieve us of the earl.'

Brown looked at her as though she had gone mad. Then he began to laugh, a dry, crackling sound. She frowned. 'I made no jest.'

'No,' he said, snuffing his laughter like a candle. 'You simply want me to order an earl – an earl commanded by Queen Elizabeth – to leave this place because a trifling laundress finds it hard to wash piss-stained sheets when he's about. That's the measure of it?'

'Well ... you got him here, didn't you? You took what I said, and they sent him.'

'I applaud your faith in me, wench. The good earl was sent to teach the Shrewsburys a lesson. No more. Secretary Cecil and the queen have been most unhappy, it seems, with the countess spending her days embroidering and chattering with a prisoner. And the earl, too, falling into sickness and letting his household run riot. Letting his slaves smuggle messages in and out – and to a duke, no less.'

'So there's nothing you can do?'

'There is nothing I can do. I only came today to tell you that our arrangement is now at an end.'

'What?' Panic rose. 'Why?'

'I have business elsewhere. Norfolk is to be committed to the Tower, it seems. That will shake his followers in the north. And the followers of those other noblemen who remain papist. They will act soon. Very soon. Your husband – have he and his priest friend said anything?'

'Not to me.'

'And what have you heard them say when you were watching.'

'I haven't. I mean, I haven't kept ears on them. So far as I know they're planning nothing.'

'Really? The last time I saw you, you begged me to protect your husband if he were found in a plot to murder our sovereign lady.'

Amy half-turned on the log. She had decided to use tears. It worked for Mary Stuart. 'I … don't … know.'

'Quit that,' snapped Brown. 'Tears will avail you of nothing by me, I promise you that. Women's false tears sicken me. If you are lying, woman – if you think that you might now cover your man's misdeeds, then it will be the worse for both of you.'

'I tell you I know nothing. They planned – perhaps they planned for the Scottish queen to marry the duke of Norfolk. That's all over now. I know of no other plan. But … what if I discover something? What should I do? If you're gone, I mean. Should I tell the earl and the countess?' Unaccountably, she wanted Norfolk to suffer, former master or not. She had no problem laying the blame on him. He started this. Her husband had fallen into some dream of chivalry because that old duffer had sought to marry the equally stupid Scottish queen. If he was locked away, the whole thing should be over.

'No,' said Brown. His voice had turned firm, colder than before. 'I want you to cease your prattling and your nosing altogether. Do you hear me, woman? Your informing is over. If you discover anything by happenstance, you keep it close until I contact you again. Here. Stay here so that I can find you if I need you.'

'But – but what if it were some great plot – something that was to be done quickly?'

'Then you trust that clever men – far cleverer than you – have it in hand. Do you understand me?'

'Yes, sir,' she said.

'Good. Do you still have that vial I gave you hidden somewhere?'

'Yes.'

'You'd better give it to me.'

'Yes. Yes, you can have it back and be welcome to it.'

'No, wait. On second thought, it cannot hurt to ensure our realm's safety. Keep it.' Her face fell. 'You remember what I told you? If there should come a day when it is in every man's mouth that Queen Elizabeth has died, or been slain, only then should you use it. Or,' he added, pinching the bridge of his nose, 'if it should fall out that the northern rebels come here and try and free the viper. Whether the queen lives or not, if an armed band breaches those walls up there and makes to take her, you must hold the witch down and force that down her throat.'

'But that won't happen, will it? The northern men – the rebels – they won't get to here.'

'Probably not. They have no one to organise them. A piffling band of trash, papist trash looking for any excuse to cause trouble. Our boys will be readied in London and destroy them when they're still saying their foolish masses in their priest holes up north. If it does, though … if it does, and you let that Scotch cow go free, I swear to you by my truth that I'll have you at the head of the crowd when your man's bowels are torn out.

'Now, I take my leave of you. Before I do, allow me to give you a little advice. If you want to make a good wife, learn to curb that tongue of yours.' For the first time, his features softened, seemingly with great effort. 'If I have been harsh with you, mistress, it was to let you know of the harshness of this world. And … my own wife would not take well to me speaking soft words in the woods with another woman, whether it was for my work or otherwise. Take my advice and do as I instruct. I wish you well.' Brown gave no bow, no other hint of farewell. He simply stalked off into the trees and disappeared from view.

Gone, she thought. Her contact with the outside world. The unpleasant brute whom she had hoped would somehow turn out to be a useful help if she ever needed one – an inadvertent hero. Gone.

Amy knew she should get back to the castle, but she could not face it right away. She sat for a few seconds and started when she thought she heard branches cracking. She turned around, thinking that Brown might be coming back. But the sound had come from the other direction. She peered through the trees but could see no one. A fox, perhaps. But it hadn't sounded like a fox. It had sounded very much like a person trying to conceal their footsteps.

***

Jack had the letter concealed down the front of his breeches. He had taken it without reading it. It had not been passed to him by Heydon, but rather by one of the queen's women – the imperious Mistress Seton, of the wigs. He had needed something to do, something to occupy his mind. For the first time he did not know that he could fully trust anyone.

Seton had cornered him in the hall outside Heydon's chamber where he had been standing, irresolute. Evidently, she had been hoping to give the letter to the priest to pass to him for safe passage out of the house, but Jack's presence had allowed her to cut out the middle man.

It was a letter to be given to the French ambassador in London. It spoke of the outrages that Huntingdon was inflicting on the household, and on Queen Mary herself, and begging for him to intercede to Queen Elizabeth and insist on the man's removal. The trick would be getting it out.

The house had really become a prison. It was a big place, but Huntingdon had posted men at every entrance and exit. Jack had come to realise that some were fairly lax. They would make conversation, ask polite questions, but ultimately let people pass. Others would push men against the wall and pat at their bodies, hoping to hear the crinkle of paper. Seton had got the letter to him concealed in a collection of reddish curls. He doubted the soldiers would have thought to put their hands inside it.

He strode along the hall, away from Heydon's office. He decided it was a good thing Seton had interrupted him. What he had been planning to say – he couldn't trust Heydon, or the men Heydon knew – not to react badly to it. He would deal with it himself, somehow.

The hall met a staircase at one end. A guard was at the bottom of it, next to the door that led into the smaller of the two courtyards. He slowed his pace, trying to sound casual. The man had let him up without searching him, but then he hadn't worried; he didn't have anything to hide. The thing about having something concealed on you was that it showed on your face. You either made too great an expression or you overdid trying to look like nothing was happening. Either way you looked guilty, like a thief trying to stroll past a constable with a stolen loaf tucked under his arm.

'You were quick,' said the soldier. He was about Jack's age.

'My friend wasn't in.'

'Oh right. Are you going out?'

'That was the idea,' said Jack. He regretted it. He didn't mean it to, but it sounded cocky, rude. The lad frowned.

'We're supposed to check folk leaving.'

'You didn't check me going in.' No, he thought. That wasn't the right thing to say either. He should have shrugged it off.

'I suppose not.' The soldier yawned. Jack stood.

'It must be as boring for you as it is for us lot, all this.'

'Ha! You've got that right.'

'Any idea how long it's all to be like this for … mate?'

'Couldn't say. We're not told nothin'. Just, well – you know what the earl's like. "I need good men to escort me to Tutbury. You, and you, and you".' He shrugged, and Jack nodded in what he hoped was a display of sympathy. He stepped away from the guard and out into the yard without another word, waiting for the hand on his shoulder. It never came.

Outside, people were milling with boxes and trunks. A general muttering filled the air, and angry looks were on every face. Soldiers walked in between them, each of them in Huntingdon's livery. 'Where do you think you're going?' Jack jumped, before realising he wasn't being addressed. 'Has this been searched yet?'

Turning, he saw an older soldier upending a man's leather bag onto the ground. Some cutlery and jewels bounced on the mud, damp from a mist of rain. 'Fine,' said the soldier, nudging the items with the toe of his boot. 'Now get out.'

'What's happening?' Jacked asked the man nearest him.

'They're reducing the queen's household. Throwing us out.'

Jack looked around. Some people were in tears, others furious. About thirty people were being evicted from the castle. He leant to the ground and began helping the man whose things had been dumped out.

'Merci, merci. Tu es un bon garçon.'

'Listen to me, sir,' said Jack, out of the corner of his mouth. He looked around, to where the soldiers were searching others. When he was certain their backs were turned, he slid his hand down his breeches and pulled out the letter. Out of the side of his mouth he said, 'from the queen. To London. Please.'

A light dawned in the man's eyes and he dropped the letter into his bag alongside a silver spoon. He gave an imperceptible nod, which Jack returned.

He returned to the soldier just inside the castle, and together they watched half of Queen Mary's household being sent packing. 'Quite a rabble,' said Jack.

'They are that,' said his young friend. 'Less of them is less trouble, I guess. Less to help the Scotch queen escape. Good thing. If she tried, we'd like as not have to shoot her. Only the cap' has a gun, right enough, and he couldn't hit a cow's arse with a lute. But the earl knows what he's doing. Least it'll be an easier thing to keep an eye on what goes in and out once that lot's shifted.'

4

'It might be a good idea to get out of this place soon,' said Heydon. They were standing in the male dormitory in the former hunting lodge. It was one of the few places that was no longer regularly searched. A pattern had emerged in the early part of October. Huntingdon's men seemed to favour turning the queen's rooms upside down. The aim, Jack guessed, was to keep her too scared and nervous to attempt anything. It seemed to be working.

Jack gulped. 'You think it's happening soon, then.' Heydon kicked out at a bundle of coverlets and moved towards a window. Since the month had dawned, a change had come over him. Barely-concealed anger had replaced cockiness.

'Fucking idiots. That damned Welsh whore, she's upset everything.' Jack almost smiled at the thought that Queen Elizabeth had upset the plan to kill her. 'She's put fear into the men in the north, and I hear she's living at Windsor. Windsor! How can we find a lodging near Windsor?'

'Well, maybe next year…'

'No! I … I can't keep the Catholic faithful in the north under control from here. They're loose, wild. It … they were meant to march only when they heard that – that our design had been executed. Then they'd have an easy time of it, marching on a headless city. But – they're ploughing their own furrow now. We shall just have to move quickly.'

Jack wondered how Heydon knew this. The castle had been all but cut off by Huntingdon's men. Yet his friend seemed privy to everything that was happening. He knew that the northern earls had been summoned to London, released, and fled home under a dark cloud, rousing their men to fear of what would be done to them next. He knew that Norfolk had failed to weasel his way out of trouble and was being conveyed to the Tower, riling up the men of his county too. Each time he imparted something, he seemed to grow angrier and more frustrated. More imperious, too. Gone were the friendly 'mates'.

'So what?'

'So we put ourselves to work. We go to Windsor if we must and you do your duty by God.'

'When?'

'As soon as possible.'

Jack folded his arms and moved towards a window recess. He sat in it, staring at Heydon. 'We can't just leave the household and go to London. Not without the earl's permission.' He hoped his voice sounded authoritative. 'We have no reason.'

'You think that matters? Do you think a pair of runaway men will matter one whit when the world turns to chaos?' Jack had no answer to that. 'If it'll please your nice ideals then I'll ... I'll request leave from the earl to conduct some business in the south. Yes, the south. The north might make him worry at this time.'

'I think,' said Jack, 'we should wait. Wait until the queen is in London, anyway.'

'It is no more time to wait,' snapped Heydon. 'Do you want to burn in hell for what you've done, or do you wish true salvation?' His voice took on a nasty edge. He softened it. 'Jack, the timing of events is key.' He looked around the empty room before continuing. 'It must be. The usurper dies. The northern men revolt against her headless government. Queen Mary is freed, and London is taken. If one of those things falls out wrong, happens in the wrong order, then the whole fails. If Elizabeth lives the heretics in London take heart and will fight the faithful. They'll march north. They might even decide to dispatch the true queen rather than chance her freedom. You can see that, can't you?'

Jack knew when he was beaten. He would go south with Heydon. He had no choice. But he suspected that when it came to it, he could not pull the trigger on Queen Elizabeth. If he failed at that, then he would find some other way to atone. He would go to Rome if he had to, and appeal to the whole college of cardinals. Or, perhaps, some divine power would surge through him on the day and he would find the strength to do it. In truth, he had no idea. Events were carrying him now.

Besides, if his wife had it in her to kill, he might find the like courage. Since he had followed Amy into the woods and listened to her calmly discuss murdering Queen Mary with a government agent, he didn't know who was capable of what anymore.

***

Amy watched Bess direct her mistress of the wardrobe to pack the bodices she had selected. The countess herself had in her hands a bodice covered in a lattice of red and gold threads. It would be slimming on her, Amy thought. 'Be sure you get the right sleeves, mind,' Bess barked. Her voice was always forthright, even when she was being kindly.

The countess seemed to remember that Amy was in the room. She reached down and grasped at her pomander, her brow knitting in remembrance. 'Of course – yes – what's your name again, girl?'

'Amy Cole, my lady.'

'It's Mrs Cole, now. You'll be my needlewoman – my seamstress.' Amy beamed. 'Take that daft grin off your face. You've never been to Court before, I take it? No, of course you haven't. Well, you've been in a duke's household. And an earl's. You know how not to disgrace yourself.' Amy bowed her head. 'That's better. My woman will tell you how to behave on the road. Now, you might borrow one dress of suitable quality. I won't have the Court think I keep my women in rags, no I won't.' She nodded at the unsmiling wardrobe mistress.

Amy's choice was limited by what the mistress would allow her. She selected a plain russet gown with rose-coloured sleeves. She had no idea if it was a fashionable thing or not, but it looked similar to what some of Queen Mary's women wore. When she had made her selection, Bess looked it over. 'Fine taste you have, my girl.'

'I like the sleeves, my lady. If I could sew up sleeves like this, I'd –'

'Very good. You can't wear this to travel. That old thing will have to do for the road. We can make you look like a woman before we reach Windsor. Right, be off with you. Go, and see to … see to it that the small things are packed. Tablecloths, anything we'll need on the road. You're no idiot – make yourself useful.'

Amy curtsied and left Bess's chambers. London, she thought. Well, not really London – Windsor. That was better. It was far enough away from the filthy streets and lousy people of the city. It was far enough away from Tutbury. Idly, she wondered if Queen Mary would ever see London. Elizabeth couldn't keep her a prisoner forever – even keeping her with the Shrewsburys since January had caused too many problems, too much illness.

She would also be leaving Jack. They had been leading separate lives, but she would have to tell him she was going south. He would be safe at Tutbury, she hoped. Under Heydon's influence, it was true, but nowhere near Elizabeth. There could be no heroics in the evil old castle. She decided to seek him out and found him leaving the earl's apartments. He looked surprised to see her. Then a smile crossed his face, his eyes brightening. They cooled.

'Wife.'

'Husband.'

'What ails you?'

'I thought I should tell you – I'm going south. With the countess. To Court.'

'What?' Jack's brow creased, his mouth falling open. 'But so am …'

'The countess is going to see the queen. To beg all of this to stop.'

As if on cue, one of Huntingdon's soldiers sauntered towards them. 'What is this, whisperin' in corridors?' he asked, a sneer on his leathery face. 'Move along or I'll report you to the earl.'

'I am speaking to my husband,' Amy said, lifting her chin. 'Does your master take such an interest in husbands and wives just talking.'

'If they're discussin' treason. Plottin'. You're right he'll take an interest, girl.'

'Treason!' laughed Amy. 'I was discussing my wardrobe, if you must know. Have you ever spoken to a woman? Or do they all take one look at your bollock-purse face and run away?'

'You little slut. I'll report you for that, see if I don't.' The soldier turned and disappeared.

'You shouldn't have said that, Amy. You're making enemies of them.'

'To the devil with them. Quick, before he comes back with someone: I just … I wanted to say goodbye to you, Jack.'

'When are you going?'

'Tomorrow. Early.' She did not like the look on his face. She could not read it. On impulse, she stood on her tiptoes and kissed his cheek. 'I love you, Jack Cole.' Before he could answer, she went off in the same direction the soldier had gone. But worry went with her. When she had told him she was going to Court, he had been about to say, 'so am I.'

***

'No, no, no!' Heydon said, running a hand through his hair before replacing his cap. Jack wondered if the document was still hidden in it. 'Stop her. Stop the whole thing.'

'I can't,' said Jack. His friend had taken the news of Amy's departure badly. He didn't know why.

'It's another … another complication. I don't like it. And … I'm sorry to say this, Jack, but I don't trust that wife of yours.'

'I do,' said Jack, his voice low. Despite what he had heard in the park – perhaps because of it – he wanted nothing more than for there to be a great distance between Amy and Queen Mary. Especially if Heydon's stories of the northern rising were true. But he had not told his friend about what he had seen. Privately he suspected that if he revealed that Amy had been a spy, Heydon might arrange for something to happen to her.

'Then you're a fool. You cannot trust her until she becomes of our faith. Until then she's steeped in heresy, wife or no wife. Tell her she can't go. Better yet, we must stop the countess from going south. We need no more complications.'

'I can't see how we can stop a countess from doing as she pleases,' said Jack. He picked up a pillow and buffed it, just for something to do. The rest of the household was at dinner, leaving them alone in the dormitory, and he felt his own stomach mewl.

'I ...' Again, Heydon removed his cap and rubbed his head. 'Very well, let them go. Yes, God has given us this challenge and we must rise to face it. In fact, we might make it work for us. You wondered how we might find license to go south. You shall say your wife has forgotten something – something of the countess's. And some papers – I'll say some papers have been neglected. A weak excuse. Huntingdon will have none of it. But he can't stop us if I can convince old Shrewsbury we must go. Right ... right ... I'm going to find something to eat.'

Heydon disappeared. Jack let his own belly growl. Why was he so intent on preventing Amy reaching Court? Might he know something of what she had been doing, of her contact with the hard-faced English spy? If he did, he certainly wouldn't want her under the same roof as Cecil and his crew.

He decided he was going to stop telling Heydon things. It only seemed to result in the man fraying further and further. And nothing seemed to dissuade him from the project he had set them.

***

Amy pulled on her travelling cloak and tied it tight at the neck. She wished she had a mirror. It wasn't that she had taken any special care over her appearance – other than her hair, which Alice had gamely curled and pinned under cap – but she felt lighter and happier knowing that she would be leaving Tutbury. She wanted to know if it showed. More, she could barely wait to see herself at Court, in her new dress, looking like a woman instead of a scrubby-faced boy.

She eased a basket up on her arm, her cutlery and some little bits of food covered by a napkin. Then she picked her way through her fellow servants. Most of them were either sleeping or sitting up, rubbing sleep from their eyes. It was still full dark outside, the candles that burned all night low.

The dormitory opened onto a wooden staircase – a rickety, temporary thing – that passed by the men's sleeping chamber. As she passed it, she thought about Jack. He would still be sleeping. She offered up a silent prayer – a wish – that he would be safe in her absence. Her previous wishes seemed to have gone unfulfilled, but there was no harm in trying.

As she reached the bottom of the stairs, she thought she could hear the sounds of grooms in the yard. Above that, a woman's voice reared. It could only be Bess. She strained to make out what was being said. So trained were her ears on the sounds drifting in from outside that she did not hear the padded footsteps coming up behind her.

Something thumped on the back of her neck. Her eyes widened, and her mouth opened, working stupidly. She did not fall. 'Wha'?'

The heavy thing, whatever it was, rose and fell again, and this time she folded to the ground, darkness creeping in at the edges of her vision. It overtook her sight entirely and her mind rose up to meet it.

5

The scuffling of the countess' stable grooms had woken Jack as they'd grunted and cursed and pulled on furs and leathers. Not that he had really been sleeping – dozing, more like. The problem was that without privacy secrets never felt safe. You might talk in your sleep. You had nowhere to be alone to think things through. Jack had been wondering if he could kill her. If he could kill her and maybe get away with it and if she would haunt him afterwards.

He lay awhile staring up towards the ceiling, listening to the sound of water eating at stone. The candlelight didn't penetrate up there. It was a pleasant oasis of darkness. He closed his eyes and tried to think of whatever it was he'd been dreaming of. It came close and then swam away again just as his mind grasped at it. He lay instead and listened to the sounds of men and boys getting ready and leaving. He couldn't see them, but his mind filled in the blanks. They were getting ready to take Amy away. Similar scenes would be playing out on the floor above him, up above the shadowy ceiling.

Eventually he gave up on another half-hour of sleep and sat up. Looking around the room, he tried to spot Heydon's berth. In the dim light he could say it, but there was no tell-tale bump. Perhaps he had been unable to sleep and had tried it on the floor of the office room. But then, surely, he would have taken the blankets with him. The wild thought struck that perhaps Heydon had decided to join the countess's people, where he might keep an eye on events. He might have realised that Jack was unfit to be an assassin and decided to do the job himself.

That idea was shattered by his friend's appearance. He slid easily into the room and wound his way between the berths that littered the floor. He was still in a nightshirt, a fur cape over his shoulders. Probably returning from the privy. Jack lay

187

back down before he could see him.

Eventually the time came when everyone seemed to rise as one – there were no bells to wake them, yet each man's body seemed tuned to the same rhythm. Jack lost no time in dressing, keeping his scarred back to the wall as always, and then made for Heydon.

'Good morrow. Did the countess get off?'

'I would guess so,' yawned Heydon. 'Been dead to the world the whole night, mate. It does a gentleman no good to rise at this hour.'

'When ... when are we setting off?'

'I'll speak to the earl after dinner today. No need to rush matters. Me, I'm going to lie down awhile longer.'

'Did you not get enough sleep last night?'

'There's not any such thing as enough sleep.' Heydon rolled over and pulled the blankets up and over his head.

Jack left the dormitory and opened a window on the landing above the staircase. Pearly morning light streamed in through the shutter, carrying the season's frosty breath. As he blinked away the pain of the sudden light, he saw that the train of the countess's attendants hadn't left yet. Instead, there seemed to be some kind of hurried conference going on. Men and women were running backwards and forwards from the doorway that lay a floor beneath him to the troupe of travellers. He couldn't see if Amy was amongst the latter or the former.

Forgotten something, shrugged Jack, turning away. Even in a great household nothing ever really ran to schedule. He went back to the dormitory. There was no sense in going down right away, not if the countess's grooms were still at work down there. Besides, someone somctimes brought in little cakes of bread from the bakehouse to provide a breakfast for the servants.

***

Amy woke not knowing what had happened or where she was. She tried to sit. Fell back. A dull ache throbbed in the back of her neck, in time with her heartbeat. Each pulse of blood brought a shuddering wave of pain through her body. As the unreality started to subside, panic struck.

She was late.

And then worse, it dawned on her that someone had struck her down. Her hands flew down to her dress, her cloak. No, she was still dressed. Her travelling cap was still tied securely under her chin, her hair pinned neatly under it. She reached out and felt around the floor, her fingers touching the basket of food. She paused to let a jolt of pain pass through and out. Where was she?

She looked around and sat up, forcing it this time. Her head struck something, and she yelped. Wherever she was it was small – confined. Breathing deeply and slowly, she moved onto her hands and knees and felt her way forwards. She didn't get far, her hand brushing wood. A door. She was in some kind of closet. With horror she realised that it was the little one that Jack had taken her into months before to make love, before workmen had converted the lodge into dormitories. The door slid open with a push, the wood scraping on flagstones. Light spilled in, making her wince.

The staircase. She had been stuffed into the tiny closet at the foot of the staircase she'd been descending. Someone had knocked her out and concealed her. But how long for? She tried to think, to make sense of it. She had heard somewhere that if someone were knocked out it should only last a few minutes. Any longer and they would die, or come back abnormal, their wits addled. She had no idea if it was true, but she chose to believe it; even remembering it meant that her mind was working well enough.

Grasping the doorframe, she eased herself upwards, letting her head hang. She shuffled forwards, out into the courtyard. Before she had got far, a voice screeched in her ear, slicing into her brain. 'She's here, the drowsy sluggard!' Someone grasped her by the elbow and propelled her forward. She let them.

'Where the hell have you been, girl?' asked Bess, already astride a horse. Reluctantly, Amy looked up. 'What happened to you? Are you unwell?'

'Sorry, m'lady.' She could hear her own voice, thick and furred.

'We were set to leave without you. You weren't in your chamber.'

'Trying to catch one last sleep with her husband, I shouldn't wonder,' sniffed another voice. Amy let her eyes languidly fall on the mounted woman beside Bess. It was one of her gentlewomen. She couldn't remember the name. Knew it but couldn't remember. Bess chortled.

'Was that the way of it?' Then, leaning down, she frowned. 'Yet … I don't think so. Can you ride, girl?'

Amy was sure that she couldn't, at least not well. Not for a while yet. But she had no choice – not if she wanted to go. With effort, she said, 'yes, my lady. If … a groom … can help me up.' An obliging boy stepped forward and hoisted her, making her head pound and spots of colour and light obscure her sight. She lurched forward and held on the bridle. Anger welled in her at the sight she must make, and she used it. 'I'll ride, my lady. I'll ride to Court this day if it pleases you.'

'You see,' said Bess, challenge in her voice as she turned to her companion. 'I told you the imp had spirit enough in her.'

'But perhaps could use a clock.' Amy didn't dare give any sauce to the scornful gentlewoman, but she shot her a look of defiance. Before they could move off, someone grabbed the bridle, tearing it from her grasp.

'This one hasn't been searched.' She looked down and saw a soldier.

'Let go of my horse, you lard-bloated ass,' she hissed. Then she glanced round, eyes wide, at Bess.

'Good girl.'

'My lady,' protested the soldier, redness colouring his broad cheeks, 'I … this strumpet must be searched.'

'Lay hands on my girl and I'll report you to the queen. The proper queen, mind you, Queen Elizabeth.' The soldier stepped back, as though the bridle had turned red hot. He spat off to his side and growled up at Amy. 'Ride on,' cried Bess. They did.

The ride was torture, but she let the pain that grew in her

legs and buttocks distract her from the throb in her head. She let her pace, too, keep up with the hoofbeats of the party.

Someone had wanted to stop her from going. She thought of Jack, but she thought – no, she knew – that he would never hurt her. Whoever it was could have killed her, but evidently didn't want to go that far. Her dead body, after all, would bring any number of problems. So who? And why? From Heydon to Huntingdon, she considered who might benefit from stopping her reaching Court. It had to be someone who could move about the household.

Well, she decided, they had failed. But that didn't mean they might not try again. And the road to Windsor was a long one.

***

'Old Shrewsbury says we can go,' said Heydon. He was not smiling. In fact, he seemed filled with restless energy. He had dressed down, wearing the rough buckram clothing of a domestic servant. 'Now. As soon as we can. Get moving.' He slung a cloak at Jack. 'It's one of my own. Put it on.'

'But – what did you say to him?'

'I'm to reach the countess with letters of introduction to some folk at Court. New friends she hopes to make in her husband's name.'

'And he thinks I'm needed for that?'

'No. I said I needed a man good with horses. Too many dangers on the roads. Get moving, will you.'

Jack threw down the brush he was holding. The countess had left thc day before. Ever since, Heydon had been in fits of manic irritation, complaining endlessly about plans going awry and muttering darkly about complications. 'It's true, too,' Heydon went on. 'There'll be soldiers on the road. Informers abroad too.'

'Are they on the rise?' He knew Heydon would know who 'they' were.

'Dunno. Nothing has come in. I'd think so. Men have been mustering up there. Couldn't delay them. Stupid bloody fools.

To wait all this time and then act in passion and fury. And I have letters from Queen Mary. To friends at Court. To tell the usurper to disregard any tales that the countess might tell of her.'

'But … the countess is her friend.'

'A prisoner can't be friends with a gaoler. Or a gaoler's wife. Her Majesty is sending out many such letters by all means she has, to the usurper herself, even. One at least will get through. Make the old witch of Windsor feel safer that her captive is behaving.' He touched a hand to his hat. 'Busy cap. Well, the more stuffing the warmer it'll keep my head. Here, we can take a pair of these brutes.' He began unlatching the paddock of the earl's reserve horses.

'Hey. Hey, Mr … sir – Jack – you can't be doin' that. Leave them, they're mine!' It was the young groom of the reserves. He had been curled up sleeping on a container of hay in a corner. He rubbed his eyes as he spoke.

'Shut your mouth, you little varlet,' said Heydon, shards of ice in his voice. 'Or I swear I'll cut your nose off it and watch you eat it.'

'Wha?' the little boy recoiled as though struck.

'I swear to you, boy.'

'Philip – Mr Heydon,' said Jack. He was surprised at the depth and strength of his own tone. 'Don't speak to him like that. He's a child.' Heydon stopped his menacing advance between the disinterested horses and turned to Jack, anger mixed with disbelief on his features. 'I mean it. I don't like seeing a child spoke to like that. It's cruel. Leave him be.'

'Very well, Jack.' The anger melted away into nothing, and a look of contrition took its place. 'Well said. Yet we are taking these brutes.' He turned back to the groom, who looked torn between fear and irritation at being called a boy. 'The carl said we could go. If he didn't say how we could go, I doubt he expected us to be walking. So we're taking these, and you can complain at your leisure, brat. I mean,' he said, with a sidelong look at Jack, 'my good young sir.'

They rode out as soon as Jack had bundled up, taking the reserves from the unprotesting but unhelpful lad. Before long, orange-tinged trees were a blur beside them. 'Hurry, hurry, will you? This is it, mate. I'm not proving your mettle this time. This time you must prove yourself before God.'

Heydon's words carried into the wind. They also chimed in Jack's mind. Divine absolution or his wife – why did he feel like he was being asked to choose? There could be only one. He would have to decide how to tell his friend that on the road.

As they rode away from Tutbury, Jack wondered what he meant by 'proving your mettle this time'. He wondered more why the countess's going had suddenly lit such a raging fire under Heydon.

They were a day behind them, but his friend seemed intent on cutting the gap.

6

Bess strode around the chamber, picking things up, inspecting them, putting them down. A candlestick. A gilt coffer. A pewter tray for sweetmeats. 'We're welcomed, then,' she said finally. A curt nod to no one in particular. 'Good.'

They had been installed in apartments in Windsor Castle, not far, apparently, from the queen's own. All were furnished, tapestries from floor to ceiling and rugs so thick Amy sank down when she stepped on them. She moved off to one side whilst the countess's other attendants saw to their tasks. There was little she could do but wait to be called, and to try and make herself invisible until then.

She watched the ritual of unpacking and preparing Bess to be undressed and changed, but her eyes didn't see it. During the days and nights on the road, and on the short journey across the river, she had thought about little but what had happened on the morning they left. Twin lumps had grown on the back of her head and lower on her neck. With the knowledge that someone had tried to stop her from coming – possibly to stop the whole party from coming – had grown a resolve. She would have to find a way to let someone know. Perhaps Brown was here. She had seen, on coming into the castle, that the place buzzed with messengers, men in travelling suits, stern-faced politicians. It occurred to her to speak to the countess and have her intercede, but she couldn't face that. It would be an admission that she had been acting secretly in the household. It would make her feel sneaky, dirty, small. Better that she find someone who looked trustworthy and whisper in their ear: a priest called Heydon was at work for the queen of Scots, and he might have some wicked design in hand. She replayed the conversation in her head for the thousandth time. 'I'm going to Court,' she had said. 'But so am I.' She was certain of it. And if Jack was coming to Court it would be with the priest. That could only be bad.

'Stop mooning, girl.' Amy's eyes focused and she looked up at Bess. 'You're not employed to stand around dreaming.' She gestured towards a door with her bedchamber. 'You don't want to stay out here with the men, do you? Get yourself in there and help pin. I can't see the queen in this.'

Amy followed and together she and Bess's gentlewoman undressed her, patted at her face and arms with damp cloths, and laced her into one of the gowns they had brought. The countess then sat on a cushioned chair whilst her woman applied powdery white cosmetics and some red paste from a silver dish. 'Shift yourself, girl,' she said out of the corner of her mouth. 'I don't want you strutting around the Court looking like a drab from Southwark.'

'Yes, my lady.'

Amy changed into her gown and edged towards the mirror, eager for a look at herself. The russet darkened her eyes and made her look quite mysterious, she thought. Almost a gentlewoman herself, were it not for the cap, still tied under her chin. 'Take that cap off,' said Bess. 'You look like a fool in it.' Amy did so and was pleased to see that her curled hair had survived the journey mostly unscathed. She had tied little strips of cloth in it carefully each night to maintain the curls. 'The queen and Sir William have graciously allowed me to call on them in the audience chamber. And the new man, Walsingham.' Bess's voice retained its usual blustering timbre, but Amy detected a note of anxiety. She was squeezing the pomander in her lap rhythmically. 'You can wait here with the gentlemen, girl. And you,' she said, slapping away her gentlewoman's hand, a small brush still in it. 'I … I will speak with them alone.'

Amy felt a wave of disappointment descend. She hadn't expected to be allowed to accompany Bess into Queen Elizabeth's presence – of course not – but it was frustrating to be so near and yet so far from the rooms in which decisions were taken. Knowledge was power, and she had that. But she could not get near the rooms in which power was turned to action.

Eventually the countess's toilette was finished, and she

marched off, out of her bedchamber and through her rooms. Her woman remained, plonking herself down on the vacated seat and beginning to make up her own face. Amy sidled towards the door, unnoticed. 'I … I'll see if the gentlemen need anything mended.' A disinterested sniff. Good.

Bess's gentlemen attendants were already at play, someone having produced the pack of cards that had made frequent appearances on the journey south. Amy walked past them, ignoring their guffaws and cries of 'cheat'. She left the countess's apartments and stepped outside, aware that she had no idea where she was going. Windows faced her, looking out on gardens. It was a courtyard, she knew from coming in. The corridor ran in either direction. They had entered earlier from the right. She went left. Eventually she found a broad staircase and climbed up it. At the top was a guard in green and white, twirling a stave. 'Are you lost, madam?'

'No.' Amy tried to fix her features into a look of nervous worry. 'Yes. I … my lady of Shrewsbury – I wait on her. She's gone up to see the queen and her ministers. I forgot to give her gifts.' The guard said nothing. 'Gifts for the queen,' she added lamely. Perhaps tears would avail her of something, but she could conjure none.

'You've to go around the staircase.' He pointed to Amy's left with his stave. Then straight ahead of you is her Majesty's dancing chamber. It opens into the audience chamber. You'll not get in there. The countess is gone ahead of you, I showed her myself. Wait in the dancing hall and pray God your mistress is in a forgiving mood, eh? Don't cry now, mistress.'

Amy smiled her thanks and hurried off in the direction he'd given. Clinking and scuffing sounds chased her – the double doors opposite the dancing hall seemed to be full of people clearing up the remains of dinner. The little hall, a frothy room painted in white and gold with stars on the ceiling, was empty save two halberdiers at a door to her left. They were small men, no taller than her, but their upraised chins tried for more.

She was at a loss, then. She had no intention of speaking to anyone in front of the countess. What she wanted was to know where the powerful people hid. She might catch one of them coming out. Not the queen, certainly, nor Cecil. They were far too frightening. But the other man Bess had mentioned – a new man – he would surely have time for her if she could make him listen, make him believe. He might listen to her worries that a priest was coming to Court – and she would have to explain also why she had left the post she'd been given as the Scottish queen's executioner.

'You cold?' She started, before realising that one of the guards was speaking to his fellow.

'A bit. It's them bloody grooms, lazy bastards. Ain't never bringin' up logs.'

'Go and get some.'

'You go and get some!'

Amy took advantage of their argument to wander into the room unnoticed, pretending that she was examining tapestries, hoping to blend into them. The black-and-white tiled floor was sanded, presumably to stop dancers slipping, and she let stepped lightly. On the same side of the room as the door into the audience chamber was a recess that led to a narrow spiral staircase. She recognised it immediately as a service entrance. When the dancing got hot, people like her could slip up unnoticed and pass around refreshments. She ducked inside and drew her back up against the undressed stone wall. She let time tick past, losing track of it. Eventually she heard the guards shuffle and poked her head out. She jerked it back a fraction as she saw Bess move past them. She was alone, and she paused for a second in the dancing hall before drawing her hand up to her brow and lowering her head. For a moment her shoulders slumped in what looked like defeat and then, overcoming it, she gave her steadying nod and departed.

But the others had not come out.

Amy swallowed. She had wasted her time. They all probably had some private means for leaving – there would surely be a private exit from the audience chamber. And now she would have to invent some excuse for having wandered away from their apartments. Then the door opened again, and she drew breath. The halberdiers fell to their knees and Amy had a brief impression of peach and cream, a cloud of vivid red surmounting it. Queen Elizabeth walked out of the chamber, a woman fussing at her back.

She knew she should pull back into the stairwell, avert her eyes, hide, but there was something fascinating about seeing the famous woman. Elizabeth paused, her head swivelling above a high ruffled collar as she made an irritated noise at her attendant. As she did so, her black eyes, glittering currants, rested briefly on Amy's. Widened a fraction. Moved on. Then she turned again and left the chamber, a ship in full sail.

So that was the great Elizabeth. Rather long faced, but her forehead was high and prominent, her nose long and thin. Handsome rather than beautiful – she had none of Queen Mary's sweetness, but a dollop more intensity about her. The guards barely had time to rise before the door opened again and two men emerged, one grey-bearded and the other solemn and, Amy thought, rather handsome. Both had rolls of paper under their arms.

Amy moved out into the dancing hall. 'Sir,' she cried, her voice coming out in a strangulated whisper. 'Sir, may I please speak with you? Please.'

'What's this, Sir William?' asked the handsome man. 'A mistress telling tales?'

'I'm busy, Francis,' said the older man, his eyes widening in bemusement. 'If our friend in France writes you, come straight to me. Now, see what she wants and send her on her way.'

***

Jack's eyes rolled over the wooden shopfronts and tenement houses of London Bridge. The usual gallimaufry of languages rose to his ears. Foreign visitors always thronged the bridge, eager to gape at the sight of the rotting heads and picked-clean skulls of the famous. The stories had spread far and wide since the days of the old king, Henry VIII. Yet even the eagle-eyed were bound to be disappointed. Queen Elizabeth was a merciful woman and the visitors often had to make do with a cold cut of pie, indifferent ale, and maggoty apples from crooked vendors. There were no heads on spikes. Would Norfolk's, Jack wondered, become one of them?

They had left Tutbury days before and headed directly for London. It was only after two days' hard ride that Heydon realised their error. Though the roads east and south were busy with messengers, none had had any word of the countess of Shrewsbury. She must, they realised too late, have led her group on a more direct southerly course, making straight for Windsor Castle. The news seemed to bother Heydon immensely. He had grown short with Jack, scolding and snapping at him to move himself, to whip his horse.

Distant church bells announced the time. Late morning. Jack and Heydon separated, the latter going off to do what he would only describe as 'transacting business'. Seizing some time alone, Jack wandered the bridge. It was here that he had been supposed to shoot at Elizabeth. He looked up at the houses. Jagged, thatched things, crooked, overhanging the water. Little alleys ran between some of them and he edged through the crowd, slipping in bits of sludgy muck that the recent rain seemed to have sloughed off the roofs.

There was no railing. At the end of the alley the side of the bridge simply dropped off into a whirling brown-and-grey void. Below him some hardy men were straining a wherry's oars, fighting the rapids. They had no passenger, and the grunting and boasting rose to meet him. A man in a leather apron joined him. 'Christ Jesus, they're going for it, those lads!' Leather apron held out a crust of bread and Jack took it, smiling his appreciation.

'They'll make it, and no mistake,' he said between swallows.

Below, the oarsmen crested a ripple of water and surged forward, into safe water. Cheers went up from other wherries and boats that had stopped to watch their vaunting. Caps were thrown in the air. Leather apron took off his, a flat brown thing, and waved it. Feeling silly, Jack did the same. It felt good, to be part of a crowd of people with nothing on their minds but the day's pleasure and foolery. The boat continued on its way, and the others got back to their business of ferrying passengers too. Leather apron clapped him on the back. 'They made it, by Christ. Brave bastards, them.' He wandered away and Jack kept staring into the water. He imagined what might have happened if they hadn't. They would be sucked under, the water forcing its way up their noses and down their throats. No one would try and help, not seriously, for fear that they would meet the same fate. Hardy men like them, of course, might make a swim for it, their muscles straining. But women, pampered people in padded clothing – they would sink to the bottom in minutes, fear crippling them.

It was wrong. The image was tinged by a visceral sense of wrongness that gnawed at him. If you believe in nothing you fall for anything, he thought. He believed now - he believed that killing Elizabeth – and maybe others – was wrong. A wrong thing to do. He clung to the growing sense of wrongness not, he told himself, because he was a coward, but because it was his. He felt it. He owned it. It was something he believed in all by himself.

'Though I'd lost you, mate.'

Jack turned to see Heydon. Under one arm was a long, thin brown chest, made of some lightweight material. 'Not easy. Lots of fellows around asking questions. Seeing if there are any strangers in town.' He lowered his voice. 'Cecil's men.'

'I can't do it, Philip.' Jack's eyes were fixed on the box.

'What's that?'

'I can't do it. I'm sorry. I won't do it.' He thought to lighten the mood. 'I mean, I couldn't hit a cow's arse with a lute, anyway.' His friend gave a ghost of a smile. 'I ... I'll find some other way to ... to God's grace.'

He braced himself for the storm. He had never seen Heydon mad – frustrated, yes, as he often was in recent days – but never truly angry. To his surprise, his friend smiled. 'Don't worry, mate. God won't ask us more than we can do in our conscience. But you'll be there if I should act? To give me strength and pray awhile with me? We are – I mean, we are brothers, aren't we, in our fashion?'

'I'll go with you. But I pray you think of some better path.

You don't have to do this either. It's … it's…'

'It's God's will. And the…' He looked around again. 'The Holy Father won't be long in making it known. You'll come with me?'

'Yes.'

'Good. We can ride once we pass along bankside. It's really in train now, mate.'

They left the alley, recovered their horses from the hitching post, and walked them into a cacophonous fury of animals rearing in different directions, curses, and whip-cracks.

***

Amy kept wanting to laugh as she spoke. It was absurd, but she couldn't seem to control the maddening itch that jerked at her cheeks. Jack's awkward grins made sense suddenly. Her husband must have been a nervous lad all the time.

The handsome man, Mr Walsingham, had led her to a corner of the dancing hall. 'And I didn't know who to speak to,' she babbled.

'Suppose you tell me what ails you, mistress.' Walsingham's voice was cool but not unkind. October sunlight fell on them from a recessed window. Outside it was just possible to make out moving figures below, tiny and insignificant.

'It's the priest, Heydon. I have cause to think he is coming here with some evil design.' Walsingham's eyes widened – she decided in shock and barrelled on. 'But I couldn't tell Mr Brown – you'll know he's gone from Tutbury, gone from watching the Scottish queen. So I was to come here with the countess, so I thought I could maybe find him, or someone, and warn you all, and you could catch him. He's using my husband as his – his groom, but Jack doesn't know anything, he's just a –'

'You say a priest is coming here with evil design?'

Amy closed her mouth, nodding in frustration. Up close, in better light, Walsingham wasn't so attractive. Somewhere under forty, his smiles seemed weak, almost false. He made her think suddenly of a household accounts keeper. Only his dark eyes and the shadowed lines around his mouth gave him intensity. 'But you know about him. Mr Brown knows about him. He works for Mr Cecil –'

'Sir William.'

'Sir William, yes.'

'The fellow who was just here?'

'Yes,' said Amy, aware that her own voice was sharpening. 'I did what I was told. I watched Queen Mary for him, as Mr Brown told me. I even promised that I would … you know, the other thing. If she ever tried to get loose or if the Catholics ever attacked her Majesty. But they might – Heydon might.'

'I know of no priest Heydon,' said Walsingham. He lifted a hand and stroked at a small, dark beard. His eyes seemed to look past her. 'Heydon. A name from the north.'

'That's right. From Newcastle Mr Brown said. An old family. He was a young son – he's about twenty-one – he fell in with the Catholics.'

'Mistress, you keep speaking of this Mr Brown. Who is he?'

'He's – why, he's one of your men. One of Mr – Sir William's. He watches the queen of Scots.'

Walsingham frowned and looked back into the room, towards the door through which Cecil and the others had left. Then he looked back down at Amy. 'I don't know what game this is, young woman. But no. No, I have an eye for names and a memory for our friends. I tell you, there is no Mr Brown in her Majesty's service. None.'

7

The words struck Amy like bullets. She spluttered for a few seconds. 'But … but … I've met him. Many times. By Tutbury, by Wingfield.'

'You are mistaken,' said Walsingham. She could hear in his voice that he was tiring of her. 'Our only man in that part of the world, he … well, I'm sure your household heard of it. He was slain. We have had no man, no Brown or any other, living by the Scottish queen. We need no sneaking spies to watch her. She is well kept, as your mistress informs us.' Something seemed to dawn on his face, turning it flinty. 'If,' he said, ice in his tone, 'you think to make trouble for the countess, young woman, you will find no succour with me.'

'No, no – the countess is a fine woman, a good woman. It's … I …' she trailed off, then with renewed vigour, insisted, 'there is a Mr Brown, whether you know of him or not. It won't be his real name of course – but you have a man up there. I know him – a brown suit and silver hair. Whether you know of him or not, I do!' You stupid old fart, she wanted to add, all sense of attraction vanished.

'Mind your tone.'

'I'm sorry, sir, but there was. He knew all about the priest Heydon, wanted him watched. For Secretary Cecil, he said.'

'Ah,' said Walsingham. He drew away from her a little, straightening the black gown he wore. 'I see. Mistress, you've been taken for a fool by a grasping fellow. Probably he sought to spend his lust with you.' He caught her horrified expression and his eyes softened a little. 'We have many men who try their luck with us. Hoping to sell knowledge. A lowly, grasping rabble. I suggest you learn not to speak with strange men. He showed you no proof of his allegiance to Sir William, I suppose?' He smiled nastily at her silence, at her suddenly averted eyes. 'No, and you did not think to ask.'

'I didn't know I should – I've never been –'

He held up a milky hand. 'Then you must learn to keep your wits about you. But … if there is some priest using the name Heydon, our men in London will inform us. Fear not, mistress – our sovereign lady is well protected. By real men. Not ghosts. I suggest you return to the countess. I shall say nothing of this … this nonsense. You might find something for your household to eat. You have missed dinner. It might explain your absence, yes?'

He bowed and walked away from her, his measured step chiming on the dancing hall floor. Her mother's old poem echoed in her head: why does evil so clearly mark the monstrous government of men?

She felt tears spring hot to her eyes. She wasn't ready to let go of the fantasy of Mr Brown, and she clung to the idea that Walsingham was simply an idiot – that Cecil kept things from him. Frantically she tried to force sense into the world. Brown had seemed to know of Heydon. She thought back, as hard as she could. What he had told her - about him coming from an old family - that could have been common knowledge. She had no way of knowing. Had he said anything - about anything - that was truly secret? Anything that only an informed and involved man would know? She couldn't think. She had trusted him, had no reason to record what he said and examine it. The house of cards fell. She knew she was wrong. She had fed information to a chancer – not to a spy or an informer, but to a trickster who hoped to become one by selling on her information.

Only – only – if that were the case, why hadn't he? Even using his real name, whatever it was, why hadn't he made himself known to Cecil and Walsingham, offering the knowledge Amy had given him?

And what of the poison he had given her? Was it some harmless concoction? Rainwater and pond scum?

Her mind whirled and, in a daze, she wandered out of the dancing hall. The sound of laughter and conversation hummed from the great hall ahead of her. Shame clawed at her and she let anger flare to meet it. A young page with a loaded trencher of comfits darted past. 'Stop, you,' she said, her voice a razor.

'Mistress?'

'Give me that.' She wrenched it from his hands. He seemed too surprised to stop her.

'But that's for Master Secretary. He missed dinner.'

'And he'll miss this. Buzz off.'

'Hey,' he cried. 'Hey, you are no lady! I'm telling on you.'

She stuck her tongue out as he ran away, knowing it was a stupid, futile thing to do. Men were going to be no help to her. She had gone to the highest and been dismissed as an addle-brained strumpet, singing her heart out to a trickster. An ugly, rational part of her mind added: that is exactly what you are, Amy Cole.

Wherever Jack was now, he was on his own.

***

The old boathouse was a meagre affair. Two rooms, the first of which had steps leading to an upper floor that had been knocked away, giving it the feeling of a tiny old tithe barn. The wood throughout was rotting and the whole placed smelt like an old, unkept fish pond. Jack and Heydon stood in the first room. The door to the second had a rusting lock on it.

They had galloped westwards, hoping to beat the sun. It had overtaken them, a surprising heat in it for the time of year. 'Not much of a place, is it?' said Heydon, a lopsided smile on his face. 'But the best I'd heard of this near to the place.' Heard of from whom, Jack wondered. 'Listen to me, mate. I have to … get all things in readiness.' He tapped the box, still tucked under one arm. 'Get this machine together. You go down to the village. Get us some meat and drink. Enough for some days. Can't say when the old bitch will take to her boat. I would … like some time to pray. To speak with God. Don't return until dark. Try not to be seen.'

Jack did as he was told, happy to get away from the shabby little shack. He considered riding down to the borough of Windsor, but it seemed a waste. Better to let his horse rest in the roofless stable that lay a short distance from the boathouse.

Windsor was a rickety town, the streets haphazard and the

buildings partially eaten away by neglect. A dismal wind whispered promises of winter through its wooden shacks. It was strange, he thought, that such a dunghill could lie so close to the splendour of the castle – in its shadow, almost. That, he supposed, was what happened to things left in the shade of greater things.

He found a selection of street vendors, their carts boasting little. There was no meat to be had, but plenty of stale bread and stoppered wooden tuns of ale. He bought up all the bread he could carry, and a sturdy wooden jug with a flat cap. It hadn't taken him long. Already the people in the streets were beginning to look at him, making him feel conspicuous. Watched. He looked up at the sky. A few clouds drifted, and the sun burned a low orange. Heydon couldn't have finished his prayers yet – Latin masses went on awhile. And he had told him to stay away until dark. Yet Jack decided to return anyway. Staying in the village could only arouse suspicion. There had to be at least one man who made his living up at the castle, and who might wander up there at any point and report a strange young man buying up provisions. Besides, his earlobes were starting to go numb.

He struck out over the unkept, dying grass towards the boathouse. As he approached the door, he thought he heard voices coming from inside and his heart skipped a beat. Caught. Caught before any diabolical scheme could be carried out. That might not be such a bad thing – although he doubted any searchers would let either Heydon or him walk away. Perhaps his friend's connections and money could get them release. He drew towards the door, setting the sack of bread and the jug of ale down and leaning close. The boards were thin enough to let him hear.

'until this evening. He believes me to be praying.'

'Still thinks you're a papist then,' spat a cold, metallic voice. A voice Jack recognised.

'Of course. Christ Jesus, could you not have found a better place? Where is the key?' A sound of movement. Jack's heart sped. Heydon's casual speech had given way to a sneering kind of huffiness.

'Have you found the wife?'

'She must be at the castle. If you had warned me –'

'If you had kept her close! You said she was in thrall to you, for the love of Christ.'

'She is a forward little bitch, I told you that.'

'And she will ruin everything. Everything. Christ, what a mess. I still say she saw me in Wingfield.'

'Bah! She is a fool. I made her think you were some woman.'

'She is not the fool he is. She is not such a fool that she would kill that Scottish bitch and without that we are lost. What use is one dead queen if the other lives, eh? An end to the unnatural government of women, my friend. Not woman. That is what you want, is it not?'

'It is not my fault she is too weak to kill, to obey. I knew a woman would not work, as foul as their natures may be. A laundress! What does a laundress know of the art of dispatch? The papist whore will die, if I have to slit her throat myself. Unnatural – unnatural it is! An end to this foolish dance between weak, crowned women.' He said 'crowned' as though it were an insult. 'A papist beldam and a woman who feigns the true faith watered with tolerance and womanly frailty. By the book, I will slit her damned throat.'

'It might well come to that, sirrah. But … we are not lost yet.' A long pause drew out and Jack heard the sharp, stuttering thuds of pacing. 'We must get her back to Tutbury. Get her back to Mary's side. Let her be seen there. And then you poison the bitch yourself. Yes – yes – and then get rid of her too. Make it look like suicide. Like she cannot live with what she has done. Same as her daft husband. But make sure the empty vial is found on her person. Then … then get yourself north. Before they shut up the borders. Get the Scotch regent told to bring the new king south before the fools in yonder castle can gather their wits. His wife will be expecting you. I told her something was to happen requiring her husband and the boy-king.'

'But … but … I'm supposed to take ship for Scotland. How am I to tell the regent to bring the babe south if I'm meddling at Tutbury and the wild north stands in my way? By the good book, how do I even get that foolish wench to Tutbury? I cannot wander into the Court and steal her away.' Jack read panic in the man's voice – or something like anger.

'Think of something, then. The enterprise stands. I have enough to do keeping the husband in check. Think of something, my dear – what is it? Mr *Brown*.' A murmur. 'Good man. Now hurry out of here. My soft-headed little friend will return soon. No doubt the moment the sun has passed. Sheep that he is. And then I shall have to take him down somehow, bind him.'

Fury filled Jack. Passed. Fear flooded in to replace it, and a desire to be away, far away from the boathouse. From the whole world, if possible. Something was going to happen to Amy. The idea struck horror into him. He would have to do something, to save her, to rescue her. He turned away from the door, leaving the food and drink, and began to walk away, picking up his pace as he moved towards the stable. To take the horse or to run?

Take it. Move.

As he stepped towards the low wooden railing, a hand gripped his elbow. 'You going somewhere, mate?' He half-turned, and something hard thumped on the back of his head. The browning grass rose up towards his face and he knew no more.

***

The countess had selected the best of Amy's selection of stolen dainties, leaving the rest to her staff. She had barely noticed her seamstress's absence and did not bother to thank her for the food. Instead, she had stormed into her bedchamber, leaving the door open. Amy had followed.

'We're staying here awhile,' said Bess. 'I don't know how long. If I go back to Tutbury, if I go back to that … that woman … By God, I think I'll take a bite out of her. Schemes and accusations, eh? I'll give her schemes and accusations. The days I've spent listening to her whine and mewl. The days

I've missed at my accounts, at my good, honest workmen. Schemes and accusations! And what we have spent on her – the *expense* of her! That ... that bud-mouthed *bitch*!' She kneaded at her forehead and then seemed to remember others were in her chamber.

'Girls. Girls, I need you to fix up something warm for me. The true queen has asked I should accompany her on the river tomorrow. After dinner. Last chance to take the air for pleasure before the weather turns. A mark of favour from a true sovereign, not a fallen one. And by God she'll hear all there is to hear about that other. I'll make my lady Majesty's ears fit to burn with the truth of that wench, by God.'

Without feeling, Amy took to a corner and began to sew a fur stole around a collar. It was pleasant, having something to do she enjoyed. In and out went the needle, rhythmically, soothingly. She might once have taken pleasure in hearing Queen Mary being spoke ill of, but she could not. All she could think about was what a fool she had been. All she could wonder was whether Jack would come to his senses. Was he in London now? Was he safe?

She offered up a silent prayer, demanding that God make things right.

8

Jack awoke to the splash of ale on his face. He smiled stupidly. It faded. As his vision returned, he saw the man who called himself Brown standing over him. Yes, it had been his voice speaking to Heydon. He recognised the grey hair, the unlined face – the one he had seen barking at Amy in the woods near Tutbury.

'Have a care, man,' said Heydon. 'That ale has to do me some days.' Brown stepped away, placing the jug on the floor by the wall. Jack's eyes followed him. He was in the first room of the boathouse. He moved and felt the binding around his wrists. His ankles, too. 'Ah, you're alive, Cole. I must say, you went down far easier than did you wife. She must have a stronger neck.'

As though in response, the back of Jack's neck throbbed. Automatically, he tried to rub it. His hands, wedged and tied behind his back, refused to cooperate. 'Now,' said Heydon, 'you will do us a favour.'

'Go to hell,' said Jack. 'You're ... you're no priest.'

'Well seen. At last. Although I did study abroad with the papists. My Latin, I think, is worthy of any Oxford master.'

'Who are you? What are you?'

'A gentleman,' Heydon smiled. 'As I said.'

'But ... you want Queen Mary dead. And Queen Elizabeth.'

'True. Stop talking. You tire me. I have heard enough of you these past months.'

'You're a Scot!' Jack cried, causing pain to crash over him.

'What? Oh. Oh, I see. No, Cole, I am no such rabble. Yet I would have the young Scotch king brought here and raised an Englishman. The Scots' leaders know the true faith, not papistry or the weak-willed softness of Elizabeth.'

Brown moved back towards them. 'The true faith,' he echoed. 'This realm will know it. The time-servers will flee. The land will be free of womanish rule.'

'Quite.'

'But … the earl of Moray, the Scotch regent. You … I … we…' He could not form thoughts, and his words stalled accordingly. 'You work for him?'

'I did,' said Heydon. 'Though you were too stupid to see it. Do you recall, Mr Jack Cole, the day the duke of Norfolk met the earl at Hampton Court? I was there. I was the earl's gentleman, though I had my beard cut off before I made your acquaintance. I saw you then, as I see you now. A simpering sheep, ripe for the slaughter.'

'Moray … the earl … he would kill his sister? And his cousin?' Heydon shrugged and got down on his haunches.

'I have known the good earl since he was an exile in Newcastle, when I was a slip of a lad. He knows nothing of this, yet he will be brought to see the sense of it. As his wife has. A good man, the earl. He knows how to play the cards he's dealt. And how to ignore the means by which the dealers shuffle.' He shrugged again, bored. 'Now, you will do us a favour.'

'You go and fuck yourself,' spat Jack. 'I'll kill you.'

'Temper.' Heydon wagged a finger. 'Has that knock to the pate shaken your humours? I'm not your father, Cole. You won't snuff the life out of me.'

'Quit playing with the whelp,' growled Heydon. 'Set him to work.'

'Yes. Cole, you will write for us a letter. To your wife. Ordering her to meet you outside the castle. Better yet, tell her to shift her narrow arse to this place. You can say goodbye, sirrah, before she goes back to the scene of her crime.'

'No, I won't. You won't touch her.'

'You'll do it, you little shit. Or I'll cut your fingers off.'

Heydon barked a shrill, high laugh that Jack had never heard before. He clapped Brown on the shoulder, but then backed away a step, as though scared. 'Now, what good would that do us? He could not write, and then when they find his corpse, they might wonder why the murderer of Elizabeth took the time to chop his own fingers off before he blasted her out of the water.' Brown made a little disappointed noise. Heydon got on his haunches and leant close to Jack. 'He has a strange love of cutting off fingers, does my friend here. I understand he did so to Cecil's man – the one sent to scout old Shrewsbury's houses.'

Heydon drew himself back up and fetched a theatrical sigh. 'I shall write the letter. I doubt his wife shall know his scrawl beyond a few words. When would that strumpet ever have cause to see it?'

Brown reached into a satchel that was lying on the floor next to the bread and ale and drew out some paper and an inkpot. Heydon set to work. When he had finished, he shook the paper carefully. Then something caught his eye and he reached into the satchel. 'Oh, Cole – you will like this, I think. Soon everyone will like of it. Copies will be thrown into the streets of London. The printers will take them up.' He withdrew another paper, cleared his throat, and read.

This day, in the year of our Lord 1569, Jack Cole, a common traitor, has slain the English queen, having gotten some weapon from friends in the low circles of his ilk. Behind him were his master Norfolk and sundry rebellious earls. His wife has slain the Scottish queen, jealous of the ecstasy of love her husband felt for that Jezebel. The damned pair have so broken all of God's laws and sought the overthrow of this kingdom that they have themselves been carried off, the fellow by his own hand and the wife struck down as she tried to escape the honest men who took her. Such was never seen in any Christian Kingdom. We cry for God's mercy to come down upon us, that we might better know his infinite love, commending ourselves unto his grace and crying for mercy. God save King James and bring us out of error and into the light of God's love.

Heydon finished with a flourish, returned the paper, then frowned. 'Of course, we shall have to change that, about your wife being struck down. As she has been so mischievous as to be here and proven herself most unwilling as an assassin. We cannot count on Huntingdon's men to hang her for a

212

murderess. But, trifles.'

'You're mad, both of you,' said Jack. Suddenly he felt tired. His words, though, had an effect on Brown.

'What did you say, you little shit? What did you call me? I'll slit your throat myself.'

'Go easy,' said Heydon, sounding a little uneasy. 'We need him alive for a while yet. Corpses cannot pull triggers. You heard me, Cole? I said that you would become a hero in this world. Perhaps you will be, one day. When the chroniclers look back on the end of popery and the English queen who halted reform and gave succour to all. You and your wife – lowly nothings who did all England a great service and rid it of two wicked and foolish women.' He turned his attention back to Brown. 'Get you gone, now – pass the letter to the wife to some slave up at yonder place.'

Brown gave Jack a hard, menacing look, before taking the letter and leaving the boathouse, the door banging behind him. When he had gone, Heydon let out a low whistle. 'That,' he said, 'is a strange fellow. Tenant of my father's. Killed his wife, you know, in Newcastle. Put his hands about her neck. I had a devil of a time getting him out of that. If only he weren't so damned full of this new faith, this hard reform. All rather boring. Ah, the things we must do to buy a man's loyalty. And a gentleman must have his own hunting hounds.'

'What? But aren't you –'

'Shut your mouth.' Heydon bent over and grasped him under one armpit. 'Get moving.' He pushed Jack towards the door; he hit the wall beside it and slid down, his head spinning. Heydon fished inside his old coat and produced a key. 'I almost forgot to ask him for this,' he said, shaking his head in amusement. When he had opened the door, he pushed Jack inside.

The second room of the boat house was as dank as the first, though much of it was lost in shadow. Pegs were nailed into the walls – for oars, Jack guessed, and a small wooden staircase led up to a landing by a large, wooden-shuttered window, presumably for watching for the boats coming in. The floor opened out where the building jutted over the water, and the smell of damp was throat-catching. As Jack looked up and around, pain stabbed at his kidneys. Heydon had punched him in the back, knocking him to his knees.

He lay awhile, winded. Whistling, Heydon went back into the first room and almost immediately reappeared, the large box under one arm and a rope laced over the other. He set down the box and worked his hands over one end of the rope, before swinging it up and over a roof beam. Jack watched, almost mesmerised, whilst he finished fashioning the noose.

***

Amy woke on the floor of the countess's bedchamber. At first, she didn't understand why – until a low, insistent rapping came to her. She thought it had been part of some dream, until sense descended. Someone was knocking on Bess's door. What time was it? There were curtains over the windows; she couldn't tell. Her only thought was to answer before Bess was wakened. Without even pulling a robe over her nightdress, she opened it.

'What is it?' She kept her voice low. 'For the love of God, why do you wake us? The countess –'

'Message come from one of the castle's folk.' It was one of Bess's gentleman. Amy narrowed her eyes as she sensed him looking up and down her body. She folded her arms over the white woollen nightdress.

'For the countess?'

'No, Mrs Cole. It's for you. From your husband.'

'What? Jack? Jack's here? Did you see him?'

'No, calm yourself, woman. It was one of the lads delivered it.' He held it out. Amy snatched it, turning back to the bedchamber. Too dark to read it in there. She stepped into the larger room, where the half-light measured early morning's progress.

There were only a few words. 'Amy, please come. Old boathouse by Windsor town. Mr Heydon at work here. Need your aid. Bring no one or I be in trouble. My love, Jack.' Ha! She thought. So finally he had come round to her way of thinking. Finally, he had seen through the appalling Heydon. But what kind of work was he engaged in, and how might it lead to trouble? She realised she was still standing in full view of the countess's male staff. 'Oh, get you all to buggery,' she hissed, turning on her heel and going back to the bedchamber.

She dressed as quickly and silently as she could. Her old dress was off somewhere being laundered by the castle's servants, so she put on her new russet gown. A good thing, too; she wanted Jack to see her looking fair and pretty.

She left the countess's rooms and wandered the castle a while, looking for a way out. Unfortunately, she came across the page boy she had stolen from, and he made a point of ignoring her. Feeling chastened, and now in a more buoyant mood, she went off and wandered further. The sun was well up by the time she had left the main buildings, the gardens and woods, and found her way on the path to the town. From there, she let the sight and smell of the river lead her to its edge where, in the distance, she spotted a tumbledown wooden shack on the same bank. Birds were singing in the trees, some skimming over the water, as she approached it and knocked on the door. It fell open and she walked straight in, his name already forming on her lips.

'Mrs Cole,' said a familiar voice. She jumped at the sight of Brown.

'You!'

'I told you to stay at Tutbury and cease this watching business.'

'You! You're a damned coney-catcher! I know all about you!'

'Stop your prattle, you stupid little strumpet.'

'Where's my husband? He's not here, is he? You sent that – he's not here.' Disappointment and anger flooded her, and she made ready to fly at Brown. His next words stopped her.

'He's in the next room. And if you want him to breathe longer, you'll do exactly as you're told from this moment onwards.'

'Let me see him. Let me see him this minute, you goddamned liar. You cheat!'

Brown took a step towards her, his face a mask of hatred. That is the real you, she thought. A monster. She shrank back. He saw her and seemed to get himself back under control. He closed his eyes briefly and took a deep breath. 'The sound of you disturbs me,' he said. 'Your filthy tongue. Wait here. I will see if your man is fit to receive you. If you run, if you cry out, he dies. It will not be a good death, I promise you.'

Brown turned and went to a door, slipping inside.

Amy brought her hands up to her mouth, resisting the urge to bite her nails – something she had not done since childhood, since her mother had put a mixture of ashes and vinegar on them. Desperately, she looked around the room for a weapon. She could tear up a floorboard, or prise a nail out of a wall, go for his eyes.

But what if Jack really was in there? She strained to hear voices. Yes! She was sure the low, muffled sound was him. If she attacked Brown, if she demanded answers as to what was going on here, she might get him killed. She tilted her head back and thought. Whatever was happening, whoever Brown did or did not work for, she was getting her husband out of there. If they had to run away together, from Brown and Heydon, from Cecil and Walsingham's whole army of men, from Mary Queen of Scots and the Shrewsburys, so be it. She would kill anyone who tried to stop her.

9

Jack had lain on the dirt floor overnight. The dampness seeped up into it from the river. He had fidgeted at his bindings now and again, even bending and unlocking his wrists and knuckles hoping that it would loosen them. It availed him nothing. His creator, he had dared hope, had given him such a freakish skill for no reason: a cruel joke.

Heydon had unpacked and assembled the contents of his gun: a matchlock caliver. Jack had heard of them, but never seen one. Was this the thing he had been expected to fire? Looking at it, at its long, thin barrel, he knew he could never have done it. Or had he never really been expected to do it – had he just been used by the false priest? The thing stood up on the viewing platform by the window, the barrel resting on a frail-looking tripod. Heydon caught him looking. 'A fine piece, is it not? Cost enough, too. Don't worry, Cole – you will be known as a man with fine taste in weaponry. I spread your name and called myself by it in every low place in the city until I found it.'

Jack said nothing, still dazed. His thoughts were now entirely upon Amy, and whether or not the letter would draw her. He no longer cared what happened to him. The noose would be welcome, as long as she could get away. He clung to the knowledge that they wanted her alive, at least until they got to Tutbury and killed Queen Mary. Surely she would find some means of escaping before then? In fact, he hoped that he would die soon, and she would know about it. Then they could not pretend that she must do as they say to save him.

He let the images of his father and of the man in the barrel shuffle into his mind, their rotting arms upraised, crying out for justice. He deserved to die, that much he knew. He had killed men, broken God's laws, and this was his punishment. It would be a blessing, really, to be quit of the world. He had never been much in it anyway.

The door opened, and he craned his neck. It was Brown. He slumped back. 'The wife is next door.'

'Good man.' Heydon kept his voice low.

'She wants to see him.'

'Of course she does. And so she must. I am not a man to keep two pretty turtledoves apart, now, am I?' He smiled at Jack, maliciousness glinting in his eyes. Then he looked up and around the room. 'But not here. If she knows what we mean to do, she will not go quietly with you.'

'That wench will not go quietly anywhere. But worry not – I have had some thoughts on that matter.'

'Have you indeed? Good. But do not hurt her. Not until she is near enough to the Scotch witch to have the blame of her death.'

'I shan't touch one hair on her head.'

'And you, Cole. You say nothing to her. If you do, I promise you that my friend here shall make her death a very unpleasant one. She can join you in the next world as gently as a feather is plucked from a goose, or she can go screaming. I assure you he can make it last for hours if it pleases him. You understand me?'

Jack said nothing.

'Do you understand me?' Heydon moved towards him and ground his boot down on his hand. Jack nodded, gritting his teeth. 'What's that?'

'I understand.'

'Good. There, you have found your voice. None of that tiresome whispering you used to use. Help me get him up.'

With an arm under each armpit, Brown and Heydon hoisted him to his feet. Brown nudged open the door, just enough to let them slip out sideways. Jack had a sudden remembrance of the man he and Heydon had killed – how they had hoisted him out through a tavern's bar. Justice indeed.

'Jack!' Amy leapt towards him. How pretty she looked. He wondered if the dead missed the living in the way the living missed the dead. Maybe that was why ghosts happened. Catholics believed in purgatory. Would he go there? Was he even truly a Catholic, if a false priest had converted him? He wanted to. He wanted her to maybe have real priests say masses for his soul. 'Let him go. You, Heydon – you're with this liar?'

'Welcome, Mrs Cole.'

'Shut your mouth. Let my husband go. I don't care two merry brown shits what your business here is. I'll say nothing. Jack will say nothing either. Just let us go away from this place.'

'Ah, if only it were so simple, my dear woman. But I do not trust you. As you never trusted me. Well, you shall have to now. Mr … Brown here would like to take you back to Tutbury. You have left matters unattended there. I shall keep Jack here until all is done.'

'No! No, I won't. I …' she trailed off, seemingly letting his words register. 'You mean, you mean to kill Queen Mary?' Heydon gave an imperceptible nod, smiling strangely. 'So you're … you're not a Catholic priest? You *are* working with the government?'

'Actually, I was ordained a priest,' he said, laughing harshly. 'In secret, you understand, on the continent. But merely so I could gather knowledge. And no, I am not working with the government. You need know no more, woman. If you want your husband to live, go quietly with Mr Brown here. If I hear you have escaped him or worse, Jack here will die in a most painful way.'

'Jack?' Amy had come close. She put a hand up to his face and he smiled at her, trying to impress love onto her with his eyes. 'Get off him,' she hissed. 'Let me say farewell to my husband, you … you great apes.' Heydon pushed Jack at her and he fell into her arms.

'I have to go Jack. Or he'll kill you.'

'I'm … dead already.' He felt his voice rattling painfully in his throat. 'But you live, please. For both of us. I'm sorry. I'm sorry, Amy, for everything. I'm sorry I wasn't a better husband.'

'I'm sorry, I'm sorry,' Brown mimicked, his voice high. He strode across the room in disgust and took a swig of ale. 'Begging forgiveness from a fucking woman. Disgusting.'

'Now, now,' said Heydon, wagging a finger in mock recrimination. 'Let the lovers say their goodbyes. It shall be awhile ere they meet again.'

'But we will meet again,' said Amy. It seemed to Jack to be half-question, half-statement.

'You have my word. As a gentleman.'

'I'm going to go now, Jack. Remember that I love you. Always. I'm sorry too. These creatures have ... they've made us fight. Not speak, as we should.'

'And how easy it was! Tell anyone what they wish to hear of themselves and they're yours!' laughed Heydon. Amy ignored him. She wrapped her arms around Jack's neck, kissing his lips, his cheeks, his ears. She lingered on the last, whispering her farewell. His eyes widened.

'Well?' she said, letting him go. 'Let's go, then. Do your worst with me. I'm not afraid of either of you. If you hurt my husband, though, I swear before God that I'll see you dead and dance a galliard on your grave.'

'I'll stop that mouth,' said Brown, steeping forward.

'I said do not hurt her,' snapped Heydon.

'And I said I shan't!'

Using strips of cloth produced from his pack, Brown bound Amy's hands behind her back. He tied the last around her head, gagging her. Heydon seemed to find it hilarious, and he put down his drink and came around behind Jack, driving his knuckles into his back as he laughed. 'How do you expect to get her back up the road looking like that?'

'I shall worry about that,' said Brown. A ghost of a smile flickered on his lips.

Jack watched as Amy was bundled out, their eyes locking one last time. He felt at peace, as though sacrificing himself might somehow buy her life. He chose to think so, anyway. 'Right, Cole,' said Heydon. 'Back we must go. We may be here some days. Until our good sovereign lady finally decides to escape the close airs of her great castle and seek pleasure frolicking with the Naiades.'

***

Brown led a gagged Amy down into the town, giving her a rough shove every few steps. She had decided at first on stony silence, given it up in favour of mouthing every swear word she knew through her gag, and retreated to silence when her cheeks began to ache. He left her standing in the street near the guildhall, where some children found and began taunting her. She had to make do with kicking stones at them, smiling like a Fury under her gag as one hit a boy on the forehead.

Eventually, Brown returned with a grizzled man, and she tried to communicate her panic with her eyes. The man looked at her with suspicion written into the weather-beaten lines of his face. 'This is the passenger,' said Brown.

'You said a passenger, not no lady.'

'She's no lady.'

'She looks like a lady, you ask me.'

'I'm not asking you. Will you take us?'

'London's too far.'

'Just as far as the Westminster Stairs. I wish to take my daughter back up north.'

'You can go north from here,' shrugged the boatman.

'I ... I have no horse. There are none to be bought in town – I always rent in London or thereabouts. You will be well paid.'

Amy listened to them barter. She was under no illusion. Brown could have taken her on Jack's horse – she had seen two in the stable outside the boathouse. He wanted her to think, though, that Jack might have the use of it. She did not trust either him or Heydon to keep their promise. Neither she nor Jack would be allowed to live if they could accomplish whatever strange enterprise they had set in motion. 'A deal well made,' said Brown, shaking the man's hand. 'We can go now?' The wherryman nodded and pointed down the street. Brown gave a tight smile, pushed her get her moving, and strode on ahead.

When his back was to them, Amy shook her head at the man, working her gag silently. 'Your daughter, you said?'

'Alas,' said Brown, looking over his shoulder, 'she was sent from the queen's own service a common scold and shrew. A great shame on us all. She is being taken home in disgrace. And I daresay the people of the town shall have great sport of her.'

The wherryman looked at her. Seemed to hesitate. Then he shrugged. 'Me wife's the same. Wouldn't mind her 'avin' the same treatment, if I'm honest. Boat's just ahead, up here. I'll have you in London before tonight.'

Resigned, Amy settled to her fate. But she had no intention of making it easy, making her body as stiff as a board and as heavy as she could so that they had to manhandle her into the back of the wherry. Brown pressed her down onto the floor between the seats, sitting himself. She did not object; she could not.

The boatman pushed away with his oar. There was little traffic this far upriver, and he set to, rocking and heaving the tiny vessel in the gentle swell. She had no idea how long it would take. The sun receded behind a thick smog of clouds, appearing again as they rocked past neatly-hedged green fields. The minutes of darkness seemed, though, to have angered the water, and the boat tumbled, rising, and falling at the front. 'Are you a'right back there, sir? She gets like this sometimes, this time o' year.'

'I am fine,' snapped Brown. Amy looked up at him as he mopped his brow.

'You sure, sir? Don't mind me sayin', but you ain't lookin' so good. Can put in and rest awhile if you like. Some folks need a rest.'

'I am quite well,' Brown hissed. 'Row on, row on.'

Amy's eyes twinkled.

*   *   *

'Why?' asked Heydon, throwing his head back and laughing. 'You ask me why?' Jack shrugged. He was interested, in a detached sort of way. 'Why, because I can, you fool. Because I can.'

By the quality of the light slanting in through the gaps in the shutters above them, morning had passed into afternoon. It was a strange thing to know that you would never see another day. To think that the sun would still rise, and other people would see it and wonder at it, but you would be gone, completely. Just gone. It might drive a man mad if he thought about it too much. It might make him rant and rail against the world for daring to go on without him. The Bedlam was probably full of such men. He wished he had said more to Amy. He hoped that she would marry again, to a better man – a stronger man. Yet he didn't want to be forgotten, and that surprised him. Maybe that was sign that hope still dwelt somewhere within him.

'Because you can,' he croaked. 'That's why – that's why this?'

'I would not expect a small mind like yours to understand me,' Heydon sniffed, wiping a hand across his forehead. 'I am from a small city full of small minds. You dare to ask me why? Because I was made to call the tunes. I was made to make men dance to them. You, yonder odd fellow, your foolish wife. And the great ones too. The Catholic rubbish in France, the Scotch queen and the northern rebels, old Norfolk. And Cecil, too. Oh, I wrote him years ago, when I was a lad, offering my services. Did not bother even to reply. Well, I shall show him. His government shall fall with his whore mistress. This land shall lose its popery and its band of scum in Whitehall and Windsor. Think they are better than me, think they can overlook me – they shall not when we have a boy king and his uncle Moray, both beholden to me. I shall see this whole realm in ruins and be a master builder in its new making.'

So, thought Jack. That was it. A vengeful scheme by a man who had been disappointed of preferment, and fancied toppling the lot and bringing in new blood. Like a servant who, ignored by his master, decided to poison the whole household, and invite a new family to govern him. Sad, really. It was sadder still to have been taken in by such a man.

'There. For a while you shall know more than any man in this realm. And then you shall die by your knowledge. I told you that the business of watching was a dangerous one.

223

Trading in secrets buys only death for trash like you.'

'You said you were an ordained priest,' said Jack.

'And so I was. And I saw all the lechery and buggery of that foul rabble. The rabble that your pretty tall Scotch wench loves, and the old harridan in the castle up yonder tolerates with a wink. All soon to be at an end.' He smiled, but it looked to be a pained one. 'Hold – what is that?'

Jack had heard nothing, but Heydon stood, stretched his legs and grimaced, and then crept up the steps, careful not to dislodge the caliver. He opened the wooden shutter a crack. 'Yes!' he hissed, 'yes! I had thought we might be here some days, or even longer. 'Bells. The stupid old strumpet is having the castle ring its bells to announce her presence abroad. And...' He leant out further. 'Music, now. That, my friend, is the sound of sweet music. Sweeter still to my ears.' Jack strained. His sight and his hearing seemed poor, driven by the rough treatment and the lack of food and water. Yet, as the seconds passed, he thought he did hear something. A haunting sound – music indeed, and the most beautiful he had ever known. He closed his eyes and let it come to him. He wanted it to be the last sound he heard, the gentle rise and fall of music, melodious and lilting. It was a sound to die by. Heydon's voice cut over it, a knife through butter. 'The queen's barge. The old jade is airing out her cunny. It will pass us – it will pass! Alas, my friend, it is time for you to make your end. I shall have you swinging by the time I shoot.'

Jack forced himself into a sitting position as Heydon returned down the few short steps. His voice, when had spoken, had sounded strained. 'No sense in fighting it, man,' he said, before clutching at his stomach. 'Christ's wounds, you would not think that I would be overcome by ill humours on this day.' He pulled Jack to his feet and nudged him towards the rope, under which he had set the gun's box. It was just big enough to stop his feet touching the ground when his neck was in the noose.

Willingly, Jack stepped up and rotated his upper body until the noose dangled before his face. 'Good lad,' said Heydon. 'I shall unbind your hands now. Try nothing.' He did, and Jack

224

didn't. 'And now your feet.' He bent and, as he did so, slid to the ground and hunched double. 'Jesus! Jesus, my belly! What … what is … ow!' Panting, he got to his knees and undid the ankle bindings. As he started to stand, Jack kicked out, hard, his boot connecting with Heydon's stomach.

He slipped away from the noose, and the box, which had been on its side, tipped, spilling whatever remained inside, little packets and hand-sized caskets. Heydon screamed in agony. 'I cannot see! What is this? I cannot see!' He choked on something, and within seconds Jack realised it was a gush of vomit, soured ale studded with chunks of bread.

'My foolish wife,' said Jack, his voice barely above a whisper. 'She's poisoned your ale.' He recalled Amy's last words to him – the words that had inspired hope when she had breathed them in his ear. 'Drink nothing.' He leant over Heydon and plucked off his cap, crinkling it in his hands. He could feel the papery resistance beneath the false lining and edged up the stairs with it. Leaning out of the window, he blinked at the brightness and then launched the cap into the river. In the distance he could see the queen's barge. Sunlight dappled its green and white pain. In the long aft section, rowers in the same colours plied their oars. Behind them the musicians played, and in the rear of the boat a covered cabin section was tenanted by a bright palette. He squinted, waiting for the reflection on the glass windows to pass, and could see the queen at the back, her seat higher than everyone else's. They were only about thirty feet away, and the barge moved smoothly, cutting through the water like a blade. No one seemed to notice the hat as it surfed the water before sinking.

Jack turned, rubbing his wrists. He had made it. Now to find Amy, to stop Brown before he could kill her and Queen Mary. In the gloom of the boathouse, he knocked over the caliver, sending it down the steps, sprinkling gunpowder as it went. Below, he saw Heydon's face blossom into light. It the glare of his tinderbox, it looked purplish. Jack opened his mouth to cry out as he saw that, whilst he had been entranced, the man had tossed about packages of gunpower. He held one the of the little casks of the stuff in his hand.

She saved my life, he thought. Thank you, Amy. I'm sorry. Be safe. Live for us both.

The room did not ignite in one blast, but in a rapid succession of them, the first flame catching its mark and eating hungrily at the fuel around it. Breeding. Setting off others.

Jack's final thought was of Amy before the world carried him off in a dull *whump*.

10

'What ails him?' asked the wherryman. He had lain down his oar and was scrabbling frantically at his jerkin. There were thick wedges of black dirt beneath his long, pointed fingernails.

'Mmph,' said Amy. The man stepped over the seating planks towards her, passing Brown, who was leaning over the side of the boat, vomiting. He pulled down her gag.

'That man is a traitor,' she cried. She was surprised at the strength in her voice. 'He's stolen me away from the queen's own palace. I'm … I'm a servant to the queen herself and he's stolen me!'

'What?' he asked, his mouthing gaping. 'What?'

'He's a rebel – a northern rebel. He means to kill the queen!' She thought about adding that he planned to kill the Scottish one too but suspected she would lose him. 'He hopes to free the Scotch queen and bring her south,' she said instead. 'He's a common traitor.'

'Is it true? What … what do I do, my lady?' Amy rather liked that.

'Put in somewhere. Anywhere. Where are we?' Before he could answer, Brown cried out in pain. He rolled back into the boat and the smell of vomit and faeces washed over them all.

'This is no sickness,' cried the wherryman. 'He has the plague – it's the plague. Oh Mary and the saints!'

Brown tried to stand. He moved towards Amy, stumbling as the wherry drifted. 'You bitch,' he said. 'I'll … ugh…' Her hands were still bound. The boatman was no use; he sat immobile, transfixed by what he apparently thought was a plague victim advancing towards him. As Brown got closer, Amy braced her back against a seat and kicked out, hitting him just below the waist. It was enough. The movement made the boat rock crazily and Brown cried out again, before careering over the side and into the water. His splash set a nearby game of swans careening into the marshy riverbank, screeching in fury.

'Mother of God,' the wherryman screeched. Amy let the momentum of the rocking boat help her stand.

'Unbind me, you fool!'

'Yes, ma'am, sorry, ma'am.' He skipped around her, one arm out for balance, and untied her wrists. She massaged each in turn. 'What should I do? I must needs report this. The water bailiff!' Amy ignored him, looking over the side herself. She could not see Brown's body. The boat was moving so wildly that it might already have left him behind. Turning, she scanned the wake. Nothing.

'Would you – return me to Windsor. Return me at once, I'll – I shall report this. To Sir William,' she added, with meaning. He seemed to understand, leaping to oars. 'Where are we?' He looked over to their left, and she followed his gaze to a stream joining the Thames. A jumble of houses lay on either side of it.

'Sweeps Ditch. Around Staines, ma'am. It'll be a journey back. Fightin' the river, like.'

The wherry turned and nosed its way back in the direction they had come. Amy kept her eyes on the water, eager to see if Brown had washed up or was floating somewhere. Hopefully he had gone straight to the bottom. She had been unsure if the poison would work, until she heard that Queen Mary's death was really intended. Probably Brown thought she had hidden it somewhere – she was sure that was what he'd instructed. If it worked so well on him, it should have done the same to Heydon – before he could do anything to Jack, she prayed. A few drops were supposed to be enough to kill, given time enough. She had upended the entire contents into the jug they shared.

If something happened to Jack first, if he were arrested for a few months' flirtation with a pretty queen's religion... Well, she would never forgive him for being so stupid. And their last proper conversation would have been a fight!

They had proceeded along some way, the minutes seeming an eternity and each bend taking an age to pass, when a larger tilt-boat slowed alongside them. It was coming from the direction in which they were heading. 'You goin' to Windsor,' its oarsman asked.

'I am that,' the wherryman answered. 'What news?'

'Bad fire up that way. By the town.'

'What?' Amy shrieked, sitting up and addressing herself to the man. 'Where?'

'Nothin' to concern yourself with, my lady. An accident, they're sayin'. Some vagabonds usin' an old boathouse. Their fire got out of hand, looks like. Queer thing, though, it looked like explosions from where I was sittin'.'

'Their? Vagabonds?'

'Rough men – masterless sorts.'

'I know what a vaga – you say more than one?'

'S'what I heard. Two men was pulled out, both burned up. Nobodies, my lady. The queen's barge was nearby, but no one of quality was hurt. Just an accident. Probably they was storin' squibs there for a pageant or that, and the fire touched them off.'

Amy had stopped listening. She collapsed on her seat, her legs shaking.

Jack was dead.

'Well, good morrow to you. Both.' The skipper of the tilt-boat doffed his cap and continued on his way. Amy's wherryman did the same.

But Jack was dead.

The sun began to wane, and she wondered if it would ever rise again.

* * *

Amy disembarked at Windsor. As she prepared to leave the boat, she found Brown's satchel, stuffed with money and papers. She took the purses and, as she did so, one of the papers fell to the floor. She picked it up, frowning and let her eyes run over it. 'By Christ's blood,' she murmured as she read the accusation against her and Jack. She quickly stuffed the paper down her bodice and gave the ferryman as little as she dared, tossing the bag into the Thames. If he was unhappy about it, the look on her face must have warned him off quibbling. She wandered towards the old boathouse and saw it gutted, apart from some timbers standing over the river, whose dampness had protected them. A couple of men were ambling around the still-glowing embers of the place, empty buckets in their hands. Smoke still drifted up, smudging the coppery sky. A man in royal colours stepped out of the wreckage and shooed them away. She decided to go no further.

This was where he died, she thought.

The horses were both still in the stables, amid kicked and smashed railings. There had been no mistake. Throughout the journey by wherry, she had been hoping that was the case: that someone else had come upon Heydon, freed Jack, and then … and then what? Blown himself and Heydon up? She knew it was a fantasy, but she had wanted it to be true. She thought back to that last kiss, the one she had left all over his face. Did that make up for the fight they had had? For calling him a nobody, a nothing?

She went to the stables and fell to her knees beside his horse. She let her tears flow, tears of disbelief, of anger. Then she hugged and nuzzled at the horse, because he had brushed it and cared for it. Her poor, lost boy, never happy. The boy she had married and promised herself she would protect.

As night fell, she began to wonder what to do. Nothing seemed possible; nothing seemed real. She took his horse and went into the town. People were still moving around the streets, wraithlike, discussing the two dead men and what they had been doing. It was mighty suspicious, apparently, happening so close by the queen's barge. And with the north said to be on the march, well – it was mighty suspicious.

She ignored all the pleas for news. Her dress seemed to attract people who thought she might know something, but her mad staring eyes seemed to do the trick. Could she return to the castle? No. She had run away again, disappeared. She could not face Bess, nor any of the other servants. They would have questions she couldn't answer. Walsingham and Cecil, too – they might be ready to see her now, after a fire and an explosion. She wanted nothing to do with either of them. Jack was dead now, and nothing seemed to matter.

She took his horse and rode away from Windsor, vaguely heading north. She spent days on the road, sleeping in strange inns and refusing company. A dim idea formed in her mind that she would just ride on until she either died or reached the end of the world. Perhaps she had to pay a penance. She had murdered two men, watched one of them writhe in agony. She would go on until Brown's money ran out, and then she would starve. Sometimes her mother's image came into her mind, but she pushed it away. She had wandered too far from the wise old woman's teachings and did not want to face her ghost.

What would Jack want her to do? Live, she thought. But how did one live with unexpected loss? Whenever she had thought about her future, he was in it. He stood at the counter of their little shop, smiling at people.

The days turned into weeks. Along the road soldiers thronged, broken up into troops. Apparently, the northern earls were revolting against Queen Elizabeth, and were marching on Tutbury. Or so people said. To her surprise, she found herself heading in that direction, albeit from the south. She had no clear idea why. Only a vague feeling drew her – a stupid idea that if she went where he used to be, he would be there.

When she arrived in the town, her dress filthy and dishevelled, she saw a great concourse of people. She ignored them, riding up to the castle under an ashy sky that was building up the courage to rain.

'You can't enter, er … mistress.'

'Let me in,' she said. 'Please. I … I am in service here. A laundress.' The guard squinted, seemed to recognise her, and drew back in surprise. 'We … we thought you'd run away. Heard that your man died.'

Amy said nothing but rode up and into the courtyard. Darts of rain had begun jabbing at the ground, washing the colour out of everything. A fitting place, she thought, seeing the familiar tomblike structure standing against the lighter grey sky. She looked at her gloveless hands, both raw and bleeding. The nails had grown ragged, too. You've let yourself run to seed, her mother's voice tutted. There were hardened patters of muck on her dress and she scraped at them, flaking them off. Then she sniffed her fingers. Winced. Wiped. 'Mrs Cole!'

Still bent, she met the eyes of Woodward, the earl's steward. The shock in them faded to cool contempt. 'Why have you come here, girl?' Something in his face softened at the sight of her and he helped her down. 'But you have brought back one of the stolen horses. I … I was sorry to hear of your husband. The countess thought you might have run mad after his … what happened. When did you last eat, girl?'

'Don't know.'

'You shall have to be brought before the countess.' So Bess was back, she thought.

'Yes.'

'But … I shall have something fetched, and then you must see her immediately. And my lord.' He gestured around the courtyard and for the first time she registered the activity. People were moving around, shifting crates and wrapped bundles.

'Wingfield?' she asked. Her voice was rusty from disuse.

'Coventry. The Scottish queen is being moved for her safety, what with these rough northern rebels on the march. Do not let it worry you. For this, my son was dead and is alive again; he was lost and is found.' He seemed to realise what he had said, and he reddened. 'I … the prodigal son, of course, the parable. I mean only – the earl and countess shall rather celebrate your return than punish you severely.' He bustled off and brought her some bread and cold meat. She picked at it before being shown into the half-stripped building, her feet dragging. Sodden leaves had stuck to the bottom of shoes which were nearly worn through.

She went before her lord and lady in a little office near his chambers. 'We thought,' the earl began, 'that you had run off.' He was seated, Bess standing behind and to his right, one hand on his shoulder.

'I'm sorry.'

'Sorry isn't good enough, my girl. I trusted you,' said Bess. 'And then I hear that your husband is blown up with a hidden

232

priest. I was on the queen's barge, if you please – I saw it all. Her Majesty was right distressed. Hates such clamours. We had to turn back – smooth her than it was some accident. And then your man was reported to the council as having wandered the streets of Southwark buying guns? You fled us - you fled the queen's castle without permission. Men came for you! After news of your husband buying guns came to Mr Walsingham's ears. And what could I say? That I'd lost my own girl! What in the name of all that's holy has been going on? The truth, girl, the truth.'

'The truth would be good,' said Shrewsbury, reaching up and patting her hand.

Amy took a deep breath and told them all that she knew.

'And you were reporting to this false madman throughout your time here?' This was Bess. Amy hung her head. 'What, was I not a fair mistress, girl?'

'You've been a fair mistress, my lady. I'm … I was a fool. I thought to protect …' She found she couldn't say his name. 'My husband.'

'And he has paid the price for your misdeeds. And his own,' said the earl. 'I do not pretend to understand any of this. Two men, one a Catholic priest and one pretending to be Cecil's man – plotting to kill the Scottish queen under my roof? Why?'

'I can't say, my lord. I only can say what I saw. I think they were in some other plot. Together, just the two of them. And they sought to use us.' Recollection pricked at her. 'Yes, they sought to use us. Blame us. Their design was not Catholic nor of the queen's faith. It was something madder.' She thrust a hand into her bodice and retrieved the paper she had taken from Brown's satchel. It was ragged now, and sweat-dampened, but she lowered her eyes and held it out. 'Being only a woman, I can't make sense of it, my lord. Only that the two men sought to use us.'

'And you let them,' snapped Bess. Shrewsbury silenced her with a soft look, reaching out for the paper.

'My word,' said Shrewsbury. A sharp intake of breath.

'What is it?' Bess gently eased the paper from his fingers

and read herself, her lips moving silently. 'Well … Hell's bloody bells. The boy-king of Scotland. Elizabeth and Mary, both dead. You the instruments. And these two men were the authors of this madness?'

'Both are dead now,' said Amy, keeping her voice brittle.

'Yes, you saw to that. And Heydon took your husband with him.'

'Yet … it seems to me that you have put an end to two wicked plotters,' said Shrewsbury. 'When Mr Walsingham would see no plot.' She thought that the beginning of a smile touched the corner of his mouth. 'His friend the good Scotch earl might have some explaining to do, having such a man ever in his service. For that we might be grateful.' It was not clear to Amy whether he meant her killing the men or embarrassing Walsingham. 'Yet for the deceit you have shown, I am afraid you cannot continue long in our service. Not when you were willing to harm our guest.'

'I was never – I thought,' she began, a little of her old fire kindling.

'Hush, girl,' said Bess. 'Just hush. My husband and I … oh, hang it all – I like you, Amy Cole. You've been an addle-pate and worse, but you've … you've lost your husband. That's a hard thing. He seemed an odd sort, but if what you say is true – about him being so treated in his past, well …' She cleared her throat. 'My lord has ships. Good ships. One of them does trade on the continent. You shall be paid your due, girl.' This time Shrewsbury coughed. 'And a little extra, we always give our folk a little extra. And you might take ship. From Kent, if you can shift yourself there. By the time you get there the ports will be open – the queen will have closed them until this northern foolery is finished.'

Amy burst into tears. At this, the earl began muttering darkly and stood, reaching for his stick and hobbling from the room. 'He … always … wanted … to … travel.' She sobbed.

Bess came and patted at her arm. 'There, there,' she began. Then, 'stop this bloody nonsense at once, my girl.' Amy did. 'You are being given a great chance. Go abroad. Your husband is dead, and his name is now stained – a man who sought weapons by illegal means. Get yourself out of England. Go, now, and find fire in Europe enough to put some back in your belly. Find strength. A new beginning for you, girl, with no one to trouble you in it.' The countess then gave her a hard look. 'You can keep the dress.'

***

Amy stood at the docks, in a mist of fish and salt. Around her sailors swore and rolled barrels along a cobbled forecourt, ignoring the mizzling rain steaming around their boots. The masts of the ships looked like a forest, and she thought of Brown, and looked away. Her eyes fell instead on a seagull as it pecked its way across the ground, its black eyes reminding her for a second of Queen Elizabeth's. It cocked its head, squawked at her, and skimmed away.

It had taken her weeks to reach the place. Christmas had passed, spent in the company of strangers at a nameless tavern in an unknown village. The time of revels and new year's gifts. Though the real new year wouldn't come for months, the people in the inn spoke of Twelfth Night as the harbinger of new decade: as different, once it settled, from the 60s as the 60s had been from the 50s. A time of peace would come after the yule weeks, they said, after ten years of uncertainty and mad events. New fashions and new ideas would arrive. The wide world was getting smaller. Then they all drank a toast to the queen, whom they said would be the one thing not to change.

Jack would see none of those wonders, though. Each passing day would simply bury him deeper under the weight of time. And so she did not want to either.

The northern rising had, apparently, been crushed without a battle, the rebels more interested in saying masses around York than organising anything properly. Where Queen Mary was, Amy neither knew nor cared. Nor did she care for where she was going. She had spent two weeks in a dockyard inn, waiting for *The Barque Talbot* to be ready to sail. Privately she had decided she would never see the new continent. She recalled thinking about drinking the poison herself once, when she had first been given it. It had been a fleeting thought then – stupid. But sometimes life did batter you enough that there was no other way out. Her mother had once told her about an Egyptian queen who had done it. The Romans, too, took themselves out of the world out of honour. But they were all pagans and destined for hell anyway. Would she meet Jack in heaven if she took her own life?

On hearing from a sailor that it would still be a while, she returned to the inn. A message was waiting for her, and as she read it, her heart began to flutter. 'Been trying to find you. Waiting in the yard at the Swan.' She grabbed the tavernkeeper's lad who had delivered it and shook him. 'Who gave you this? Where is he?' The boy wriggled free, looking at her as though she were demented.

'Some feller in a brown suit. Said he's been on your trail a good while,' he said, and darted away.

Amy went to meet him. In her sleeve, she had hidden a knife bought from the innkeeper himself.

The Swan was a rival inn, frequented by sailors rather than the ambassadors and foreign visitors in the one Amy had chosen. She wandered into its yard, keeping her back to the wall of the building. She knew how silently and quickly Brown could more.

And then she saw him. He turned and saw her.

Within a second Amy had thrown herself into his arms. 'How? How?' The knife slipped from her sleeve, clattering to the ground with a tinny splash.

Jack eased out of her grip and leant in, kissing her. She let him, and then felt angry tears spring our of her eyes. She began to pummel his chest, and he winced. 'How?' she asked again. 'You're dead.' He smiled his old, stupid, moon-man smile. 'How are you here?'

'I … wanted to see you. To find you. I'm supposed to be dead now, the world's to think – but I got away. I mean, I jumped from a window. Heydon burnt the place.'

'But – they found bodies. Two!' Anger and joy fought for her. It seemed like, for months, some cruel, evil joke had been played on her, and Jack had been in on it.

'They found me. I … I must have been knocked out. Guards from the castle. When they heard the explosion. They took me, and they took what was left of Heydon. My arm was broken. One of the queen's bonesetters fixed it.'

'But why – I've thought you were dead – I wanted to be dead myself. I was going to jump into the sea from that ship. Why did you not find me? I went to Tutbury, where I thought you might be!'

Jack sighed. 'Amy … I've been locked up these past months. They told me that from now on Jack Cole was dead.' He lowered his voice. 'Sir William Cecil and the other man, Walsingham – they kept me locked in a cell. Asking me questions every day.'

'Did they hurt you?!'

'No. No, they kept me well enough, fixed me up. But in a room, all alone. I told them everything and they believed me.' Absurdly, she thought: of course they would listen to a man. 'About Heydon and Brown. About their plan for the Scotch prince, too, and the earl of Moray. I think that fellow will find himself watched from now on. I …' he grimaced, 'I betrayed the men of the north. The good, true men – the ones whose names I heard Heydon speak. I had to – I … I had to.'

'To hell with the north. To hell with Cecil and Walsingham.'

'Amy, quiet.' He tossed his head, making his fringe bounce. It had grown back straighter.

'I've been quiet enough! I … am I dreaming?' She had had similar dreams in past weeks, although always taking place in Tutbury or Wingfield.

'No. No, this is no dream. I've … I've been turned. I think. They want me to go to Europe. They don't care what I believe, so long as I inform them what the Catholics are doing. They think the pope will attempt something this year. Maybe this month. So they put me in this suit and told me to go – and to know that I'd be watched.

'But I said I couldn't without you. So they made what they called enquiries, and found you were being sent on the earl's ship out of the country. I've been chasing you since. We're both to go abroad, then. Jack Cole is dead. They said I can choose whichever name I want in the world, so long as they know it. I didn't,' he added, 'tell them what I heard. You and that Brown man – about killing Queen Mary.'

'You knew – you heard? I wasn't. I never was - it was - a fantasy. I could never have carried it through, no matter what he thought.'

'I couldn't either. I couldn't kill Queen Elizabeth. Not in cold blood, not even for forgiveness. I'm not made for an assassin. I'm not … you're a diamond, Amy. Made like one. Not like me. Not wax.'

'A diamond,' she smiled. She would take that. 'Yet you've lived through a madman's fire. No man of wax does that. So who are we then, husband? Adam and Eve?'

'I don't know. You decide.'

Epilogue

They stand on the deck of a ship, two nameless people. Elizabeth's England has disappeared from view. Neither miss it. On the horizon is the coast of France, or Belgium – neither know. They have discussed their future, buried in a tiny cabin in the deck below, where they laugh and cry and make love. A single berth again, no dormitories or separate beds.

They are to be watched people and watching people from now on. Or they might disappear in some unknown village, learn the language, and be known as the émigré couple who fled the horrors of a heretic queen's England.

She continues to care nothing for religion. She is willing to go where he goes and practice whichever happens to be the faith of their chosen homes. She talks a great deal, and the sailors on the ship have already started whispering that the silent young fellow has married a shrew and will repent of it, if he does not already.

He continues to believe in the Catholic faith. The confessional side of it appeals to him. He knows he was taught the tenets of it by a dead charlatan, and that he is now expected to betray those of the faith. But he might not. He might seek forgiveness instead for betraying England's northern men. Guilt is addictive, he thinks. When you relinquish it for one thing, for one act or other, you seek it for another as a drunk seeks the bottle. He tells her, grudgingly, about his childhood, and then finds he cannot stop. It seems odd to him – sinful almost – that he kept it from her before their marriage. To his horror – at first – he finds that she already knows. And then he loves her more for her silence. For knowing about him and marrying him anyway. For loving him still.

She thinks about the men she has killed. There are no regrets. Honour is a man's burden. A married woman can do as she pleases if it helps him. If she had the opportunity to relive the past, she would do it again. She considers the future, though. In her private thoughts, she realises that she sees the future every single day. Everyone does. Would the twelve-year-old her have been able to understand or imagine her murdering two men – planning and doing it – and then finding herself on a ship to the continent? Of course not. Absurd. Yet here she is, seeing the future.

He thinks about the men he has killed, and he is sorry for it. As his wife's thoughts turn to the future, his turn to the past. He has spent too long seeing it every day. When he realised that he could not run from it, whenever that was, he chose to be trapped in it. He considers that everyone lives in the past, replaying it in their head, letting it chip away at them. Some let it help them grow, others let it hold them back. Some people just plain outgrow the world, wanting to change in a world that remains sluggish and stubborn. He realises that he is not his past, and that he is not hollow. With her, he is himself in the present and the future. He has found what he wants and what he needs - and he believes in it.

The boat docks and they disembark in a strange town, not knowing the language. To her chagrin, he finds that he can pick up foreign tongues easily. She used to call him a chameleon, so it should not surprise her, but her own lazier ear irritates her, sparking her anger. When she feels an argument brewing, she reminds herself that he might have been dead. And then she argues anyway, because that is part of living, and she has to remind herself that it is all real.

And so they go on living, their lives and their identities traded in for a new beginning.

Author's Note

In her correspondence, Mary Queen of Scots always referred to her arrival at Tutbury Castle as the beginning of her imprisonment. She had been found not guilty of her second husband, Lord Darnley's murder by the English Privy Council in January 1569. Her accuser had ultimately been her brother, the earl of Moray, who had assumed the reins of government in Scotland after she had fled in May 1568. Moray, who had been investigated simultaneously for rebelling against his sister, was likewise found not guilty, although he was permitted to return to Scotland and continue ruling in the name of Mary's son, the infant James VI (and later James I of England). Throughout the whole bizarre charade, Queen Elizabeth (and the English government) had assumed the role of impartial mediators in a Scottish domestic affair. Rather than risk destabilising things north of the border further, the English decided to keep their hard-Protestant and rather deferential friend Moray in charge of Scotland, and the deposed Catholic queen in honourable confinement in England. Those interested in Mary's life are best served by Antonia Fraser's *Mary Queen of Scots* (Philips Park Press, 1969) and John Guy's *My Heart is My Own* (Harper Perennial, 2004). Moray's life is covered in Maurice Lee's study of the Scottish Reformation, *James Stewart: A Political Study of the Reformation in Scotland* (Columbia University Press, 1953) and my own *Blood Feud: Mary Queen of Scots and the Earl of Moray* (Sharpe Books, 2018).

During the first year of her imprisonment, Mary was put under the guardianship of George Talbot, 6th earl of Shrewsbury and his countess, Elizabeth Cavendish Talbot (popularly known as Bess of Hardwick). Bess's life is masterfully recounted in Mary S Lovell's *Bess of Hardwick: First Lady of Chatsworth* (Abacus, 2005). During the first months of their custody of the Scottish queen, relations between the Shrewsburys and their charge were largely congenial. However, Shrewsbury soon tired of her tears, and Bess engaged in spying on Mary (which Mary seemed to realise, writing to Elizabeth in October 1569 to beware the countess's 'scheming and accusations' during the latter's visit to the royal court). Joining Mary in her shadow royal court were a number of women, from ladies-in-waiting to friends and lower servants. Rosalind K Marshall's *Queen Mary's Women: Female Relatives, Servants, Friends and Enemies of Mary, Queen of Scots* (John Donald, 2006) is an excellent resource for those interested in figures like Mary Seton, the queen's long-time friend and hairdresser, and the countess of Moray.

Mary did not engage in plotting during her first year of captivity. Instead, she conspired at marriage with the 4th duke of Norfolk, England's premier peer. This appears to have been an open secret amongst Elizabeth's privy council, with members divided on when and how to tell the queen. Mary, however, seems to have been convinced by Norfolk that Elizabeth would approve the match between Protestant peer and Catholic queen, likely believing that the parsimonious English monarch would welcome a transfer of responsibility for a deposed queen to someone else. When Elizabeth found out, however, in September 1569, she was furious and ordered Norfolk's arrest. He was sent to the Tower in October, though later released (whereupon he resumed his marriage plans with Mary, not content until he actually lost his head in 1572). These events are covered in detail in Jane Dunn's study of the queens' strained relationship, *Elizabeth and Mary* (Harper Collins, 2004) and David Templeman's exhaustive study of Mary's captivity, *Mary Queen of Scots: The Captive Queen in England 1568-97* (Short Run Press, 2018).

During that first year, too, dissatisfaction spread in the largely-Catholic north of England. The earls of Northumberland and Westmorland and a number of lesser gentry raised arms in November, having been spooked by the privy council's quizzing of the two magnates (and Norfolk's arrest; they had swung behind the marriage plan). This resulted in the only real revolt of Elizabeth's reign: the northern rising (or revolt of the northern earls). More detail on the rising can be found in George Thornton's *The Rising in the North* (Ergo Press, 2010); Anthony Fletcher and Diarmaid MacCulloch's *Tudor Rebellions* (Pearson, 2008); and Krista Kesselring's excellent *The Northern Rebellion of 1569: Faith, Politics, and Protest in Elizabethan England* (Palgrave Macmillan, 2010). It was from the latter that I drew the names of Philip Heydon's network of contacts, as well as a sense of the uncoordinated and stuttering nature of the revolt. It should be noted that Mary Stuart did not approve or endorse the rising, seeing it as a potential roadblock to her marriage plans.

Mary's marriage plans were apparently initially endorsed and then rejected by her brother, Moray. Having told the duke at Hampton Court's park that he would support his sister's marriage, the earl betrayed him in the summer of 1569. He not only did not wish his sister restored to authority (which Norfolk would have wanted, desiring a reigning rather than a deposed queen for a wife) but he wanted her kept in England. Elizabeth, to his chagrin, toyed with the idea of sending Mary back during the same year. There is no evidence, of course, that Moray wanted either his sister or Elizabeth dead – although, if that had happened, there is a real possibility that the baby James could have been sent south to be raised as England's king, with his Anglophilic uncle as his guardian. Nor was there a secret document, written by Margaret Tudor or anyone else, which proposed that Scotland was a vassal country of England. However, the idea is inspired by Henry VIII's frantic searches for exactly such a document when he was pressing those claims himself (which he did intermittently during his reign). Work on this area is currently being undertaken by Professor Lorna Hutson, with a proposed monograph entitled *Shakespeare's Scotland*. The project promises to 'reconceive the question of Anglo-Scots relations in the period before James VI's succession, not as a "succession problem", but as a complex transformation, through English literature, of the older Anglo-imperial claim to sovereignty over Scotland by means of the medieval legendary "British" history of Brutus and King Arthur'. At any rate Moray himself was assassinated by gunshot – the first in British history – in January 1570.

Religion loomed large in the 1560s, as it would throughout the early modern period. Scotland had been reformed along Calvinist lines at the start of the decade, while the English lived in varying states of tolerance under Elizabeth's 1559 settlement. The latter was a genuine attempt to foster a peaceful compromise between Catholicism and Protestantism. Unfortunately, tolerance was an ugly word in the period. Catholics were dissatisfied (as evidenced by the northern rebellion) and staunch, Calvinist-leaning Protestants thought the settlement an exercise in appeasement. Later in the queen's reign, 'hotter' Protestants would evolve into Puritans. In early 1570, the pope would declare Elizabeth excommunicate and issue a papal bull releasing those who killed her from any spiritual punishment. This largely ended the 'nudge and wink' policy that the queen had tried, with the best of intentions, to maintain up until that point.

In this climate, spies flourished. However, the famous network and elaborate system made famous by Sir Francis Walsingham was in its infancy in 1569. Walsingham himself was a relative ingenue in the art of what was called spiery. His life and career are well told in John Cooper's *The Queen's Agent: Francis Walsingham at the Court of Elizabeth I* (Faber and Faber, 2012). My favourite biographies of the queen he served are Anne Somerset's *Elizabeth I* (Phoenix Press, 1991) and Alison Weir's *Elizabeth the Queen* (Random House, 2011). A shorter, highly enjoyable biography can be found in Helen Castor's *Elizabeth I* (Penguin Monarchs, 2018).

What made people turn to spying, and what kind of people did it? Answers can be found in Stephen Alford's *The Watchers: A Secret History of the Reign of Elizabeth I*. It was Alford's recognition that 'servants made the best spies' that gave me the idea for this book. Service itself is an overlooked part of the well-thumbed pages of early modern history. A good overview of how servants were considered, how they dressed, what they ate, and how important they were to their masters and mistresses' image, can be found in Jeremy Musson's *Up and Down Stairs: The History of the Country House Servant* (John Murray, 2009). Servants were people. They listened, they helped, and they were privy to all kinds of secrets.

The idea of the gentleman spy has died hard, if it had ever died at all, but many of the tales of Tudor-era spies do involve disaffected or wandering gentlemen. A gentleman, however, might expect to have serving men about him, and those serving men often had wives and families of their own. The Renaissance is often considered to be the first great age of self-fashioning – or constructing public personae. The period coincided with a blossoming in self-reflection and examination of the soul and conscience. Whether nobleman or playwright, queen or laundress, early modern people began to consider themselves as individuals with a duty to make the most of their own humanity, of their own consciousness, and of their own abilities. I find it conceivable that some would become lost in this cultural shift, especially in service, where identity continued to be tied to the master of the household. The seminal text on this idea is Stephen Greenblatt's *Renaissance Self-Fashioning: From More to Shakespeare* (University of Chicago Press, 1980), albeit recent scholarship has widened its horizon beyond the confines of the great personages of the age.

For the geography and layout of various places in the novel, I drew upon Liza Picard's *Elizabeth's London: Everyday Life in Elizabeth's London* (W&N, 2013) and Ian Mortimer's *The Time-Traveller's Guide to Elizabethan England* (Vintage, 2012). Simon Thurley's *Houses of Power: The Places that Shapes the Tudor World* (Random House, 2017) was also invaluable, particularly in providing floorplans. Any errors made are my own.

Jack and Amy Cole are last seen starting a new life on the continent, away from the faction and drama of Britain's reigning and captive queens. Unfortunately for them, Europe was itself in the throes of religious and civil strife. The 1570s would see the St Bartholomew's Day massacre of Huguenots in France, the battle of Lepanto, the succession of Pius V, the siege of Sancerre, the death of Charles IX of France, and a plot to assassinate John of Sweden. Whether the Coles – or whatever they end up calling themselves – will become entangled in any of these events, or simply retire to a shop in a rural town, remains to be seen.

If you enjoyed their story or would like to question anything – from customs to character – feel free to get in touch on Twitter @ScrutinEye.

*

Printed in Great Britain
by Amazon

72884270R00151